GOODBYE
CHAIRMAN MAO

GOODBYE
CHAIRMAN MAO

*

CHRISTOPHER NEW

THE
COMPANION BOOK CLUB
LONDON AND SYDNEY

THE COMPANION BOOK CLUB

The Club is not a library; all books are the
property of members. There is no entrance fee or
any payment beyond the low Club price of each
book. Details of membership will gladly be sent
on request.

Write to:
The Companion Book Club,
Odhams Books, Rushden, Northants.

Or, in Australia, write to:
The Companion Book Club,
C/- Hamlyn House Books, P.O. Box 252
Dee Why, N.S.W. 2099

---

*Made and printed in Great Britain
for the Companion Book Club
by Morrison & Gibb Ltd, Edinburgh*
6008 72513
480/351

Prologue

St. Anne's Church in Wardour Street was built in 1642. Over the centuries Soho grew densely round it, hemming it in. It was less than a hundred yards from Piccadilly Circus, but by 1940 only a few taxi-drivers, streetwalkers and policemen could have found it without trouble. Now nobody could. For in 1940 German bombs fell on it. The church was completely destroyed except for the west wall, which somehow survived, erect if not intact.

St. Anne's was never rebuilt. What was the nave is now a parking lot. What was the churchyard is now a little park. By day, the iron gates to this little park stand open. Office workers sit on the wooden benches and eat sandwiches off their laps, while pigeons flutter round their feet for crumbs. At night, the gates are locked, to keep out prostitutes and tramps. The heavy wooden doors in the gaunt west wall are always shut. The windows are blind, the stonework worn, bleak and grimy.

London, Tuesday, 29 June 1971
Chan paused anxiously to listen. There were steps behind him, coming closer. He walked on faster. The steps went faster too. He glanced fearfully back up the empty, dark alley. There they were, passing through a dim pool of lamplight. Four of them, striding silently after him. About thirty yards away. His heart thudded unsteadily in his chest. He began running, quite slowly at first, as if he were merely in a hurry, not frightened for his life.

For a few seconds he heard no footsteps but his own. He

felt a sudden, incredulous lightness of relief – perhaps they weren't out for him after all. But then came the muffled sound of other footsteps, running footsteps. With a lurch of panic then he knew for certain they were hunting, knew for certain he was their prey. He ran his fastest, dashing round the corner into Wardour Street, down towards Shaftesbury Avenue. Their steps raced behind him.

Two hundred yards to go. His hammering heart made breathing harder, his fear weakened his legs, but he forced himself on. They were gaining on him. He could hear the swift padding of their feet drawing closer. *Soft shoes*, he thought, *they knew they'd have to run*. He flung himself forward desperately, heart pounding, legs aching, gasping for breath.

One hundred and fifty yards. His eyes picked out useless sights like an indifferent camera and his brain numbly registered them – the darkened, blank windows of a strip club, a cat arching its back against an overflowing trash can, a lightless streetlamp with a broken glass. His brain numbly registered them and numbly yet rapidly wondered whether these were the last things he would ever see, while his aching, tiring body lunged on towards Shaftesbury Avenue.

One hundred yards. If he could only get across into Gerrard Street he'd be safe, his own people would be there. He forced his legs, he strained his lungs, for one more burst. He was keeping his distance, he was beginning to go ahead, he felt again the brief wild buoyancy of hope. But then the shadowed wall of the ruined church in front of him stirred. Three figures stepped across his path. He was trapped.

His legs gave up. The chase was over. He staggered back against the church wall as if for sanctuary, panting and aching for breath, his mouth gasping and dry. He heard the men behind him coming closer. They too were panting. The others blocking his way stepped briskly forwards. He wanted to turn and hide his head, but with a last effort he raised his arms against them hopelessly, wearily, sickened with dread. *Let it be quick*, he thought pleadingly and heard himself sob as they paused, all of them, gathering themselves together.

Then they closed silently round him. For a terrible long second he could see the face of the one nearest him, see the bright indifferent eyes watching him alertly, hear the breath hissing through the half-open mouth. Then he pushed out blindly against him with his hands, screaming a wordless scream. Still nothing happened.

Let it be quick, let it be quick. Then at last came the sudden sear of knives plunging into him and he felt himself falling, *let it be quick,* surprised that it didn't hurt when his head thumped against the stone pavement, surprised that dying gave him time to notice such things. Then the knives were plunging into him again and again and his body was jerking and twisting in agony, an agony that grew duller, though, with every stab. Soon he ceased to feel anything. He heard his voice screaming and choking, saw his body twitching like a slaughtered sheep, but he felt only a dulled numbness. His eyes had grown filmy. Why was breathing so difficult and yet so painless? Someone was pulling at his clothes and he wanted to protest, but his hands wouldn't move and he couldn't speak. It was like a dream, yet he knew distinctly that it was not, that he was dying. He could feel the world draining away from him more swiftly now, so that it didn't matter after all that they were pushing and pulling his body like a sack, going through his pockets. Whatever they did to him, it wouldn't matter any more.

And now, with a flicker of lucidity, he realized why he couldn't breathe. He was drowning in his own salt-tasting blood, while his body was jerking uncontrollably, twitching and quivering. He could hear his breath whistling and gurgling through his severed windpipe. It was growing dark, darker than the night, darker than it had ever been before. The gurgling and whistling became a wind, a typhoon howling, and then a quiet wailing. It became the wailing voice of his mother beating her head on the ground at his father's funeral in Hong Kong, beating it until her white mourning headband came undone and fell limply on the dark ground beside her, while the firecrackers banged and smoked all round to drive away the spirits of the dead.

Go search for people who are hurt by fate or nature. . . .
It is sad indeed, and humanly shallow – but we are
obliged to profit from it.
General Sudoplatov, Sometime Head of the
Special Bureau, Russian Secret Police

Chapter One

On 1 October 1949, Mao Tse-Tung proclaimed the formation of the People's Republic of China, with himself as chairman of both the Republic and the Chinese Communist Party, and with Chou En-Lai as prime minister. Mao's power then was supreme, but by 1965 it seemed to be waning. His 'Great Leap Forward' campaign to industrialize China overnight had been a failure; he had been replaced as chairman of the Republic by Liu Shao-Chi and he had been criticized openly in the Politburo meeting of November 1965. The revolutionary ardour that had spurred the people on in time of war was a disturbing liability in the more sedate years of peace. Or so the pragmatic bureaucrats thought, as they sat down at their desks and tried to direct and control their vast, unwilling and unready land. Liu Shao-Chi was the leader of the bureaucrats. Chou En-Lai remained prime minister.

Mao retired to Shanghai, apparently finished. In reality, he had merely retreated two steps in order to advance three. Six months later he launched the 'Great Proletarian Cultural Revolution' to regain his political power. The magic of his name alone enrolled millions of young supporters into unofficial armies of 'Red Guards' who denounced and pilloried everyone he chose, and some he did not. Liu Shao-Chi was disgraced and died soon after. The nerves of the party organization were convulsed, then paralysed, and Mao's Red Guards, drunk with the power they had only just tasted, rampaged through the cities out of control. Anarchy and civil war threatened. Marshal Lin Piao, the defence minister and China's most famous general, made an alliance with Mao to restore order. Most of Mao's enemies were purged, but the Red Guards were taken over, disciplined and finally disbanded. Then the party organization was slowly revived.

Lin Piao had his reward. He was formally appointed Mao's successor in a draft constitution approved in 1969.

Chou En-Lai remained prime minister.

These three ruled the largest and potentially the most powerful nation on earth. It was a gerontocracy – Mao was seventy-six, Chou seventy-one, Lin sixty-two. Yet it was the youngest of this ageing triumvirate, 'Tiger Cat' Lin, who seemed the least healthy. Nobody looked less like a tiger cat. He was frail, slightly stooping, bespectacled, and he suffered from tuberculosis as well as a painful chest wound inflicted during one of his campaigns against the Japanese. Mao, on the other hand, showed no sign yet of the Parkinson's disease that was stalking his body, Chou no sign of the cancer cells secretly massing in his.

Tiger Cat Lin was the heir apparent, but he didn't look likely to succeed for several years to come. How many years did he have himself? He wouldn't have been human if he hadn't pondered this question. All of them had survived plots against their lives. None knew where the next was being hatched. All of them had their supporters too – criss-crossing networks of old loyalties and new coalitions that they spun like spiders' webs throughout the army and the party.

Mao was fond of the hot spicy food of his native Hunan province, while Lin Piao liked fried yellow beans and Chou was a discerning judge of wine. They didn't always have the same tastes in politics either. Mao wanted to reform human nature now; Lin wanted to reform the army now; and Chou – Chou alone of them had been born a mandarin and was too polite to show what he wanted. Perhaps, though, he wanted to reform Mao.

London, Wednesday, 7 July 1971
The chargé d'affaires of the People's Republic of China sat stiffly on the edge of the capacious leather chair, inducing a

mild uneasiness in the British foreign secretary about his own indolent, legs-crossed posture. His parliamentary private secretary, Harry Maguire, however, was leaning forward alertly in his seat, so perhaps that would be enough. After all, the foreign secretary excused himself as he listened, his back *was* playing up.

'The government of the People's Republic of China,' the chargé d'affaires was saying, 'is seriously disturbed at this brutal murder of a Chinese compatriot in the heart of London and requests the British government to take the most urgent steps to apprehend and severely punish the culprits.'

'Ye-e-es,' he shifted his back a little against the cushion. 'I am informed the police are doing everything in their power to trace the murderers.' And then almost as an afterthought, 'It's most distressing, of course.'

The compact, stiff little Chinese listened with his head cocked on one side like a sparrow, his rimless glasses glinting briefly in the light. When he was quite sure the foreign secretary had finished speaking, he leaned forward a little further, resting his fingertips rigid and claw-like on his knees. 'My government does not share the view expressed in your newspapers that robbery was the motive of the crime.' His singsong intonation gave his voice a birdlike quality, further strengthening the image of a sparrow that had drifted across the foreign secretary's mind.

'Indeed?' He allowed his eyebrows to lift faintly. 'Which newspapers?' And he glanced at Maguire. Maguire thought he saw the brown Chinese eyes flicker as they registered that glance.

The chargé d'affaires ignored the foreign secretary's inquiry. 'The victim was a patriotic Chinese and an admirer of the immense achievements of the Chinese people under their great leader Chairman Mao Tse-Tung.'

'Quite so, quite so,' the foreign secretary responded non-committally.

Again there was that polite pause until it was clear the foreign secretary had finished and then, with a slightly forced

13

hardening of the voice, 'My government takes steps to ensure the safety of foreign nationals living in China and it expects the British government to do the same.'

'I should perhaps remind you,' the foreign secretary smiled the dimpling smile that made him look almost boyish despite his scant grey hair, 'I should perhaps remind you that the victim was a naturalized British subject. He emigrated to Hong Kong in the er . . . late fifties?'

'Nineteen fifty-eight,' Maguire responded to the foreign secretary's questioning look.

'Yes, nineteen fifty-eight. He emigrated with his family in nineteen fifty-eight and he was naturalized in nineteen sixty-eight. Then he came to London to work in a travel agency in . . .' he hesitated to say 'Chinatown' in case that sounded patronizing.

'Gerrard Street,' Maguire prompted him.

'Yes, Gerrard Street, in Soho.'

The Chinese glanced from the young Maguire to the old foreign secretary, then spoke into the space between them. 'The People's Republic of China regards Hong Kong as an inalienable part of Chinese territory,' the words tumbled off his tongue clumsily yet pat, like a schoolboy's recitation learned by heart, 'and therefore repudiates absolutely the absurd view that it has no concern with the victim's death. Besides,' he added almost mollifyingly, 'he had relatives still living in China and they have asked the appropriate department of the foreign ministry to pursue this matter.'

'Ah. Well,' the foreign secretary rose with a grimace of pain as the chargé d'affaires stood up, 'no doubt the question of Hong Kong will be resolved at a later date.'

The Chinese inclined his head. He looked still smaller, still more compact, beside the bony length of the Briton.

'As to this other business, though, I can assure you the police are making every effort to er . . .' The sentence was completed with a wave of the hand. 'And we will keep you informed of course, in view of your government's . . . interest in the matter.'

The chargé d'affaires again inclined his head, signifying

14

comprehension rather than acknowledgement. He gave them each a limp formal handshake by the door. Maguire noticed how neatly the Mao jacket fitted his body as he walked away.

'They must have good tailors in China,' he said as the chargé d'affaires closed the door.

'Oh first class, first class,' the foreign secretary stood absently by the tall curtained window, fingering his pointed chin. 'Shanghai tailors . . . first class in the old days . . .' He was watching the traffic crowding slowly and impatiently along Whitehall.

The noise sounded muffled but steady through the gently rattling windows, like the rumbling engines in some vast ship. *An old ship, a tired ship*. He waited until he could see the black diplomatic car bearing the chargé d'affaires away down the street, while the image of a rust-streaked, red-and-black-funnelled liner floated dimly behind his eyes. *An old ship, a tired ship*. Then he braced himself and turned. 'Well what did you make of that, Harry?'

'Did you notice how he avoided your question about the newspapers?'

'He knew as well as we did that nobody has suggested any motive for the murder. He just wanted to let us know that *he* didn't think robbery was the motive. But why?'

'Perhaps the man was one of their agents?'

'Yes?'

'And they're telling us they want the people who killed him caught?'

'Why would they want to tell us that?'

Maguire shrugged.

'No country acknowledges it's got agents in another country, not even as indirectly as our friend did just now.'

'Perhaps he was hinting it's about time we cracked down on the Nationalist Chinese in Britain?'

'Hm . . .' the foreign secretary smiled his boyish dimpling smile again. 'But why should they be bothered about that? It isn't as though the Nationalists were very active here. . . .' Then he began massaging his back, reaching up inside his jacket and wincing with pain. 'I really must give up politics soon, you know.'

'Bit of a mystery.' Maguire had learned to ignore the hints of retirement that the foreign secretary let fall on bad days.

'Hm . . .' he sat slowly and carefully down behind his desk, then sighed with relief. 'Well, I suppose we'd better pass the word on to intelligence. No doubt they'll have some extravagant theory to explain it all.'

'I'll have a memo sent, then, shall I?'

'Mm?' he was frowning down at his diary through his half-moon glasses he always wore halfway down his nose. They made him look like a scholar, which he had no claim to be, rather than a politician. 'Yes, would you do that, Harry? Perhaps they can put the pieces together.' And his mouth snapped shut with an unexpected finality that reminded Maguire of the jaws of an elegant, if antique, trap.

Chapter Two

The Amur and Ussuri Rivers are not yet familiar names to Western students of diplomacy or war, but the day will surely come when they are. They mark, or fail to mark, most of the border between the Soviet Far East and the People's Republic of China. The Amur wanders for hundreds of miles through the mountains bordering northern China until it turns aside to Khabarovsk, headquarters of the Russian Far East Military Region. From Khabarovsk it flows away from China into the sea of Okhotsk, north of Japan. It is the Ussuri River that marks the rest of the border, running almost due south to Vladivostock, headquarters of the Russian Far Eastern Fleet. Peking, in the north of China, is never more than a thousand miles from the Russian border. A thousand miles is a long way, but it is only one-fifth of the distance from Vladivostok to Moscow.

Much of the Soviet Far East was seized from China by nineteenth-century imperialist czars. The Chinese do not recognize the 'unequal treaties' by which these lands were ceded to Russia, but the rulers of communist Russia have no wish to give them up.

Moreover, the Ussuri River is wayward and shifting. It often changes its course by as much as a mile. Disputes arise as to where the true, if unequal, boundary lies. Between friendly states, such disputes could be settled smoothly, or at least peaceably. But Russia and China, although they are both communist, are not friendly states. When Mao won the civil war against the Nationalists led by Chiang Kai-Shek, Stalin was surprised – he had expected Mao to lose. Perhaps

17

it piqued him to be wrong. After a few years of superficial friendship, the real antipathies between the two nations became apparent. To the Chinese, Russia was revisionist, no longer truly revolutionary, interested only in hegemony over other communist states and the consolidation of its empire. To the Russians, China was a dangerous, naïve, unruly giant, threatening by its opportunistic manipulation of the Third World to oust Russia from the position it had enjoyed since 1917 as leader of the communist bloc. The Chinese have a saying, *There can be only one sun in the sky*. The Russians would have agreed.

Under Khruschev, the Russians abruptly withdrew all their aid to China, hoping to teach the unruly Chinese a lesson. And so they did, but not the one they intended. The Chinese made a virtue of the self-reliance they had to practise of necessity. Instead of collapsing, their industry slowly recovered from the Russian withdrawal. Gradually they developed their own guns, their own planes and, eventually, their own atomic bombs. Six months before the assassination of an obscure Chinese agent in London, China conducted a series of nuclear tests in the atmosphere over Sin Kiang – tests which sharply and precisely foreshadowed the day when China would be as strong a nuclear power as Russia. When that day came, the Russian Far East would cease to be a threat to China and become instead a hostage.

The Amur and Ussuri Rivers are not yet familiar names to Western students of diplomacy and war. But they are very familiar to Russian and Chinese generals, soldiers and diplomats. Heavy battles have been fought, involving infantry, tanks and artillery, over their frozen banks. (Yevtushenko, the establishment anti-establishment Russian poet, has celebrated the death of a Russian soldier at one of the Ussuri battles. It is not one of his better poems.) Only a hurried meeting between Chou En-Lai and Leonid Brezhnev prevented one long battle from blossoming into the open war which neither side was ready for – yet. A commission of Russian and Chinese officials was set up. It met weekly in Peking to discuss the border, while the soldiers of both sides

18

looked down their gun barrels at each other. The Russian officials drank vodka and offered token concessions. The Chinese officials drank tea and refused token concessions.

The talks dragged on. Skirmishes and incidents occurred almost weekly and the Russians watched the Chinese growing stronger. It would have been strange if they hadn't made some plans.

Moscow, Monday, 12 July 1971

There are hotels in Moscow which do not accept Russian money. To have a drink in the bar you must pay in dollars, pounds or marks. Since most Russians have only roubles, they cannot be served, and that means these hotels are patronized almost exclusively by foreigners – which conveniently insulates all but the most persistent foreigners from all but the most persistent, and therefore easily observable, Russians.

One of these hotels is the National on Gorki Street, the oldest hotel in Moscow. John Pritchet, the Russian correspondent of the *Guardian*, sat in a corner of its little bar, half watching two bored American tourists – elderly, paunchy men who sagged over their bar stools at the counter, drinking whisky and exchanging bored comments on the details of their trip.

Pritchet was new to Russia himself. He had been in Moscow for only one week. At four o'clock the press attaché at the British Embassy was coming to take him round the suburbs. He spread an Intourist map of the city out on the little table in front of him and studied it perfunctorily – he had never been good at transposing the information laid out in maps into the solid visual images of land, rivers and buildings.

The Americans hadn't liked their hotel in Leningrad, it seemed. Apparently they liked this one better. The Intourist guide had spoken perfect English according to one of them, but the other thought she had an accent. They argued about it desultorily, then relapsed into bored silence.

Pritchet was bored too. He looked up from the map to the

19

barman who was leaning on the counter at the far corner from the Americans, chin on hand, suppressing a yawn. Pritchet glanced down at his map again and wondered how he would last two years in Moscow. He sipped his vodka, which, he already understood, was the quality ordinary Russians could not get, then slid his glass back and forth across the bit of red formica tabletop not covered by the map. Back and forth the glass slid and the clear vodka slopped up and down the sides with each movement.

A man sat down at the table next to him. Pritchet slid his glass faster, until the vodka washed right up the sides of the glass, up to the top.

'Are you a correspondent?' the man beside him asked abruptly. 'Newspaperman?'

Pritchet looked up and nodded. The man wore the thin jacket and trousers of poor, shapeless quality that were the mark of a Russian. 'Yes,' he nodded again.

'I have something to tell you. You must pass it on to your embassy.' The man spoke almost casually, so that for a moment Pritchet thought he must be an Intourist official with some routine message. But then he noticed the tightly clenched fist on the table, the knuckles showing white. He glanced sharply at the man's face. The Russian was middle-aged, his dark hair thinning, his face narrow rather than broad and Slavic. He had spoken deliberate but good English.

'Almost impossible to meet the people . . .' one of the Americans was saying.

Pritchet waited, no longer sliding his glass, while the man looked at him measuringly, then licked his lips. But Pritchet never found out whatever it was he had to say. Two Russians in suits walked into the bar and spoke quietly to the man. The Russian's expression did not change as he answered them, but he stood up as if in respect. The two newcomers glanced at Pritchet almost apologetically. One of them touched the man's arm and they walked out together. Pritchet noticed a crumpled scrap of paper drop onto the floor from the man's clenched hand as he walked away.

20

One of the Americans was going to look at Moscow University tomorrow on the Intourist tour bus. The other thought he'd give it a miss and look at the shops instead. They hadn't noticed what had happened.

The barman came slowly from behind the counter and unnecessarily wiped the table where the man had sat. Pritchet put his foot out and covered the scrap of paper with his brown suede shoe. 'What did he want?' he asked the barman, jerking his head at the door which was still swinging gently.

The barman shrugged. 'Too much drink.' He went back to the bar, flicking his cloth morosely.

Pritchet waited until the barman's back was turned before he stealthily picked up the paper and folded it inside his map. He finished his drink as casually as he could, went to his room and opened the map away from the window. The paper slipped out. He smoothed it down and studied it excitedly. It was the size of a small postcard and contained several rows of Russian letters written in ink. He folded it up again and slipped it into his pocket.

The press attaché laughed at his story, which Pritchet had saved until they'd got out of the car and were alone outside a large new apartment block. 'Either drunk or a bit cracked,' he said, unfolding the flimsy piece of paper in his hand and smiling down at it. 'I'm afraid you won't get any drama out of that one.' And he crumpled it up into a little ball.

As they walked back to the car the press attaché was about to throw the paper away, but a vestigial sense of shame at littering foreign streets, and perhaps some deeper sense of hesitancy, restrained him. He smoothed it out, slipped it into his breast pocket and forgot all about it until he found himself standing next to the military attaché at a cocktail reception for the British trade delegation a few hours later.

Chapter Three

In the first week of July, President Nixon's Assistant for National Security Affairs, Henry Kissinger, arrived in Dacca for talks with the Pakistani government. On ninth July it was announced that he had left Dacca for a short, private holiday in the hills, so that he could relax undisturbed, away from prying reporters. His 'holiday' was in fact a secret flight to Peking, where he met Chou En-Lai for the first time. In two days' time they completed a year's devious and guarded negotiations which had begun in a dowdy room in the Rumanian foreign ministry in Bucharest, a room dominated by a vast oil portrait of President Ceausescu.

Kissinger did not meet Mao or Lin.

On fifteenth July it was announced on television by President Nixon and simultaneously by a special announcement in Peking that Premier Chou En-Lai on behalf of the government of the People's Republic of China, had extended an invitation to President Nixon to visit China at an appropriate date before May 1972. The meeting between the leaders of China and the United States, the announcement went on, was to seek the normalization of relations between the two countries and also to exchange views of concern to both sides.

Perhaps the only other government in the world that had regular information about the furtive diplomacy which led to this announcement was the government of Russia. Rumania let the Russians know, at first only in guarded terms, that things were happening. Then President Ceausescu visited China, a month before the announcement was made; on his way back to Bucharest he held 'brief discussions' with Kosygin and Brezhnev in Moscow, in which he told them of Kissinger's forthcoming visit to Peking. Relations between Russia and Rumania had been cool for a long time and Rumania's acting over the years as a go-between for the United States and China had done nothing to warm them. But Ceausescu had judged, correctly, that, since the Russians would find out exactly what the Americans and Chinese were up to anyway, it was best they found out earlier from him rather than later from someone else. A prudent policy, making himself useful to everyone.

London, Friday, 30 July 1971
Brigadier Stuart's right leg had been shattered by shell splinters outside Rome in 1944, when he was only twenty-three, and he had spent six months in a military hospital. Coming from a soldiering family, he had refused to accept it when doctors told him he would have to be given a medical discharge from the army. He wangled himself a job in intelligence and so discovered by accident what his true vocation was. He had a capacious, penetrating and patient mind, the value of which was immediately recognized when he was put to work interrogating suspected Nazi war criminals. He rose quickly through the obscure and uncertain hierarchy of the intelligence services until in 1964 he became head of one of its most important branches. Though he was gazetted as a brigadier with staff duties at the War Office, in fact his salary and responsibilities were more like those of an army commander. Because of his injured leg, which was two inches shorter than the other, he had an elevated shoe and usually walked with a cane.

At exactly three o'clock on tenth July, he limped into the cabinet room at 10 Downing Street carrying a large, worn leather briefcase under his arm. Except for that limp, he looked much like any other senior army officer in mufti.

The prime minister sat at the head of the long table, with the foreign secretary on his right and Maguire next to the foreign secretary. Stuart was familiar with the room, as he was with prime ministers. The first time he had been there was in the Cuba missile crisis of 1962, the last time two weeks ago. He sat down as usual on the prime minister's left.

'I think you all know Brigadier Stuart?' the prime minister asked perfunctorily.

'Mr Maguire does not know me, sir,' Brigadier Stuart laid his cane on the floor and his briefcase on the table. 'Although I know him . . .' He adjusted himself comfortably on his chair, his bad leg straight out in front – so the prime minister found he couldn't stretch his own legs out – took the three identical files out of his briefcase and silently passed them across the table. His unblinking blue eyes gazed at each of them in turn, lingering reflectively on Maguire's thin face with its narrow, brown eyes and still youthful, dark hair.

He closed the briefcase carefully and placed it deliberately beside his chair. The prime minister's fingertips drummed with impatience on the polished table, which reflected them hazily in its rich brown surface. Brigadier Stuart would not be hurried, though. He glanced at them each again – his heavy, squarish face, framed by short, sandy hair turning grey at the sideburns. Then, placing his palms on the table, he began speaking in a slightly brusque, lowland Scottish voice.

'At approximately two fifteen on the morning of twenty-ninth June, a Chinese male was found murdered in Wardour Street with twenty-three stab wounds in his body. A patrolling police car apparently disturbed the murderers while they were going through the man's pockets. They ran off without being identified and no clues have been found. However, we know the man was an agent of the People's Republic of China. There was nothing in his pockets except a torn piece of paper about two inches long with some capital letters on it. The Chinese chargé d'affaires later expressed rather obvious concern about the man's death.

'On the assumption that this was an espionage assassination, which seemed most likely, we considered the scrap of paper might have some significance. It could have been part of a coded message which was taken from him by the people

24

who killed him. We didn't think it was planted on him, by the way, because it had his fingerprints on it and in any case we have no idea what the code means. If it had been a plant, whoever planted it would presumably have wished to mislead us with it. But if we don't know what it means, we can't be misled. So we were reasonably confident it was a genuine coded message, the rest of which had been taken by the assassins. But as to the nature of the code, its source and its significance – we were completely in the dark. In fact, we even made the mistake of thinking the letters were in the Roman script when, as it turned out, they were not.'

Maguire noticed how Stuart's eyes constantly but slowly travelled from face to face as he spoke. They were slightly protuberant, the whites a trifle bloodshot at the corners, and when they moved the rest of his face remained still.

'We didn't have any idea of that, though, until just over a week ago, when we got a report from our embassy in Moscow. Apparently, a correspondent of the *Guardian* was approached by a man in a Moscow hotel bar who said he wanted to pass something on to the embassy. The man was jumped by Russian plain-clothes men – presumably KGB – before he could deliver the message, but he dropped a scrap of paper which the correspondent picked up. He gave it to the press attaché, who fortunately showed it to the military attaché. A photocopy of this paper and the other piece is at the top of page two of your files. You see they each contain the same letters. They are – what we didn't realize at first – letters of the Russian alphabet. What we took to be a capital P is in fact the Russian R. What we took to be a capital H is the Russian N. The other four letters happen to be the same in both the Russian and Roman alphabets. The correspondent has now had a look through the photographs in our files and he's fairly confident the man who approached him is a Russian-Jewish dissident physicist named Girov. Girov is quite well known to Feodorev, the aeronautical engineer who defected at the air show in April. There's no doubt he was genuine. So now we know that the Chinese agent and this man in Moscow were both carrying a coded

25

message in the Russian alphabet. The question, of course, is why. If you will look at page three, I will summarize our present analysis. There are altogether five points to take into account.'

He cleared his throat while the pages rustled.

'One, President Nixon has announced he's going to visit Peking next year and Russia doesn't like that at all.

'Two, the Russians have been building up their forces along the Chinese border ever since the military clashes began in 1968. This build-up has been intensified in the past six months. They now have about three hundred long- and short-range nuclear missiles, fourteen hundred tactical strike aircraft and twenty-five battle-ready divisions in position along the border from Vladivostok to Khabarvosk.

'Three, China's military and industrial power is growing. The recent nuclear tests in Sin Kiang were apparently successful. And China will soon have a credible nuclear arsenal, although less sophisticated than that of the Russians.

'Consequently, four, if Russia contemplates any military action against China, between now and late September might be the best time. If they don't act soon, winter will prevent them. And next year Nixon will be in China. They wouldn't want to embroil America in any action they take against China. That would increase the risks for them incalculably. After that, China's nuclear power may make the game not worth the candle.

'Five, Chinese agents are anxious to get hold of a message in some Russian code, and a dissident in Russia was anxious to give the same message to the west. The Chinese are very keen to know who it was that killed their agent here. So keen, they don't mind almost admitting he was an agent.

'All this suggests that the Russians are preparing some action against China. And that the Chinese have got wind of it. It could be a limited strike across the border, a plan to destroy the Chinese nuclear capacity or something else. There must be a great many disaffected people in China now, especially after the shake-up of the cultural revolution. Some of them might be looking for Russian support to topple Mao.

It seems likely something's going to happen – we just don't know what.'

Brigadier Stuart indicated he had finished by leaning his elbows on the table and resting his fingertips against each other.

The prime minister was drumming on the table again. 'Isn't that rather a lot to build on the evidence you've got?'

'It's unconfirmed, certainly,' Brigadier Stuart nodded slowly. 'We need to know more about their code before we can confirm it. But everything points in the same direction. We know the Russians are worried about China. We know now's the best time for them to strike, if they're going to strike at all. I'd say we've as much evidence now that the Russians are planning something for China as we had that the Germans were planning something for Poland in 1939.'

'Oh come, now,' the foreign secretary chided gently, smiling his dimpling smile.

'Some people didn't believe it then, of course.' Brigadier Stuart outstared the foreign secretary, who they both knew had been one of them. 'No doubt some won't believe it now. But in my view the question is not *whether* they're preparing something, but *what* it is and *when* it might happen.'

The prime minister had begun doodling on his pad. 'How can you find out?'

'Breaking the code will help.'

'And how long will that take?'

Brigadier Stuart's palms lay flat and inert on the table again. 'Without more messages, it's hopeless. We need a string of messages. About two thousand letters. Then we can get started. We're listening for them with all we've got, but so far we haven't heard a thing. That probably means it's not come into general use yet. When it does, things will be happening very fast and we won't have much time. I suggest, sir, that the Americans should be informed of the developments to date.'

The foreign secretary glanced at the prime minister.

'I don't propose to pass on mere speculation to the Americans,' the prime minister said tartly. He resented

27

Britain's client status and wanted to show his independence where he could.

Brigadier Stuart had expected this. His cool, slightly bulging eyes contemplated the prime minister's face. 'It is my duty to tell you, sir, that in the event of a Russian nuclear strike on China, there is a very real danger that missiles intended for Canton might overshoot and destroy Hong Kong. Also, missiles intended for targets in Fukien province could overshoot and even reach Taiwan. In that second eventuality, the US Seventh Fleet would be at risk as well as Taiwan, and the Americans might retaliate at once, on the mistaken assumption that the rockets were intended to land where they did.'

'Hm. *If* there is a Russian nuclear attack on China. But that is a mere hypothesis.' He tapped the open file in front of him. 'Pure conjecture.'

But Stuart was persistent. 'Any war between Russia and China could escalate into a nuclear war very quickly. I must warn you that the danger of a nuclear war is greater now, in my judgement, than at any time since the Cuban crisis.'

'All because of a couple of scraps of paper.' The foreign secretary crossed one leg over the other in his usual indolent pose.

'Brigadier Stuart, you must get us some harder evidence,' the prime minister leaned back, irritation sharpening his voice. 'Why do we have all those agents in Russia? Why can't you get them to work on that code?'

One of Stuart's most valuable traits was that he never lost his temper. 'Our agents are not cryptoanalysts sir,' he explained patiently. 'And nobody can do anything with the letters we have so far anyway. But I do have a suggestion to make about the code. If and when we get messages coming through in it, we shall need to break them very quickly. I would like to get the best people working on it without delay.'

'Well?'

'Some of the best people in cryptoanalysis are civilians. There is one in particular we ought to recruit who had a great success with the field code the Russians used in Hungary in 1956. If you would turn to page five of your files . . .'

Maguire saw on page five the name of the man who had taught him philosophy at Oxford. 'Good God,' he looked up, 'John Coomb.'

'Precisely, Mr Maguire,' Brigadier Stuart was regarding him with those cool, protruding eyes again. 'With the prime minister's permission, I'd like to ask you to stop over in Hong Kong and approach him on your trip to Tokyo next week.'

'Hong Kong? What on earth's he doing in Hong Kong?'

The prime minister had shown his independence by stubbornly resisting the first of Brigadier Stuart's suggestions. So he felt he could give a little on the second – to strike some sort of psychological bargain with Brigadier Stuart. Perhaps Stuart was intuitively aware of what had happened, but the others were confident they were guided solely by reason and fact.

TOP SECRET

M1/S10/C/71/203

Report No.: 71/7/75
Compiled on: 28.07.71

Subject: Coomb, John
Date of birth: 3.06.29
Place of Birth: Islington, London N1.
Father: Coomb, Wilfred. Nationality: Brit./Eng.
Mother: Coomb, Lucy. Nationality: Brit./Eng. (maiden name: Smith)
Father's occupation: Clerk. Retired, 1962.
Mother's occupation: Housewife. Deceased, 1954.
Present Address: Tai Peng, Lamma Island, Hong Kong. British Crown Colony.
Personal data:
   1939–45 Islington Borough High School.
   1945–47 National Service. Trained as cryptoanalyst, attached BAOR (service reports at Annex I).
   1947–51 Balliol College, Oxford University.

1951–60 Fellow of Magdalen College, Oxford.
1958 Married Suk-Yee Chan, Hong Kong Chinese (Annex V).
1960–66 Professor of Logic, University of London.
1961 Daughter, Sarah, born.
1966 Resigned from London University and went to live at present address. No paid occupation since 1966.

Religion: None.
Health: Good.
Political affiliation: See Special Remarks.

Special Remarks:

(i) Daughter suffers from a form of leukaemia, allegedly contracted from involuntary exposure to radioactivity in USA. Disease first diagnosed in 1964. It is regarded as incurable (Annex IV).

(ii) Gave 'personal reasons' for resigning from London University – probably daughter's illness. Lives mainly on wife's income, who is daughter of Chinese manufacturer in Hong Kong (Annex V).

(iii) Since resignation has been involved in peaceful activities against nuclear weapons and atomic power stations and in 'ecological' movements (1968 onwards). No record of extremism. No affiliation to normal political parties at any time. Has visited China with his wife for three weeks, June 1970. Met and corresponded with Soviet and East European academicians at Philosophy and Logic Congresses held in 1959, 1963, 1967, but no evidence that anything except academic matters was discussed. Surveillance until 1967 did not reveal any suspicious contacts. Has been invited to attend Congress in Moscow in August 1971. Has accepted.

(iv) Has been suing government of US and the US Atomic Energy Commission since 1965, alleging negligence in radiation control as cause of daughter's illness.

(v) Has published two books on mathematical logic and seventeen papers in professional journals. Since resignation from London University has published only three articles on environmental matters (Annex II). Is now completing a book on environment/ecology for publication by W. H. Allen in 1972.

(vi) Prior to marriage was consulted regularly about analysis of codes used in intelligence operations of other powers. Instrumental in breaking Russian field code used in Hungary in 1956 (Annex I). Not consulted since 1956 owing to marriage to a Chinese, which was considered to indicate security risk. Case reviewed annually, but risks judged to have increased marginally with involvement in environment/ecology movements.

Character analysis:

(i) Potentially unstable, but controlled. Unsociable: has only one known close friend, a fellow of Magdalen College, Oxford, whom he usually visits when in UK (Annex VI). Rarely visits widowed father, writes approximately once every two months. Regarded as unapproachable by most colleagues.

(ii) Generally held to have done his best work before he went to London. Involvement with environment/ecology groups may be motivated by desire to excel that was frustrated in his profession, but major motivation can be traced to sickness of child.

(iii) No deviant habits known. No criminal record.

Chapter Four

Chinese and Russian soldiers watched each other through their glasses along the banks of the Amur and the Ussuri. Every few days they clashed, warnings were shouted, shots fired, blood stained the sand or snow. Chinese loudspeakers broadcast accusations in Russian of Russian revisionism. Russian loudspeakers broadcast accusations in Chinese of Chinese intransigence. Behind the front lines lay the command posts, where skirmishes were recorded and sometimes prepared. Behind them lay the divisional and army headquarters of each side, where tactics and strategies were being developed and reviewed. And behind them lay Moscow and Peking, where different voices prevailed at different times, urging either peace or war. For policies were never settled. They changed with circumstances and the power of factions.

In Moscow, the hawks considered war with China inevitable and the moment opportune and the doves thought war would bring about a Russian Vietnam, which had to be avoided at all costs. In Peking, the purists thought war with Russia inevitable and victory certain and the pragmatists insisted war would destroy Chinese communism and be the ultimate annihilating disaster. On both sides, there were those who, for their own differing reasons, watched the approaching reconciliation of America and China with apprehension and misgiving. In Moscow, there was the fear of the unspeakable – an eventual Sino-American alliance. In Peking there was a corresponding fear – that the anticipation of such an alliance might lead the Russians to attack before China was strong enough to resist. And on both sides, there were those who wondered whether it was even necessary for the two great communist powers to be in opposition, whether some compromise couldn't, after all, be worked out.

Mao, Lin and Chou ruled China. They didn't always have the same tastes, either in politics or in food. The fourth most powerful man was Kang Sheng, head of the party's intelligence and security affairs department. He was always called 'Old Kang' even by Mao and Chou, who were several years older than he.

Peking, Monday, 2 August 1971
Chairman Mao waved Lin to his customary seat on his right, and Kang Sheng sat down on the Chairman's left. They watched the Chairman's favourite green tea being poured into the delicate rice-pattern cups and, following the Chairman, sipped it silently until they were alone.

Tiger Cat Lin glanced, his eyes mild under his bristly brows, at the signs of age in the Chairman's face – the deep lines, the sinking flesh, the loosening folds of skin, the slackening mouth and drooping lids. And yet beneath those drooping lids, the little eyes were still alert and shrewd. The Chairman was old, yes, but not decrepit. Even his scant hair was not yet grey. He dominated both the other men still and it was no formal courtesy that prompted them to wait until he chose to speak. Lin glanced from Mao's face down to the brush and ink on the table. Some strokes had been made on the paper and he felt a twinge of envy that the Chairman's calligraphy was still so bold and firm.

'Another poem,' Mao said in his thick Hunanese accent, divining rather than observing Lin's glance. He put his cup down, licking his lips. 'As I grow older, I wish I had more time . . .'

Kang Sheng and Lin smiled simultaneously. 'When we are old,' Kang blinked with watery eyes behind his thick lenses, 'we shall still not have the talent, even if we have the time.'

The Chairman laughed, a rumbling laugh that started deep in his belly. '*When* you're old, Old Kang? You've been old for fifty years.'

Kang Sheng blinked again behind his glasses. His high, domed forehead, wispy moustache and watery, myopic eyes gave him the appearance of a benign, rather owlish uncle, which was why he had always been called 'Old Kang'. His eyebrows were usually raised, corrugating his brows, so that he seemed to suffer from a condition of chronic perplexity.

Lin was wondering if it would seem extravagant to suggest it was time to publish an edition of the Chairman's later poems. But Mao turned to business now, glancing at him with those tiny sharp eyes which he seemed to keep sheathed behind their heavy lids.

'As it is a security matter you want to discuss,' he smiled, so that his face became a wrinkled mass of skin in which the eyes almost disappeared again, 'I've asked Old Kang to come as well.'

'Of course,' Lin nodded quickly, 'I expected he would be here.'

But Old Kang only gazed at them both owlishly, as if, despite the Chairman's explanation, he was still surprised and even embarrassed to find himself there.

'It is also a military matter, though,' Lin went on in his reedy voice.

'Well?' Mao turned the full bland oval of his face towards Lin. 'Do you think the Russians are likely to attack, then?' It was the thought in all their minds.

Lin glanced round the walls of the study as he answered. Mao's books were marshalled along each one from floor to ceiling in silent grandeur, somehow reflecting the imposing stature of their owner. Outside the window, two guards patrolled beneath the trees, red Mao badges poised like spots of blood over their hearts.

'They are ready,' he nodded slowly. 'And if they are going to make a full-scale land attack, they will have to do it in September at the latest.'

'And if not a full-scale land attack?' Mao's eyes were interrogating him still. He knew the answers, but still he wanted to hear them said.

34

'A strike against our nuclear sites.' He coughed, a tight, hard, painful cough. His chest wound always bothered him in the humid summers. 'Or against Peking itself.'

The chair groaned slightly as Mao turned slowly to Old Kang, hunched behind the thick walls of his glasses.

'What the Russians want is a change of government,' Old Kang blinked straight ahead, his brows rising still higher. 'There are those in China who also want a change of government . . .'

'Ahh . . .' the Chairman breathed rather than spoke. The chair groaned again as he reached slowly for his tea. He sucked it up with thoughtful but noisy relish.

Old Kang was still blinking puzzledly into space. 'The main danger is from an attempt to seize power by people who would then make a deal with the Russians. The policy of normalization with America could provide an excuse.' His eyes seemed to grow vacant, as if he were actually seeing into the future now, not merely guessing. 'It could be said that the leadership had betrayed the revolution by moving closer to the arch imperialist and capitalist power. Friendship with Russia could be said to be the natural state, which the new government would restore. It could be said . . .' He stopped and looked at the Chairman, blinking circumspectly.

The Chairman put his cup down slowly. 'It's easy to see you were trained in Moscow, Old Kang,' he said drily.

Old Kang's brows seemed to lift still higher and he peered now at Lin, as if puzzled by this last remark. 'Tiger Cat Lin has spent more years in Russia than I have. I think he will agree with me.'

Lin nodded, fingering the little round Mao badge in his lapel. 'The Russians might not want a prolonged war, but an adventure like that could be successful. That is why your personal safety is so important.'

The Chairman stroked the mole on his chin, turning his keen little eyes from Lin to Kang and back to Lin. 'Well?'

Lin coughed and went on. 'I propose a special combined force, to be composed of army and air force units. Their job would be to protect you and remove you to a place of safety if a threatening situation ever developed. They would be hand-picked, trained – '

'What is the 8341 Legion for?' the Chairman interrupted.

'They are your personal bodyguards, but we need more than bodyguards. We should have a unit of brigade strength with a squadron of planes deployed solely for your protection. The 8341 Legion has essentially a police role. What I am thinking of is a combined military operation. The group would have to work with the 8341 Legion, of course, but their roles would be different.'

'Hmm.' The Chairman fingered the mole on his chin again. *A block of granite with a wart on it*, Stalin had called Mao once, with mixed respect and scorn.

'This is a matter of political, not merely personal, significance,' Lin persisted in his high, nasal voice. 'The security of the revolution is bound up with your own security.'

Old Kang was peering into the future again. 'Who would command such a force?'

Lin looked at the Chairman.

'It should be considered,' Mao nodded at last.

'Who would command it?' Old Kang asked again.

'A good tactician with staff experience . . .' Lin began slowly.

The Chairman waved a limp hand. 'It should be considered,' he repeated. 'Draw up a plan and send it to me. Send me all the details.'

Mao's secretary came in and whispered to him. The Chairman had another appointment. Kang and Lin stood up while Mao remained seated, gazing down with hooded lids at his tea. 'What do you think now,' he asked slowly, 'of this business with America?' The question seemed addressed to both of them, but it was at Lin that he glanced first.

'I accept the decision that has been made,' Lin said after a moment, 'but I do not like it. The Russians may be provoked by it, but' – his cough interrupted him and he spluttered the last words – 'but the Americans won't give us missiles to fight them with.'

'You should take care of your cough.' The Chairman

looked down again musingly. He picked up the brush that lay beside his tea, dipped it in the ink and held it too long poised over the paper. A drop gathered, trembled and fell, making a large wet blot. The Chairman didn't seem to notice. 'It was hard for me to accept, too,' he muttered almost to himself.

'With my son killed in Korea, as well. But we must use one enemy against the other, one against the other . . .' He looked up suddenly at Kang Sheng, his voice rising with unexpected strength. 'Eh, Old Kang, isn't that right?'

But Old Kang merely raised his brows a little higher, his watery eyes blinking back at the Chairman. 'It is the policy,' he acknowledged vaguely.

Mao didn't look up when they left and didn't press the bell on his chair. His eyes, hooded again, gazed down at the tip of his brush, where another drop of ink was forming like a black tear. The tear shivered and fell, enlarging the pool made by the first drop. He gazed into the glistening surface of the pool, seeing faces pass across it like reflections in an autumn pond. He saw the face of his first son, An-Ying, killed by American bombs in Korea, the face of his second wife, shot by Chiang Kai-Shek, the face of his third wife, whom he divorced against everyone's will to marry his fourth, Chiang Ching. And the face of Chiang Ching herself, whom he no longer loved nor even trusted. But then, whom could he trust?

He'd climbed to the summit of power again, he'd gained a last chance to mould China before he died, but still he didn't really know how many of his comrades shared his vision, how many he could trust to pursue it until the thing was done. Lin? Was Lin really with him? They marched in step now, but when Lin succeeded him, would he change pace? Chou? No, Chou was always dragging him back, forcing this American policy on him against his will, for instance. Lin was right there – Chou was pliant, persuasive and persistent. No, they'd never really agreed. Though each needed the other to survive, they were like dog and cat and trusted each other no more than dog and cat. Old Kang? Old Kang was a functionary – his loyalty was to offices and roles, not to people. He could serve Lin in his time as loyally as he'd served him, no matter what Lin's policies were.

And Chiang Ching and her lot. How could it be that he felt he no longer knew her mind, that he couldn't trust her? She'd fought beside him like a tigress in the cultural revolution, and yet there had been things done behind his back, against his will, which he couldn't forget. How could he lose trust in his own wife? He watched another black tear fall from his brush onto the page, breaking, then widening the surface of the glistening little pool. Suddenly his lips puckered wrily and he snorted at himself. 'How could he lose trust in his own wife?'! What a question to ask. Wasn't that the predicament of every husband?

He sighed and pressed the bell at last. No, there was only Chan Tung-Hsing, commander of the bodyguards. He was loyal all right. But Chan was just a fighting dog, loyal to his master without caring what his master thought. Or even understanding. His son's face appeared again in the shiny black pool of ink. *I've never seen his grave*, he thought as he heard the door open. *Perhaps I shall leave nothing behind me after all. Perhaps it will all vanish in the dark.*

Chiang Ching was frowning as she sat down.

'What was so important that I had to be kept waiting half an hour?'

'Old Kang and Lin.'

She reached across and twisted the paper to read what he'd written. 'And what did they want?'

'That doesn't concern you,' he said brusquely, laying the brush down at last. When he'd married her, he'd promised them all he'd never let her take part in politics. In big things he'd broken his word, but in small things he still tried to keep it.

She shrugged off the rebuke. It made no difference, she'd find out anyway in the end. 'You've blotted this,' she held up the paper so the ink ran and became suddenly ugly. 'Look, it's spoiled. What was it, a poem?'

'A melancholy one,' he answered shortly. 'Or it would have been. Throw it away.'

Chapter Five

At breakfast time, the VC10 was flying over the central plains of India and Maguire was drinking his second cup of coffee. He looked down thirty thousand dizzying feet at the plane's shadow rippling effortlessly across the folded brown hills and scorched barren earth, where half a million starving, unseen people looked up vacantly and starved.

The pretty Chinese hostess leaned across to take his empty cup. Her graceful, pale-skinned fingers reminded him of a Chinese scroll that had hung ever since he could remember in the hall of his home in Yorkshire. He glanced back down the aisle to the economy-class cabin, where his secretary, Jane Wellcome, sat. She was dabbing her mouth with a napkin. Her fingers looked pink and stubby. So ungraceful, so well adapted to the typewriter.

When he was twenty-six, Maguire had succeeded to his father's safe rural seat in parliament, from which he would never be dislodged except by revolution. He had been treasurer of the union at Oxford, made thoughtful speeches and inherited his father's political friends as well as his house, his investments and his seat. So he had risen swiftly in the party without any great effort, or even ambition, of his own.

As parliamentary private secretary to the minister of state for foreign affairs, he was being tried in office for the first time. And he had begun to feel vague, uneasy stirrings of disenchantment and futility. He had come to believe less fully in the policies of the government he had joined, to sense

39

more strongly the incapacity of politicians to change, or even comprehend, the stream of history on which they drifted. He had begun to feel less and less comfortable acting out his role in what he half-consciously regarded as something of a farce. Yet he lacked the certainty, determination or energy to be critical or to resign. So he had gone on, passively acquiescing to what he could not change.

But Brigadier Stuart's briefing had disturbed his usual passivity. The prime minister and foreign secretary had scoffed at Stuart's analysis because they didn't want to believe it; Maguire had believed it because he didn't want to scoff. Not that he had any more reason to believe than to scoff. Certainly not that he grasped what it would mean for Russian nuclear warheads to fall on Chinese cities – perhaps only the few survivors of Hiroshima could grasp that. Only that at last he had begun to feel free from that indistinct sense of drift and futility. At last a clear issue seemed to lie before him, in which what should be done was also clear. So clear that he'd even written a memo to the foreign secretary the next morning, strongly recommending that the Americans should be informed of Stuart's assessment after all. The foreign secretary had phoned him in the afternoon and told him urbanely that it was out of the question. Never mind, he was acting, doing – that was what mattered. It was a release, a catharsis. He'd broken out of the cocoon of helpless ineffectiveness in which he'd gradually been suffocating.

He'd arranged another briefing with Brigadier Stuart and gone through Coomb's file with an intense meticulousness, adding to it all he could remember of him as his teacher at Oxford. What he recalled was daunting. Coomb was rude, impatient and unfriendly, but that only made the task of recruiting him more challenging. Brigadier Stuart had said Coomb would be invaluable if they could get him, but he was afraid they couldn't. Maguire had almost promised they would. He was excited, fulfilled. One of his uncles had won the Victoria Cross at Ypres in 1917. Perceptive and sophisticated though he was in some ways, in others Maguire was naïve – he wanted to be a hero too.

The plane's shadow rippled across the brown hills and barren earth of India, where half a million unseen people looked up vacantly and starved.

It was after tea when the VC10 tilted into its approach to Hong Kong.

'You can see land if you look out.' Jane brushed past the hostess into the first-class compartment, carrying a tea-cup and dabbing at her lips again. A smudge of cherry lipstick stained her cup.

Maguire raised his blind and looked down. Little rocky islands, covered with dense, vivid green foliage. Wooden junks with stiff, winglike sails, rust-red and grey, immobile on a glittering blue sea. *Like toy yachts*, he thought, reminded of the paper boats his grandfather used to make him on summer afternoons at Scranton. He saw himself for a moment pushing them out across the little lake that seemed so vast and deep then, saw them floating stiff and still on the glassy surface. Then he noticed the plane's shadow again, flitting beneath them over the waveless China sea.

The undercarriage went down with a shuddering thud and the engine note changed to a high-pitched whine. Maguire felt that faint lurch of apprehension in his stomach, that primal fear of falling, which he had to conquer every time he flew.

'What time is it in Hong Kong?' he asked Jane quickly, glancing at his watch.

She was going back to her seat, obedient to the *Fasten Seat Belts* sign. 'They're eight hours ahead of London.'

The plane sank lower. Over little islands, jagged shores bordered with surf, green jutting hills with clusters of white houses on them. Then more junks, dozens of them now, and at last land again, factories, crowded streets, acres of concrete blocks. Suddenly, as they seemed about to touch down, they were over the sea once more, sinking rapidly. Freighters in the harbour slipped by at mast height. Maguire's palms moistened and his fingers tightened around the arm of his seat, but then he felt the rescuing solidity of a runway beneath them like a road in the sea and the plane settled

41

back, bounced, fell gently down again and ran smoothly on along the tarmac.

'Half an hour late,' Jane chirped. 'I suppose they'll have air-conditioning things? I wonder what time the shops shut. You won't need me tonight, will you?'

'Your first visit to the East, I believe?' the political adviser inquired blandly. He ushered Maguire from the VIP lounge into first the oppressively humid heat of the open air, then the cool of an air-conditioned black Daimler. He was a little older and far more assured than Maguire, and he'd handled the press with nonchalant ease, steering the junior minister out of the room as soon as he'd uttered his rehearsed piece. The purpose of his stopover was to acquaint himself with Hong Kong's special trading position in preparation for his forthcoming talks in Tokyo, Maguire had said. A group of glum reporters, Chinese and European, had looked him over indifferently and a few cameras had flashed. 'As I understand, you'd rather not attract too much attention,' the political adviser had murmured suavely. 'I hope you won't mind the rather muted welcome we're giving you.'

The Daimler moved serenely away and the political adviser slid the glass partition across, insulating them from the Chinese driver in his white drill uniform. Maguire, one hand on his briefcase, watched the crowded, shabbily colourful streets pass by the window as if through a smoothly changing kaleidoscope. Garish shop signs hanging out across the streets, covered with Chinese characters; women in wide straw hats humping hods of bricks at a building site; men in neat, dark suits carrying neat, dark briefcases; raucous street markets, squalid tenements, ostentatious hotels; arrogant traffic policemen in khaki shorts and shirts, with revolvers at their belts; red London double-decker buses passing stringy men pulling rickshaws. Everywhere noise and crowds.

'I've warned Mr Coomb you're coming,' the political adviser was leaning back in his corner. 'He's expecting you to give him a ring tonight, after dinner. The governor hopes you'll be able to have dinner with him, by the way.'

Maguire nodded, 'That's very kind. How did he take the news that I was coming?'

'Coomb? I've only spoken to him on the phone, of course. And I was deliberately . . . noncommittal. Just said you were an old friend and you'd like to meet him as you were passing through.'

'Not really an old friend. Only a former pupil.'

'Ah.' The political adviser seemed uninterested in the distinction.

'How did he take it?'

The political adviser waited until they'd passed a pneumatic drill blasting at the pavement before he answered. 'Well, he seemed a bit surprised, that's all. Nobody knows much about him here. He's written tiresome letters to the press about pollution and that kind of thing. But nothing that brings him exactly into my sphere of activity. Bit of a crank, by the sound of it, but, like many cranks, I gather he may have his uses?'

Maguire glanced at his briefcase. 'He may indeed.' And he secretly welcomed the interested look the political adviser threw him.

'I asked if he'd like us to pick him up and bring him to meet you in government house, incidentally, but he seemed to prefer *being* visited to visiting.'

'I'm not surprised; it's in character so far as I remember him.'

'He was rather blunt, in fact,' the political adviser chuckled. 'Said he'd no intention of coming to government house to meet anyone. Ever.'

'Hm. He's a blunt man. His child is seriously ill of course.'
'Yes?'

'But he's always been blunt,' Maguire cancelled the implied excuse. 'At least, he was when he was my tutor at Magdalen, which must have been long before his child got ill. Before she was born, even.'

'Ah. When were you up at Magdalen?' the political adviser sensed a topic they could explore comfortably and safely until they reached government house.

43

Chapter Six

Peking, Tuesday, 3 August 1971

'Engineering Project 571 is going ahead,' the stocky Korean repeated woodenly in his stilted Chinese. He nodded emphatically as he spoke, and with every nod he memorized a word. He closed his eyes, saw the words printed on his mind and looked at the hooded man again.

'But there must be no more leaks in the pipes,' the Chinese voice went on, muffled through the black hood. 'Otherwise we may have to abandon it. They must see there are no more leaks.'

Again the Korean repeated the words, nodding them into his memory. 'Anything else?'

'No. Not yet.'

The Korean glanced at the figure behind the desk. The dark hood hung loosely from the man's shoulders, concealing his arms and body in a baggy anonymity. Only his shoes were visible under the sack, small and black. The anonymity didn't prick the Korean's curiosity. Not much did. Once he had gone a whole year hearing messages on one phone and repeating them into another, without having any idea either who was speaking to him or who he was speaking to. There were usually other things on his mind; there were now. 'I would like a Japanese camera', he said abruptly. 'To reach my home in Pyong Yang. A Minolta SL.'

The eyes flickered behind the hood. 'You have been paid already. You have had furniture, equipment, dollars – '

'It isn't much,' the Korean interrupted sullenly. 'Don't

44

forget my tour with the embassy ends this month. I won't get another chance.'

'You may have to stay until the end of September. It has been arranged with Pyong Yang. You can expect a promotion when you get back, incidentally.'

The Korean's eyes narrowed slightly. He hadn't realized he was dealing with people who would fix things like that. But he persisted stolidly after a moment. 'It wouldn't be much trouble to arrange a camera for me.'

The hooded figure sighed and nodded acquiescence at last. 'Very well. Write down the name and model. I'll see what can be done.'

'I've got them here.' The Korean took a slip of paper out of his pocket, unfolded it and placed it with both hands on the desk. It occurred to him that the man was small and spare – something about the way the hood hung down in loose folds from the narrow, angular shoulders. But the thought slipped out of his mind unheeded. 'And the usual payment?'

'It has already been made. You will find it in your account for this month.'

'Ah.' The Korean didn't doubt him. He had found spymasters the most reliable of employers. They never bilked. The penalties were too high.

'We shall tell you in the usual way when we need you,' the hooded head nodded dismissal.

Outside the house was a paved courtyard. The Korean walked quickly across it, paused by the old wooden gate, then let himself out. The slightly stooping Chinese, who had taken off the hooded robe and now held it over his arms, watched him through the narrow slats of the shutters upstairs. The gate opened onto a dusty lane. The Korean walked down it in the shade of the peeling wall, towards the street at the end.

The street teemed with cyclists on their way home from work, men and women alike in their blue overalls, faces sweating in the slanted afternoon sunlight, tyres sizzling on the burned, dusty tarmac. He made his way across the road and down to the number 47 bus stop. A throng of workers was waiting there patiently beneath a red placard inscribed with golden characters, *Study and Carefully Apply the Principles of Mao Tse-Tung Thought.*

The stocky Korean waited patiently too, thinking of his Minolta camera.

Chapter Seven

The only dead man Maguire had ever seen was his father, whose heart had simply stopped beating while he slept. Maguire was intelligent, sensitive and humane. He knew that war was terrible, and he thought it appalling that two-thirds of the world's people were undernourished and that between ten and twenty million of them were born to starve each year. He carried in his briefcase terse, factual projections of dead and injured if one Russian rocket strayed into Hong Kong, or if there were merely a limited nuclear exchange between the great powers, or if general nuclear war developed.

But all this knowledge was detached. The millions of deaths and the devastation of the earth foretold so matter-of-factly stirred his imagination no more than the thought of a thousand dead flies and a bonfire. 'Nothing ever becomes real,' Keats said once, 'till it is experienced.' And the trouble was that Maguire had not experienced enough. The thought of death for him was merely the almost cosy thought of an elderly rich man lying well-fed in bed. No matter how well he knew the picture was false, his imagination had nothing else to feed on. And so the figures in his briefcase were inert abstractions.

What stirred him now was what he experienced now – the glamour of a special mission, the prospects of success and praise, the excitement of the extraordinary. And after all, as the political adviser had said, it *was* his first visit to the East.

47

Lamma Island, Hong Kong, Tuesday, 3 August 1971

Coomb's voice had sounded as curt over the phone as it used to fourteen years ago when Maguire knocked on his door in Magdalen and waited for an unwelcoming shout to call him in. Maguire's confidence had ebbed after the phone call, but now, as he stood in the cabin of a dark blue police launch, watching the sunset melting the flawless sky, it began to rise again. The launch cut through the placid sea, leaving a widening streak of foaming wake behind it. Maguire, still gripping his briefcase, leaned out to feel the salty air blowing on his face. Twenty minutes after leaving the landing dock in Hong Kong, he stepped ashore onto a narrow wooden jetty on Lamma Island. He followed a lithe young Chinese detective up a stony path to the top of a little hill.

Again the thick sultry heat, the lifeless air oppressing the land. He had changed into an open cotton shirt and trousers following a hurried dinner at government house, but after a few yards he could feel his clothes beginning to cling to him as his body sweated. The detective walked on briskly, waiting for him at the top of the hill. Maguire noticed with chagrin that his olive skin looked cool and dry. A bulge under his loose, orange shirt suggested he was more than just a guide.

The hill rioted with green. Shrubs, creepers, elephant grass, a matted green jungle with scarcely a flower or tree. Green pressed upon green, except where the path had been hacked out of it, or where huge brown-grey granite rocks poked through like bones.

The detective nodded down the other side. A narrow bay, already shadowed by the hillside, a few junks and sampans resting motionless on the still water, a single line of white-washed stone houses fringing the beach. They walked down, out of the last light of the sun into the sudden-falling dusk.

'That house there, sir,' the detective pointed to a large house at the far end of the village. 'I wait for you here.' And he leaned against the hull of a boat rotting on the beach.

Maguire nodded. 'I hope I won't be long, Inspector er . . . ?'

'Detective Inspector Tsang.'

'Inspector Tsang, I hope I won't be long.'

'Never mind, sir.' He took a cigarette from his shirt pocket.

A little path wandered along the edge of the beach to Coomb's house. Four or five boats were moored near the shore, and two men in shorts squatted in one of them, stowing away some fishing nets. The sea hardly sounded as it unfurled on the beach and drained away in the wet sand.

The houses were small and shabby, plaster and whitewash flaking off the walls. Dogs barked as he passed, children and women peered out at him from open doorways. Paraffin lamps glowed in the darkness of the bare little rooms, which had shutters but no windows. The smell of cooking fish drifted out to hang in the torpid air. Maguire sensed the slow monotony of time here, where life was governed by poverty, the sea and the sun. He wondered absurdly for a moment whether there was a sewage system and, if not, where their sewage went (it went into the little garden at the back of each house) and then, more sensibly, what would have induced an intellectual like Coomb to bury himself alive in such a place.

A large dalmation suddenly bounded up to him from the side of Coomb's house, barking deep-voiced and loud. Maguire stopped, holding his briefcase out for the dog to sniff, then walked on. The house was larger and newer than the others, reminding him briefly of the manor house in an English village. It was freshly painted in white, with green window frames and doors. The windows were large. Lights shone in every one, upstairs and downstairs, the warm yellow glow of oil lamps. A long green veranda ran the entire length of one wall. The door was open. He walked towards it while the dog trotted at his heels, alternatively sniffing and growling. There was the sound of voices and then Coomb appeared, framed in the doorway with the light behind him.

'Ah,' Coomb glanced at his watch as he called the dog off. 'You're punctual, Mr Maguire.' And Maguire remembered at once the chilly remoteness of Coomb at Oxford, his formality – or was it sarcasm? – in always calling him *Mr* Maguire while every other tutor called him either Maguire or Harry.

They shook hands awkwardly on the doorstep. Coomb had aged. His brown, scrubby hair was still rebellious and brown, his grey eyes still pale and cold, but his face had grown thinner and was scored by deep lines. Maguire had forgotten that he, too, must look older, but Coomb reminded him brusquely.

'Politics seems to have aged you Mr Maguire. You looked less careworn as an undergraduate.'

'It's nice to see you again,' Maguire began lamely, but Coomb was already leading the way into a large room on one side of the hall – white walls hung with oriental rugs and scrolls, windows open to the veranda, oil lamps hissing, cool, tiled floors.

A slim Chinese woman came towards him from the veranda, dressed like Coomb in sandals, cotton shirt and trousers.

'My wife,' grunted Coomb, not troubling to introduce him to her.

The woman smiled. They shook hands. Maguire thought she had strong, rather beautiful, features. She looked many years younger than Coomb.

'You used to be a student of John's?' She spoke with an American accent.

'Not a very diligent one, I'm afraid.'

Coomb grunted again, assenting. 'Didn't want to bother with serious work. That's why he's gone into politics, I suppose.'

She laughed, gesturing Maguire to a seat. 'What do you know about it, John?' She sat down composedly in a bamboo rocking-chair and asked Maguire about his journey. Coomb interrupted his answer to offer him, in his boorish way, a drink.

'Whisky or beer? That's all we've got.'

Maguire chose whisky and water. Coomb strode out, his sandals slapping on the floor. Maguire noticed a green mosquito coil smouldering in a saucer in the middle of the room, a plume of thick, incense-like smoke streaming straight up from its glowing tip, then curling and drifting away. He nodded at it. 'They have them in Italy, too.'

'Yes. Serpenti.' She said the word in Italian.

'You know Italy?'

'I lived in Florence for a time, yes.'

'A beautiful city.'

'Yes.' Her face softened as she smiled, as if she were remembering. Maguire guessed the strength he had noticed in her features was learned rather than natural.

A grey-haired servant shuffled in, carrying two whiskies on a little wooden tray. Coomb's wife spoke to her in Chinese, and the woman answered with the easy familiarity which old family servants – he could still just remember from his childhood – often acquire. She wore baggy black trousers, black pointed slippers and a white high-necked tunic. Her grey hair was plaited in a long queue which hung down her back.

Maguire took his drink. The servant spoke again, looking curiously from Mrs Coomb to him, and Mrs Coomb laughed as she answered.

'She wants to know why you haven't got a uniform on. She knew you were from the government in England.'

'Oh, I must be a disappointment to her.'

'No,' and she laughed again. 'Well, yes, frankly.'

'She's been with you a long time?'

'Ever since I was born. My mother got her to look after me and she just stayed.'

'Ah.' Maguire lifted his glass and then –

'Where's your wig?' Coomb's voice grated harshly behind him. Mrs Coomb's eyes tensed, the servant turned and Coomb's voice grated again.

'Wig on, Sarah!'

Maguire turned too.

He saw a completely bald girl of about nine or ten standing in the doorway looking at him. She was wearing a white vest and pink shorts. Her skin was a very pale, nearly transparent,

51

olive colour, as if the blood had been drained away beneath it. She was thin, a little round-shouldered, with pale lips. Her eyes seemed very large in the soft lamplight. She was gazing at Maguire with a curious, luminously patient gaze. Her face was neither Oriental nor Western – or rather it was both.

'Hello,' she said and smiled.

Maguire must have absorbed this almost instantly, for within a second or two the servant had shuffled towards her, hissing strangely under her breath, Mrs Coomb had said 'Sarah' in a mildly remonstrating tone and Coomb had swept the girl up with an almost brutal tenderness and carried her off in his arms, followed by the shuffling servant.

The girl questioned Coomb and he answered gruffly as his feet clumped, sandals slapping, up the wooden stairs. Maguire turned back, the image of the small, round, bumpy skull slowly fading from his eyes.

Mrs Coomb's face was arranging itself again. 'Are you married, Mr Maguire?' she asked tranquilly after a moment.

'No, I . . .'

'That was our daughter.'

'Yes?'

'Sarah.'

'Sarah?'

'She's not very well, I'm afraid.'

Maguire looked down at the rich, tawny whisky in his glass, uncertain whether or not to tell her he already knew about her daughter.

'But I expect you noticed that?' She smiled as he nodded, then got up. 'Excuse me a moment. I'll just settle her down. John's kind of heavy-handed. I expect you've noticed that too?'

Maguire rose, smiled, listened to her sandals slapping up the stairs and sat down, looking round the room again.

The rugs on the floor were Persian and Chinese. There were three more hanging on the walls, with ragged tassels. He glanced without understanding at the scrolls hanging down between them. These were the only luxuries in the room. The furniture was all simple bamboo and rattan, the chairs with bright orange cushions on them.

He got up and walked out onto the veranda. Another green mosquito coil was smouldering on the floor, giving off the same heavy, fragrant scent. He gazed out over the beach and sea, already darker now. A mile or two away, the lights of Hong Kong island gleamed and twinkled in the humid air, some in dense clusters and rows, some strung out like beads across the dark shapes of the hills. His eye followed a long, looping thread of orange lights marking some road. Over the denser clusters, the sky itself glowed faintly, reflecting the lights beneath. The image of Coomb's pale, bald daughter hung in the back of his mind as he looked out across the quietly breathing sea. Baldness made her look prematurely aged, and the large Eurasian eyes gave her a gentle, vulnerable look. There had been a long blue vein running over her head, he remembered. Maguire wondered whether her hair had been shaved off for some reason or had simply fallen out. He tried to imagine a million people looking like her, the survivors of nuclear war, slowly dying of radiation sickness. But all he saw was Sarah's pale face and her large eyes, in itself neither ugly nor even sad.

Coomb's sandals slapped down the stairs and into the room. The dog's claws clipped over the tiles beside him.

'A nice view, Mr Maguire.' He took his glass from the tray and joined Maguire, thumping rather than patting the dog's bony head.

'Your wife told me your daughter was ill,' Maguire turned, 'I'm sorry.'

'Did she?' Coomb gazed past him into the night, ignoring his condolence. 'Well, what brings you to these parts?'

'I was on my way to Tokyo and, as I heard you were in Hong Kong . . .'

'You wouldn't have heard unless you had some reason to find out.' He closed his eyes as he gulped his whisky. Maguire noticed again how deep and long the furrows were in his face. Coomb smacked his lips with deliberate vulgarity. 'So what is it?'

Maguire glanced back at his briefcase lying by the chair. 'I have something for you to look at.'

'It's leukaemia, by the way.' Coomb was examining his glass, his head to one side.

'Yes I know. I'm sorry.'

'Ah.' Coomb was still examining his glass. 'So you've been reading some file on me, eh?'

Maguire hesitated, then went to get the briefcase without answering.

'I suppose it's a code?' Coomb followed him inside.

'Yes.'

'Hm.' Coomb swallowed the rest of his drink. 'Why now, after so long? I haven't touched a code for years.'

'Apparently it's your kind of code.' Maguire handed the file across to him and unclipped a black fountain pen from his shirt pocket. 'Would you mind signing that official secrets form first?'

'Ha, official secrets!' Coomb snorted, but signed.

'Well it's quite a serious business. As you'll see.'

'Hm. Another drink?'

'Oh. Yes, thank you. With a lot of water.'

Coomb called something in Chinese. Without knowing a word of the language, Maguire could hear that his accent was atrocious. The servant shuffled in and took their glasses, Coomb started reading the file holding it towards the lamp, ignoring Maguire. Maguire felt as if he were an undergraduate again, waiting uncomfortably for his tutor's comments on an essay he had written. But he had not written this one. It was all Brigadier Stuart's work.

Coomb sniffed, turned a page, sniffed again, then looked up at him. 'Come, come Mr Maguire,' he spoke in a tone of brusque weariness. 'I'm sure there are dozens of professional cryptoanalysts who could do this job. Why me?'

'A very special request was made for you by intelligence.'

'Hm.' He sniffed and went on reading. Maguire still stood awkwardly. The servant shuffled in again with their drinks. Maguire sipped his. It was nearly all whisky, with only a dash of water. Coomb sipped his too and grimaced, then called out irritably to the servant. She muttered back at him imperturbably from the kitchen and brought a bottle of water, which she placed with a slight but definite clunk on the table, still muttering as she shuffled out. Coomb helped himself first, then handed the bottle to Maguire. Maguire poured, watching the water swirl into the oily richness, then put the bottle down again. Coomb turned a page.

His wife's sandals sounded on the stairs. She came in and sat down in her rocking-chair again, lifting her bare feet out of the sandals. 'Why don't you two sit down?'

'Mm?' Coomb was still reading.

Maguire sat down. 'Has she gone to sleep?' he asked quietly.

'Sarah? Going. Did you give her her pills, John?'

'Mm?' Coomb looked up, frowning. 'Yes, of course, I'll take this into the study. It's too noisy here.'

Mrs Coomb laughed at him again, as if he were a child. 'Why must you be so cantankerous?'

Coomb grunted and walked out, followed by the dog. As Maguire went to shut the door after him, she raised her hand.

'No, leave it open, please. It's cooler.' But he realized that wasn't the real reason. Really, she was listening for any sound from upstairs.

She turned her head back to look out over the veranda, tipping her chair very gently back and forth with one foot. I'm sorry he's such a boor,' she spoke in a low, calm voice, although there was a slight frown on her forehead. 'Was he like that when he was teaching you?'

'I'm afraid he was, yes.'

Her lips pulled down into a smile. 'I'm always telling him about it, but it doesn't do any good.'

Maguire watched her from his chair. She didn't turn to him when she spoke, but gazed straight ahead so that he saw her in profile. Her American accent sounded incongruous, coming from that Chinese face. He took in the lines of her high cheekbones and slanting eyes, emphasized by the upward sweep of the black hair knotted severely on top of

55

her head. A pearl glistened in the lobe of her small and delicate ear.

For some time they sat without talking, listening to the wash of the waves on the beach. She seemed undisturbed by the silence between them, her face almost masklike in its watchful repose.

'Is it important?' Still she didn't turn her head.

'Why I came here?'

She nodded.

'Yes, it is.'

She nodded again, more slowly.

He drank from his glass and leaned back. Suddenly his eyes blurred for a moment, and he realized he was tired – his flight had lasted eighteen hours. He shifted in his chair. 'You can hear the sea here,' he said inconsequentially.

'Yes. Our boat's on the shore.'

She stopped rocking her chair. It creaked two or three times and then was still. 'Yes, it's very quiet,' she said, as much to herself as to him.

'You don't find it lonely, living here?'

She glanced at him before answering. 'I suppose we won't live here much longer.'

'Oh?'

'Sarah will have to go into hospital in England, soon.'

'I see.'

'They have the latest things there.'

'Yes.'

She spoke with such a detached calm that Maguire felt he wouldn't be trespassing if he asked more.

'Has she been ill for long?'

She didn't answer at first and her face remained immobile, only tensing faintly underneath the skin. Then she nodded. 'She's always had it – did John tell you what it was?'

'Yes.'

'She's always had it. Always.' Her voice had tightened slightly too, but on the surface she was as calm as before. 'She was exposed to it before she was born. I was working on an atomic power project in the States. I didn't know I was

56

pregnant. I didn't have more than the permitted dose of radiation, but it was too much for Sarah . . .' Her hand rose and fell limply on the arm of the chair. 'She had it before she was born.'

Maguire nodded, looked down at the floor, wondered what to say. His eyes watched the smoke curling up from the mosquito coil.

'The permitted dose is much too high anyway. A lot of scientists have said so, but they won't admit it.'

'They?'

She shrugged. 'The US Atomic Energy Authority. They don't want to admit they've made a mistake, I guess.' She laughed curtly under her breath. 'John's got an action going against them, as if that would be any use . . .' Her cheek twitched a moment and then her face was still once more.

Maguire drank again. The sea washed on the beach. The lamps hissed in the room.

'That's where we met,' she raised her brows reflectively. 'That's where I met John. He was spending a semester in the States.'

'Is there – what are the chances of a cure?'

'Today, none,' she shrugged briefly. 'Tomorrow, who knows?' Then, after a pause, 'It can be arrested for a time. We just have to hope, from one day to the next, one month to the next.'

Again they were silent, without any uneasiness between them, as if silence were the natural state, as perhaps it was for her, living on this remote island.

The sea washed on the beach, the lamps hissed in the room.

'No, I'm not lonely here,' she resumed the thread she'd let fall a few minutes before. 'There's quite a lot to do with Sarah, and she has to go for treatment a few days every month anyway, so I'm not here all the time. You can see the hospital lights over there.' She nodded out over the sea. 'Besides, I'm kind of a solitary person anyway, I guess.' Again the incongruity of the perfect American idiom and the Chinese face. 'And John's become a recluse too. He can work here without being disturbed.'

57

Maguire was glad to be able to steer their talk away from her child. 'I gather he's given up logic and philosophy?'

'He's gone into other things, yes. He seems to think the world's ending,' she laughed, looking at Maguire at last. 'Well I guess it must end some day, mustn't it?' There was a rueful humour in her eyes. Her lips, Maguire noticed, were full and sensuous, though pale.

'How far has he got with it?'

'The book? Nearly finished. There's a final draft on the table over there. You should take a look at it. He'd be flattered, secretly.'

'Have you read it?'

She shook her head briefly and gave a wry smile. 'I've got other things on my mind.'

Maguire nodded again. He was beginning to think her face had a statuesque kind of beauty after all, as well as strength. He wondered whether she could influence her husband.

'Is he very busy now?' he began warily.

'John? Why?'

'Well if he agreed to help the government, he'd have to spend a few weeks in London. But if he's very busy, I expect he wouldn't want to.'

'Is it a code?' she looked directly at him again.

'Yes.'

'Well, one of the things he'll forgive me for,' she smiled, 'is that he wasn't asked to help with any more codes after he married me.'

Before he could answer, a faint coughing sounded from upstairs.

With a murmured 'Excuse me,' she got up and slipped out of the room, leaving her sandals on the floor. Her empty chair creaked as it rocked back and forth.

Maguire's eyes felt misty and blurred again. The humid air seemed to press down on his tired lids. He forced himself to get up, finished his whisky and wandered round the room, fingering the silken rugs that hung on the walls. There was no sound from upstairs, nor from across the hall, where Coomb's study presumably was.

58

He walked to the table. A large porous stone from some beach stood as a paperweight on the sheaf of typed pages she had pointed to. He lifted the stone and started reading. The first page was heavily corrected. He recognized Coomb's spidery scrawl at once, looping over the lines, deleting and changing words, scribbling abbreviated notes in the margin. It was hard for Maguire to find his way through the corrections as he read.

Preface to the Collapse of Industrial Civilization

The decline and fall of industrial civilization is imminent, though not inevitable, and the main stages of the decline and eventual collapse are already clear. While no one can say with certainty when the first stage will occur, what that stage will be, and what the next, can already be safely predicted.

The new age which daily approaches, and which we have the power but not the will to avert, will be one in comparison with which the Dark Ages were a glorious dawn. If it comes, it will come in two or three generations. The children of children now living may perhaps look back on our present age as on a golden age and marvel that man's highest civilization passed so quickly from the face of the earth. Perhaps fading memories of that golden age will rub bitter gall into the sores of hunger, disease, poverty and wolfish war that will be the common destiny of mankind. Will they seek for bizarre explanations, incredulous that so much could have been destroyed and lost only by obtuseness, apathy and greed? . . .

. . . The simple truth is that industrial man is invisibly destroying the things by which he lives. When they are gone – as they surely will go, unless he changes the manner of his existence now – he, too, must go. We have only to continue as we have in the past to cause our own destruction. What was the recipe for yesterday's success will be the formula for tomorrow's disaster. Obtuseness, apathy and

greed will in all likelihood prevent men from seeing, let alone avoiding, the impending catastrophe, until suddenly it will be too late. . . .

. . . One thing alone can prevent the accelerating progress of our collapse, but that thing demands from men now in power qualities of vision, energy and unselfishness which they do not possess. . . .

Maguire put the stone back and stood gazing down at the typescript. The sombre rhetoric, moulding itself round the hard lines of Coomb's usual bony style, for some reason brought the image of Sarah's skull back into his mind. He riffled the pages with his thumbnail, then riffled them again.

The sea washed on the beach. The lamps hissed.

Gradually, he noticed another sound, the quiet, melancholy strains of a mouth organ. It came from the back of the house. He hesitated, then walked down into the kitchen. It was empty. A tap was dripping in the new, stainless-steel sink unit. A large brown cockroach scuttled across the floor, into a cupboard beneath the sink. Maguire walked across to turn the tap off harder, thinking as he did so that this must be the only house in the village that had plumbing.

The music was coming from outside. He went to the open door, quietly pushed the fly-screen open and looked out. The servant was squatting at the other end of a little stone yard, beneath the large, torn, floppy leaves of what he assumed was a banana tree. Her hands covered a mouth organ as she blew pensively on it, the lamplight from the kitchen falling across her face. Her eyes regarded him with a sort of neutral watchfulness, neither welcoming nor hostile. She was playing a tune he'd never heard before, unlike a Western melody. He listened and watched her while she watched him and played. Her hands moved as her mouth passed over the holes. After a while, she stopped and looked away from Maguire, gazing unseeingly in front of her.

He let the fly-screen close quiety and walked back along the little hall. The mournful tune began again. He had never seen a woman playing a mouth organ before.

60

The room was still empty. He noticed a little green lizard on the wall, as motionless as a stone.

He walked out onto the veranda again. The lights of Hong Kong gleamed brightly across the sea. The mast lamps of a junk were moving slowly across the bay in front of him. Still the faint wailing of the mouth organ continued. Maguire went back to the table, picked up Coomb's typescript in one hand, the stone in the other, and sat down in his chair. He started reading, cursorily at first, then with growing absorption. As he read each page, he laid it face down on the floor with the stone on top of it. He didn't notice when the mouth organ stopped. He forgot his tiredness. He didn't notice that the mosquito coil had gone out or that he was being bitten.

He read one and a half chapters in all, which, though they impressed him vividly at the time, he remembered only indistinctly afterwards. The theme was one that became increasingly familiar during the next five years – the ability of the earth to sustain its doubling human population; the impossibility of continuous economic growth; the vast and radical social changes that will have to occur for what we know as civilization to survive; and the psychological and institutional forces that obstruct these changes and will probably prevent them from taking place.

The things that distinguished Coomb's book from later ones, at least in Maguire's partial and uncertain recollection, were neither merely the deft command he seemed to have of every aspect of his subject – he was as much at ease with mathematical models as with marine biology, with economics as with political science, with psychology as with sociology – nor the clarity and succinctness of his arguments. Those Maguire would have expected. It was his all-pervading sombre sense of doom, of morose, sardonic hopelessness, of enjoyment, almost, and relish in despair that set Coomb apart. Several times, as he read, Maguire was reminded of an Old Testament prophet calling down, rather than warning of, the angels of famine, plague and death hovering over mankind. Whether his impressions would have been confirmed by other readers will never be known. For there were

61

no other readers. The book never reached the publishers. Coomb began it soon after his daughter's illness was diagnosed in nineteen sixty-four and worked on it unremittingly for six or seven years. All that survived those years of his life was a fragment of the preface. That, and the text of a paper which he delivered to a bewildered and uncomprehending congress of mathematical logicians.

Chapter Eight

It was over an hour later when he heard the study door open. Coomb's sandals slapped heavily and the dog's claws clipped lightly, over the floor. Maguire got up.

'I shall have to think about this, Mr Maguire,' Coomb tapped the file with his middle finger, then stopped, frowning at the papers in Maguire's hands. His lips pressed together. 'I should prefer it if you ask my permission before you read my work.'

Maguire looked at him in embarrassed surprise. 'I'm sorry, your wife suggested I should look at it.'

'She shouldn't have.' Coomb stooped to pick the type-script up from the floor, took the unread pages from Maguire's hand and gave him the file in return. 'Sorry to be so brutal about it,' he looked through the pages suspiciously, 'but I didn't think you'd go in for snooping in other people's private papers.'

'I can assure you I had no intention of snooping – '

'If you go on like this, you'll be prying in the prime minister's desk next.'

'Your wife suggested I should read it – '

'Don't suppose he'd take kindly to that, would he?'

Maguire felt his cheeks smarting. 'You know perfectly well I haven't been prying in anyone's desk. I've already told you twice it was at your wife's suggestion that I read it.'

'If my wife suggested you should inspect my bank statements, would you do that too?' Coomb shrugged irritably, turning his back on Maguire to replace the papers on the table. 'I don't expect to have to lock everything up just because you're coming, you know.' He slapped the stone down on top of them. 'Only hope you haven't mixed the pages up.'

Maguire gazed stiffly at his back. 'I think you'll find they're all in order.'

'Hmph.' Coomb turned round again. 'All right then, I'm sorry. Sit down. I'm touchy about these things. Sit down.' He bent over to light the mosquito coil with a match. 'You've let this go out too. It's a wonder you've not been eaten alive.

The apology was given so brusquely, and was so clearly thought to close the matter, and the next rebuke had come so quickly after it, that Maguire's resentment only grew stronger. But he remembered what he was there for and sat down, steadying his voice as he picked up the file. 'Er . . . you said you wanted to think about it?'

'Another whisky?'

'No, thank you.'

'No? What did you think of it?'

'This?' Maguire raised the file.

'The book.'

'Oh.'

'How far did you get?'

'About forty-five pages, I think.'

'What do you think of it?'

'Well, I must admit I was impressed,' Maguire spoke grudgingly.

'But?'

'Well, I didn't get very far, of course, but I wonder what the other side would argue.' He was groping for something negative to say, yet something that wouldn't make Coomb bristly again. Words came into his mind. *It's all too lurid: you're unbalanced.* He pushed them quickly down again and tamely repeated himself. 'I just wonder what the other side would say.'

'Indeed?' Coomb's voice edged.

'I mean, there must be another side to the argument, I assume? It seems, well, too one-sided as it stands.'

'Hmph.'

'But it certainly was impressive, what I read.' *It's all too lurid. You're unbalanced.*

'There is another side, Mr Maguire. And it's pitiful.' Coomb's grey eyes regarded him, unblinking. 'That little business you're worrying about in that file – it's nothing compared to what will happen in the next fifty years or so, if we don't look out. Nothing at all. Total collapse will begin in a couple of generations or so, total irreversible collapse.'

Maguire looked away from Coomb's uncomfortably direct gaze. 'But surely the possibility of a Russian nuclear attack on China can't be considered nothing, by any standards?'

'Quite frankly, Mr Maguire,' his eyes caught Maguire's and held them again, 'a little nuclear war now wouldn't be as bad as a bigger one twenty years from now. It might just bring a few people to their senses.'

The man's a lunatic, Maguire thought, leaning back in disbelief. 'You're surely not proposing a preventive dose of nuclear war?'

'Don't be daft, Mr Maguire. I'm not proposing, I'm predicting.'

Maguire paused, nonplussed. 'Well, if you want to think about it,' he started weakly, 'perhaps I can clarify any questions you may have? The government's willing to pay a large fee and all expenses, of course.'

The dog had lain down beside Coomb. He rubbed its ear with his bare toe. 'My wife's inherited a perfectly comfortable income – isn't that on my file? I'm not for sale, you know.'

'Well, are there any questions I might be able to . . . ?'

'I merely want to think about it. I always sleep on something before I decide.' Then he frowned. 'Well there is one question.'

'Yes?'

'I've been invited to attend a conference in Moscow.'

'Yes.'

'You knew that too? My file must be pretty well thumbed, Mr Maguire.' He paused, but when Maguire only lifted his brows in acknowledgement, went on. 'I take it I should have to cancel that?'

'It would hardly be safe for you to go, under the circumstances.'

'Hmm.' He scratched the dog's ear again.

'Does that bother you?'

He shrugged. 'I particularly wanted to go, but . . .'

Maguire thought of his assurances to Brigadier Stuart. 'I wonder how many children would get leukaemia as the result of even a limited nuclear war,' he hinted cruelly.

Coomb stood up. 'The answer is calculated in an appendix to my book, Mr Maguire. And you can't get at me like that, so don't waste your breath trying. Particularly in such an obvious manner. I can also tell you how many people will get leukaemia this year, by the way, simply as a result of the nuclear tests that China and France have carried out in the past twelve months. You can't teach me anything about that.'

Maguire stood up also, putting the file back in his briefcase. 'I didn't presume to teach, only to remind.'

'No reminders are necessary,' Coomb answered bitingly. 'Surely you realize that?'

'I'm sorry. But we do need your help.'

The dog stood up too, shaking itself and stretching. Coomb thumped its head again, heavily. 'What I need time to think about is whether your intelligence people are being just alarmist or realistic. Who's in charge of all that, by the way?'

'Brigadier Stuart.'

'Stuart? Brigadier now, eh?' Coomb sounded unexpectedly respectful. 'Used to be a colonel when I knew him. Well he's no fool. Used not to be, anyway.'

They were walking out to the front door. 'How long do you need?' Maguire asked.

'When are you leaving?'

'Eleven o'clock tomorrow morning.'

'I'll phone you at nine.'

'I'm surprised you've got a phone in such a remote place.' Maguire held out his hand.

66

'For our daughter,' Coomb said gruffly. 'It cost a hell of a lot, too.'

The detective rose silently from the shadow of the rotting boat, where he seemed to have been smoking all the time. He dropped his smouldering butt in the sand, churned it in with the toe of his shoe and pulled a small torch out of his pocket. 'Watch out for snakes,' he warned, shining the torch on the rough path back up the hill. 'Many snakes on Lamma Island.'

Maguire looked back at the dark and silent houses of the village. He saw the lights go out one after another in Coomb's house, until only one was left, upstairs. Across the whispering sea, the lights of Hong Kong glittered just as brightly as before. He turned and walked on, the detective lighting his way. He began to feel sweaty and tired again. The large, uneven globe of the moon was rising over a dark, distant hill. It was almost red. A three-line lament, quoted by Coomb in his book, slipped into his mind – three lines scratched on a clay tablet by some survivor of Ur.

> *O my city which is no longer, my city.*
> *Attacked without cause,*
> *O my city, attacked and destroyed.*

Ur, man's first great city, destroyed in the year two thousand before Christ.

Maguire shook his head suddenly. *No, the man's a lunatic*, he decided again.

Coomb stood in the doorway to Sarah's bedroom. His gaze passed slowly over her long, spindly legs, up along her narrow back to her slightly rounded shoulders and thin, outflung arm. Then back to her neck and softly moving throat, to her pale, waxen cheeks, one puffed up where it lay on the pillow, to her shadowed eyes with their long dark lashes, to her round, bald, bumpy skull. Her dark brown wig,

67

matching her eyelashes, lay on the chest of drawers, beside the plastic medicine bottles and pill containers. He fingered the wig thoughtfully.

The bamboo bed creaked in the adjoining room as Suk-Yee, his wife, lay down. Coomb pulled the sheet gently over Sarah. There was a dew of sweat glistening on her head. He left the door ajar and went in to Suk-Yee. She lay with her hands folded under her head, her long hair combed out, gazing reflectively up at him. He got his large, red toothbrush from the bathroom, squeezed a snake of toothpaste onto the bristles and started brushing his teeth, pacing up and down the bedroom.

Suk-Yee was still gazing at him. 'What are you thinking?'

'Mm?'

'What are you thinking?'

Coomb pointed at his mouth, covered with white foam from the toothpaste, then went into the bathroom and spat. He rinsed and spat again, then came back to the bed, turning the lamp down on the way. 'I was thinking,' he said slowly, 'that our daughter might have grown into a beautiful woman.'

He stretched himself out on the bed beside her, sprawling with one arm and leg across her. She didn't move except to shift her head a little so that she could look down at him. His body was fair-skinned and still firm, hers pale brown and slim. 'If we had another', she said calmly, 'it might be beautiful too.'

He shook his head vigorously against her shoulders. 'There are too many people on earth already.'

'I thought it was all right if everyone had two . . .'

'Well *we're* not going to have two,' he shook his head again, impatiently. 'You must be mad to want to go through all this again.'

She looked towards Sarah's door. 'It wouldn't be all this again.'

'It might be.'

She sighed. 'About some things you're the most stubborn, irrational man I've ever met.'

'Rubbish. I'm the soul of reasonableness.'

Suk-Yee looked away out of the open window. The moon was rising large and red, sailing through a puff of cloud.

'One day I shall end up hating you,' she said simply.

He grunted mockingly. 'How could anyone hate me?'

She lifted his arms off her for answer and turned on her side away from him. 'Are you going to do it?' she asked after a time.

'Do what?'

'Work for them.'

'Don't know yet. I'm thinking about it.'

'Is it important?'

'Could be.'

'How long would you be away?'

'Don't know. A month or so, I suppose. If I go.'

'You're thrilled by it, aren't you?'

'No. Why do you say that?'

She shrugged. 'Of course you are.'

'I caught him reading my book, by the way. He said you told him to.'

'Isn't it meant to be read?'

He sensed she was smiling now and lifted himself up on his elbow to look at her. She was. He pulled her round onto her back.

'Admit it,' she challenged. 'You're stubborn and vain and thrilled that they've asked you.'

'Well . . .'

'And flattered that he was reading your book. Was he impressed by it?'

'Of course – not that he wanted to admit it.'

For a moment, as he looked down into her eyes and felt her body move beneath him, he was stirred by the old desire. But then there came a half-wakeful moan from Sarah's room and he rolled off her and lay on his belly while she went to see what was wrong.

At nine the next morning, Coomb phoned Maguire to tell him he would work on the code. Suk-Yee was still sleeping.

Sarah had had a restless night and Suk-Yee had stayed up with her.

Maguire cabled London immediately.

As they boarded the plane, Jane Wellcome told him about the beaded dress she'd bought in a shop near her hotel. Maguire clenched his moist hands as the aircraft soared off the runway, then slowly relaxed them as they circled and climbed. He looked out over the dipping, silver wing tip, trembling and glittering in the morning sun, as the plane set course for Tokyo. Somewhere beyond that curving hazed horizon lay Peking.

Chapter Nine

The Russian embassy scowls out on Peking from barred windows and grim, bare walls. Once the most populous and busiest embassy in the capital, since the rift with China it has become almost desolate. The red flag droops from a pole which needs painting, a few taciturn faces move glumly behind the windows and many of the once frequented rooms are shuttered and locked. Apart from playing card games there isn't much for the few remaining Russian diplomats to do except attend official functions, often merely in order to stalk ritually out of them at their Chinese hosts' ritual condemnations of Soviet revisionism.

The consular section isn't quite so dull as the rest, though. There's always an erratic trickle of East European and Asian visitors to China who need a visa for Russia or have some inquiry about their Intourist itinerary. So there's usually someone ringing the bell during the brief period the office is open each day.

Peking, Wednesday, 4 August 1971
The stocky Korean passed the papers across the desk to the surly Russian. 'The details of our engineering group.' He spoke in Russian now. 'They're touring Tang Shan at the moment.'

'Oh?' The Russian's tone registered disapproving surprise.

'We'd like them to be able to go on direct from Peking to Russia, if that can be arranged.'

'They must enter Russia from Korea,' the Russian said gruffly. 'What do they expect to see in Tang Shan, anyway?

It's primitive; they're wasting their time. They must fly to Irkutsk from Pyong Nang. Look, it's all down here, why do they want to change?'

'It would save time and money if they could fly directly from Peking,' the Korean shrugged. 'But if it's difficult – '

'Impossible. Only diplomats can go that way.'

'Ah, well . . .' the Korean shrugged again, indifferently.

The Russian pushed the papers back across the counter, speaking a little less gruffly. 'Sorry, there's nothing I can do about it.' He watched them disappearing into the Korean's briefcase. 'Are those the people working on your new petro-chemical plant, by the way?'

'Yes, Engineering Project 571, that's right.'

'Uh-huh.' The Russian glanced ostentatiously at his watch. 'Going on all right, is it?'

'Yes, it's going ahead, I believe.' The Korean, too, seemed uninterested. 'Provided there aren't any more leaks in the pipes. Otherwise they may have to abandon it. There mustn't be any more leaks.'

'Ah, well,' he stood up as the Korean went to the door. 'Sorry I couldn't help. Frankly they're wasting their time in China, though. We're technologically years ahead of them in Russia. They'll see that when they get there.'

The Korean nodded a perfunctory goodbye.

It was a few minutes to twelve. The Russian glanced in the dingy waiting-room. It was empty, as he'd expected, so he closed the office early for lunch.

Chapter Ten

Coomb left for London by BOAC on the afternoon of August the fifth. Suk-Yee and Sarah went with him to the airport. He lifted Sarah up to hug her, gave Suk-Yee a single red rose, as he always did when he went away, then walked through the departure gate. At the immigration desk, he looked back. Sarah was waving, pale and wide-eyed. She was taking her new medicine quite well, and the white cell count in her blood was going down, but still she looked a frail, sick child. Suk-Yee stood beside her, rose in hand, with lips that were smiling and eyes that were not.

The VC10 flew over East Pakistan, where Pakistani troops were looting, raping, torturing, massacring and enjoying what other peacetime distractions the Bengali population could afford them. It flew over India, where half a million people were starving to death and Indian staff officers were discussing plans for the invasion of East Pakistan. It flew over the Middle East, where Arabs and Israelis were sleeping, as a rest from fighting. It flew over Europe, which was enduring the longest peace it had ever known.

London, Friday, 6 August 1971
Coomb had been booked into the Hotel Russell, in Russell Square. He got a phone call in his room half an hour after he arrived. A voice told him to walk through the main gates of the British Museum when it closed at six o'clock, where a man would give him a message. Mystified, Coomb obeyed. He walked through the gates as the museum disgorged its chattering tourists and wan-faced scholars. A man in a

checked sports jacket asked him if he could change a pound note. When Coomb opened the folded bill the man gave him, he found a slip of paper inside on which were printed an address in Piccadilly and the instruction to ask for Mr Stuart there at seven-thirty that evening. No reason was given for this unusual reception of a mere civilian adviser on cryptoanalysis.

The man who had met Coomb followed him secretly, to ensure that he was not being trailed by others. Coomb went to the address. It was a small club. He asked for Mr Stuart, and in a few moments Brigadier Stuart came downstairs, leaning on his cane and wearing a fawn raincoat.

Brigadier Stuart raised his cane, shook Coomb's hand and led him outside again, steering him across the road. 'There's a nice pub down here; we can have a quiet drink.'

'What's all this cloak and dagger nonsense for?' Coomb asked irritably. And then, when Stuart didn't reply, he added grudgingly. 'You've grown more distinguished looking.'

'I regret I can't say the same of you,' Stuart appraised him in mock distaste. It had begun to drizzle, and he turned up the collar of his coat. 'I'd be ashamed to be seen with you, but for the fact you might be useful to us. But you're not indispensable, so don't push your luck, laddie.'

Coomb had to smile. They hadn't met for fifteen years, and he was relieved that they could at once resume the old bantering tone they'd come to use during the Russian invasion of Hungary and the Suez crisis. It revived something in him that had atrophied, he realized in a fleeting afterthought. He'd felt a sense of release just then because he'd been so utterly insulated from other men during the past five years, so absorbed in his gloomy concern for Sarah and in the incessant labour of his book. Perhaps even schoolboy humour was better than none.

'And how does Britain strike you,' Stuart interrupted his thoughts, 'after so long an absence?'

Coomb snorted. 'As well as can be expected for a nation living on handouts.'

74

Stuart's eyebrows lifted faintly, but his only answer was a half-assenting rueful grunt.

They went into the saloon bar. It was small and empty. Coomb sat in the corner by a window while Stuart waited at the bar. When the barmaid, a tired-looking woman of fifty or so, at last appeared, he ordered two double whiskies.

'How did you know I'd want whisky?'

'Eh?' Stuart eased himself down beside him, thrusting his bad leg out under the table. 'You forget I'm paid to have a good memory. I recall very well how you downed your whiskies when we were working on that Hungary affair.' He laid his cane on the table and lifted his glass. 'Cheers. I was very sorry, by the way, to hear about your daughter.'

Coomb's eyes stiffened. 'Does everyone in the War Office know about my daughter? Do memos about her health pass back and forth for every clerk to read?'

Stuart looked up at him from under his sandy brows. 'Your file is known to four people only.' He took out his pipe and worn tobacco pouch, slowly and deliberately. 'As I've got no children, I don't suppose I can know much about what it means to you, but – '

'Never mind.' Coomb muttered and drank sullenly. 'For a moment I'd forgotten all about it. You brought it back before I was ready.'

'I'm touchy when people express concern about my leg.' Stuart fed the shaggy brown tobacco into the blackened bowl of his pipe and stuffed it down, then looked up at Coomb again with his slightly protuberant blue eyes. 'It's strange how we resent even the mildest kindness, isn't it?'

'The kindness I'd appreciate would be if you didn't mention it.' Coomb's lips pressed together a moment, then he shrugged. 'To business.' He drank again, smacking his lips.

Stuart lit his pipe and drew on it for some seconds reflectively, then leaned forward. 'I gather you've been invited to a learned conference of some sort in Moscow?'

'Logic. Well?' Coomb waved the thick blue smoke away,

screwing up his face in distaste. 'Why don't you give up that filthy habit?'

'Of course, if you were working on a Russian code for the British government, it would be a bit risky to go to Moscow too,' Stuart went on unperturbed, but holding his pipe a few inches further away.

Coomb drank again. 'So I should suppose.' The drizzle outside had turned to a steady rain. He heard it pattering on the fogged window while Stuart spoke.

'Nevertheless, I'd like you to go to that conference.'

'Oh?' Coomb looked askance at Stuart. 'I seem to detect some inconsistency. I thought you wanted me to work on the code?'

'There's nothing to work on yet.'

'No more messages?'

'Not a single one.'

'But why should I go to Moscow? Does the government intend to give me a paid holiday? A somewhat surprising resort to choose for me in the circumstances, I should've thought.'

Stuart lifted his glass and turned it round in his hand. Coomb noticed for the first time the light, sandy down sprouting on his knuckles.

'Who was it invited you to the conference?'

'The secretary. Valentski.'

'Whom you've met before?'

'Years ago, yes.'

'You haven't published any work in logic for several years?'

'No.'

'Don't you think Valentski knows that?'

'Well, yes, I suppose he does, but . . .'

'Why have you been invited then?'

Coomb shrugged. 'Because I'm the author of Coomb's Paradox,' he said with a touch of pride. 'Which is still unsolved.'

'Perhaps. But we think there's another reason.'

Coomb looked away at the window, frowning. Hesitant

trickles of rain ran erratically down the glass. 'What are you getting at?' he asked at last, hesitant himself.

'We have some reason to think Valentski is not entirely happy with the Russian government. And he may have some important information he wants to pass on to us. Through you.'

'Me?'

Stuart nodded. 'The KGB has penetrated our little ring of agents in Russia. None of them can be trusted now. Valentski knows that. At least, we think he does. We think he wants to pass something on to you. All we want you to do is to go to this conference and see what happens. You'll act exactly as you would have if we'd never sent for you about this code business. You'll be absolutely safe – provided you do what we tell you.'

Coomb sniffed his whisky, holding the glass up to his nose. 'I suppose that's what you say to everyone you get to work for you?'

'You're rather different. They've invited you themselves.'

Coomb felt a disturbing feeling, something between excitement and fear. He felt, as he glanced again at the English rain trickling down the English window, that he was being induced to make a life or death decision, yet at the same time it all seemed so ordinary that he couldn't believe anything of the kind. 'But I sent off a letter a couple of days ago saying I wouldn't be able to come.'

'We intercepted it.'

Coomb whistled aloud. 'You'd better do some explaining.'

'You see, that's why I arranged this rather discreet way of meeting.' Stuart glanced round the still empty room again. 'We didn't want you to simply walk into the War Office tomorrow morning. Someone might just have spotted you.'

'That's not the explanation I want. Besides, you shouldn't split your infinitives, even in intelligence.'

Stuart nodded and smilingly corrected himself. 'Simply to walk in, then, if you must be such a pedant. Let's have another whisky each.' Then, as Coomb offered to pay, 'No, no, it's HM's money.'

When he returned, Coomb was tracing the meandering track of a raindrop trickling down the outside of the window. 'Tell me,' Coomb said, without looking round, 'how serious do you think this whole business is?'

'It could be serious or it could be very serious,' Stuart slid Coomb's glass across the polished table. 'What it couldn't be is not serious at all.'

'Hmm.' Coomb looked down at his glass, running his finger round the top. 'Why me, though? You'll have to do a lot of explaining, you know.'

Stuart nodded again. He explained for over an hour, buying three more rounds of whisky. The bar slowly filled up, but nobody came to sit near them and they talked on undisturbed. Coomb grew very tired and a little drunk, as Stuart had hoped. At last they stood up to go.

'I'll think about it tonight.'

'Of course.'

'I always sleep on a thing before I decide.'

Outside the pub, it was still raining. Stuart hailed a taxi. He took Coomb back to his hotel, said goodbye from inside the cab, then gave the driver an address near Baker Street.

Intelligence analysts work in the way Coomb did when he traced the raindrops trickling down the window of the pub in Piccadilly. Drops of information trickle fitfully and erratically before them, get confused with each other and often lost. Brigadier Stuart, however, had had the luck to see a fairly clear track and that was why he had changed his plans for Coomb.

In March that year, Feodorev, a Russian aeronautical engineer attending the Farnborough Air Show, had defected and sought political asylum in Britain. During his intelligence interrogation, he had casually mentioned the name of an eminent Soviet academician, Leonid Valentski, as someone he thought was uneasy about the Soviet government's policies. Going through Coomb's file and security check report several months later, Stuart noticed the name Valentski again. Something prompted him to ask for a full report on Valentski, and in that report he discovered that Valentski's daughter was married to a colonel in the signals section of the Russian military headquarters in Moscow. Before Maguire had packed his bags to fly to Hong Kong, Stuart had instructed the chief of his Moscow agents to approach Valentski, in the hope of learning something about the Russian code.

The approach wasn't the subtle one that would have been adopted if there'd been more time. Valentski was walking in the grounds of Moscow University when a man asked him for a match. Valentski handed him his matchbox. The man lit his cigarette (a British one) and, saying he had something important to tell Valentski, led him to a stone balustrade overlooking the whole of Moscow. There he told him that his association with Feodorev would be revealed to the KGB unless he agreed to pass on certain technical information which might become available to him. Valentski protested he had only met Feodorev once, but the agent assured him Feodorev had made a lengthy statement about him which would incriminate him hopelessly with the KGB. The balustrade was at the top of a hill used for ski-jump practice in the summer, and Valentski, watching Muscovites one after another slide down the ramp, soar into the air and swoop down again, felt as if he too were falling – but further, far further. The agent left him with a friendly clap on the shoulder, saying his government would be willing to pay generously for the little piece of information required.

While Maguire was eating his dinner on the plane to Hong Kong, Valentski met the man again at a bus stop near the Kremlin. They boarded the bus together and bought tickets to the Tretyakov Gallery. While they walked together in the basement, where official ideology had banished all the early Christian icons, Valentski was told what information would be needed. He was warned again that Feodorev had said things which would certainly incriminate him with the KGB. He was offered money once more, and he was promised he would never be troubled again. He was given a time and place for their next meeting and then left alone. Valentski sat down with trembling knees before a Christ the Saviour who could not save.

At that time, Stuart had no thought of using Coomb for any purpose except cryptoanalysis in London. But the chief of the ring had reported during the night that the KGB had picked up three of their agents and that it would be dangerous for anyone to approach Valentski again. Stuart sat looking at his files until four in the morning. He needed a contact for Valentski whom the Russians would not suspect. His instructions were sent out at five-thirty. Valentski was met once more by the British agent. He was told to give the information to Coomb. The agent again borrowed a match-box from Valentski, giving one back that looked the same but carried instructions and some tablets inside it. The man, who held a nominal post in the embassy, left Moscow the next day with 'suspected appendicitis'. He never returned to Russia. Stuart could only hope the KGB had no inkling of Coomb's association with British intelligence fifteen years earlier.

Little of all this was divulged to Coomb. Stuart told him that Valentski was a secret dissident from the regime, who had volunteered to pass on information which might prevent a war between Russia and China. And why pass it on to Coomb? Because, Stuart said, judiciously blending truth with fiction, it would be safer for Valentski that way.

The next morning Stuart telephoned Coomb. Coomb said he would do it. He had his own reasons for wanting to go to Moscow, although he didn't tell Stuart that. They arranged to meet the following Tuesday. If there were any change of plan, they agreed, Stuart would phone a message to his hotel. Otherwise, Coomb should behave as if he'd come to London merely to see his father and to look up some friends before going on to Russia. The conference was to start in ten days time. Until then, he should enjoy himself – Stuart didn't say how.

Intelligence operations usually go as slowly as single raindrops trickling down a window pane. But sometimes several drops run together and their weight pulls them down straight and swift. Never before had Brigadier Stuart had to make so many decisions so quickly. Never before had he recruited an agent so abruptly, or prepared to send one off with so little training. He wasn't a natural gambler.

Chapter Eleven

London, Saturday, 7 August 1971

The day had been alternately rainy and sunny. Now it was
sinking into a chill, grey evening. A gritty wind rustled scraps
of paper and tickets along the unswept gutter. People hurried
past Coomb wearing shapeless raincoats and holding um-
brellas ready, their faces pinched and pale. He had slept after
Stuart's phone call, woken up at three, walked in Regent's
Park and at last taken the underground to visit his father. He
was treading the familiar streets from the station now, grim
with ingrained poverty, and as each turn came, it was as if his
feet knew before his eyes which way to go. He had trodden
these streets every day as a child. The deepest traces in his
memory sprang up fresh and vivid as he passed the shops, the
church, the pillar-box, the few stunted trees along the way.
Each one had its own place in history, its own special
significance.

The clouds closed over the watery setting sun, and a few
heavy drops of rain splashed onto the broken, grey stones of
the pavement. Coomb hated it all, hated the spotted pavement, the mean little houses and the mean little lives that
were imprisoned inside them. He hated their shabby poverty,
their lower-middle-class complacency, their closed and petty
interests. He hated the grey depressed chill of hopelessness
in the streets that seeped up into his bones like rheumatism.
Perhaps above all else, he hated decay.

He turned the last gritty corner, passed the last green
lamp-post, with two stale brown dog turds neatly coiled
beside its base, and walked down the little terrace of

mouldering Edwardian houses. He knocked on the familiar, peeling green, door, last but one of the row. There was no sound from inside except the blurred, vapid noise of the television. A woman was pushing a pram past on the other side of the road, glancing sideways curiously at him. Perhaps he'd known her as a child. Perhaps he knew her mother. He looked away. The noise from the television grew louder. He pictured his father coming from the tiny back room, leaving the door open, shuffling down the hall, his swollen, knobby knuckles at the latch.

The door opened stiffly, and he remembered that too.

'Well, here I am,' Coomb said abruptly.

'Hallo, son.' His father looked older and frailer than he'd expected. He was unshaven. A loose, stained cardigan drooped from his shoulders. His stubbly cheeks were pouched with food. 'Come in, then.' He went on chewing. His mild rheumy eyes avoided Coomb's. He rubbed his arthritic hands up and down his cardigan, uncertain whether or not to shake his son's hand.

'Get my card, did you?'

'Eh?'

'Get my card?'

'Oh, card, yes. Yes, I got that all right. Come in, come in.' He turned and shuffled back down the hall in his slippers. 'Raining again, is it?'

'Spitting a bit, yes.'

'Eh? Only spitting, is it?'

The same wallpaper in the hall, peeling at the corners, mildewed. The same smell of old, unidentifiable food. Coomb leaned back against the door to close it, remembering to push hard when it scraped against the jamb as it always had. Everything was familiar. Nothing had changed; nothing would ever change. Whenever he came back it was the same. It was as though he was twelve years old again, coming home from school.

His father's wispy grey hair drifted round his bald head like an ancient shred of dirty cotton wool. His unbuttoned shirt collar was rucked up under his cardigan, his grey trousers baggy, worn in the seat. 'Well, how are you, John?' he asked in a weak, phlegmy voice over his shoulder, as he shuffled into the back room.

'OK. How are you?' Coomb dropped his bag by the old sideboard where he used to leave his school satchel.

'Mustn't grumble,' his father eased himself with a sigh into the armchair opposite the television, which was booming at full volume in the corner. 'I was just watching that Great War series on the old telly.'

The table behind him was laid for tea – bread, margarine, jam, standing in a semicircle round his plate and cup. 'Like a cup of tea? Should be one in the pot.' He turned back to the television. 'This programme finishes in a few minutes.'

Images of the Russian Czar, of cossacks charging, of Lenin in a fur cap, flickered across the bluish screen. An actor's well-tempered baritone spoke a grandiloquent commentary, full of second-hand sonorous phrases like 'impending doom', 'the sword of Damocles' and 'the empire's vanished glories'. To Coomb, it seemed obscene that these grandiose sentiments, these stirring magnificent scenes, should echo and glow in this shabby little cell with its damp walls and lonely, failing inmate.

He felt the teapot, remembering the stained chipped spout as he did so. It was still hot. He went back into the kitchen where his cup hung on its hook in the pantry, untouched perhaps since he'd put it there on his last visit two years ago. It was grimy with dust. He rinsed it under the tap. The sink was stained, the morning's tea-leaves still soggy by the plug-hole. Breadcrumbs lay scattered over the draining-board and a piece of eggshell crunched under his foot. His father didn't move when he came back into the room. He was absorbing the television's message about a new brand of soap-flakes as intently now as he'd earlier absorbed its rhetoric about the Great War. Coomb poured himself some tea.

His father turned the volume down at last. 'Get that series in Hong Kong, do you? The Great War?'

'We don't have a television where we are.'

'No telly? Don't you?' His voice rose and cracked with incredulity. 'No telly at all?'

'Not where we are,' Coomb sipped the tea, thick and stewed. 'Too isolated.'

'Too isolated, eh?'

'Of course, most people do,' he added soothingly.

'Oh. Most people do, eh?'

'Yes. Shall I pour you a cup?'

'Nah, had three cups already.'

He turned back to the screen, but it was only another commercial. 'Well, how's the family?'

'OK.'

'Sarah getting on all right?'

'Yes.' Coomb had never told his father what her disease was. He pretended it was some mild form of anaemia. 'I see you've still got the same teapot,' he added quickly.

'Eh? Yes, that's right.' His eyes twitched back to the screen again. 'So the family's all right then, eh?' He never mentioned Suk-Yee's name. 'When are you going to bring Sarah to see me, then?'

'Oh, maybe next time.'

'Ah. Next time, eh? What're you doing here this time? Staying long, are you?'

'Not long, no, I'm on my way to a conference.'

'A conference, eh?' His eyes glimmered with a moment's pride, and Coomb remembered with sad near-unbelief how proud he once would have been to see that glimmer. 'Where is it then? Not in London?'

'No it's in Russia, actually. Moscow.'

'Russia? Whatever next? Watch out those old commies don't get you, eh? Here, just a minute,' he leaned forward to turn the volume up again. 'There's a new comedy series just starting. Got that Richard er . . . Richard what's 'is name in it. A real scream, he is, a real scream.'

'I er . . . brought this for you.' Coomb took a slender packet out of his pocket.

'Eh?'

Coomb raised his voice. 'I brought this for you.'

'Oh.' His father turned. 'What is it, then?'

'It's a letter opener.' It had been made somewhere in China and exported to Hong Kong, where communist shops sold thousands like it to passing tourists.

'Oh yes, a letter opener. So it is. Thought it was a knife at first. Thank you, John.' He smiled shyly and awkwardly. 'Thank you. Very nice. Won't have to use the bread knife in the future, will I? Not that I get many letters, of course. Still, thank you.'

For a moment their eyes met and then, embarrassed, they looked away. A catchy tune rang in the new comedy series and his father laid the letter opener down on the worn arm of his chair. 'Have a good look at it after this,' he apologized. 'Just see what this is like first. He's a real scream, this Richard er . . . he really is a scream . . .'

The next morning, Coomb cooked porridge and eggs, made tea, washed up, swept the kitchen and left his father 'just looking through' the *Daily Mirror*. He laid an envelope with a cheque inside it on the dusty sideboard, beside the photograph of his mother taken in an Islington High Street studio during the war. His father noticed, but said nothing, too shy perhaps, rather than unwilling, to thank his forbidding and alien son. The letter opener still lay on the arm of his chair – he meant to have a good look at it when he'd finished with the paper.

On the unswept, ticket-littered steps leading down to the underground, Coomb saw a newly pasted poster asking for contributions for the fight against cancer and leukaemia. It showed a little girl sitting up in a hospital bed with an attentive nurse beside her.

We never admit at first that the worst will really happen to us. When Coomb learned what the doctors suspected, he woke up every morning before it was light and felt his heart turning over with dread, yet he believed against the odds that the test results would be negative. Even when the diagnosis was confirmed, it was no different for a time. He woke up before light to the same silent churning of horror and despair, but still he couldn't bring himself to believe it really was leukaemia. He couldn't stop thinking some mistake would be discovered in the laboratory tests and it would turn out all right in the end. He was even able to pity other parents with their worn and anxious faces at the hospital, because their children were so obviously worse than his.

But his self-deceptions couldn't last for ever. Slowly, imperceptibly, the defensive walls he had thrown up in his mind crumbled away. The doctors' words were eventually given their full weight, the truth was gradually accepted. And, strangely enough, now that he faced the fact that she was incurably ill, the horror and dread diminished. They were slowly transmuted into a dull, numb ache which, though it was always present, was never intolerable. Life went on – complicated by the routines of hospital visits and circumscribed by Sarah's weakness – but otherwise as before. Only heavier. There was an intangible burden that could never be put down. For Sarah, it was easier. She was never conscious of herself except as a sick child, so she never knew what she'd lost. And, of course, the ultimate prognosis was always kept from her.

But then had come the suggestion, which Coomb treated as a certainty, that Sarah's illness was caused by the inadequate safety regulations of the US Atomic Energy Authority. Then his numb acceptance gave way to a bitter anger that was only strengthened by the bland evasions or silences that his protests drew from the Authority.

Coomb couldn't cure his daughter, but he could turn his pain into anger; he could fight; he could struggle. He began a hopeless lawsuit, advised by a lawyer who was well aware of his wife's fortune. And it was while he was collecting material for this legal battle that he was gradually drawn into the investigations that led him to write his book. Of course, many scientists had been warning of the earth's creeping ecological crisis before Coomb. But none with such single-minded passion. Coomb became a prophet of doomsday, all because his daughter suffered from leukaemia. A mono-maniac. Prophets usually are.

As for Suk-Yee – her daughter was going to die, her husband was immersed in what she could only consider remote abstractions and he wouldn't give her another child. She grew strong, she was already patient, she waited. But behind her reposeful appearance, she was growing desperate. To her fell the main duties of daily nursing while her husband worked. To her the protracted hospital visits, the broken nights, the sight of newly bereaved parents being led away from curtained beds, the waiting for X-rays, for blood tests, for marrow tests, the waiting for new drugs, the waiting for radiotherapy, the waiting for inevitable death. And Sarah didn't behave like a martyr. She behaved like a child who was going to live. She was cross-tempered when she felt unwell, which was often; she was isolated and bored, perverse, as any child will be. She played her father off against her mother. She didn't lack any of a child's instincts; she merely lacked a child's health. And a child's beauty. Acute illness brings out tenderness; chronic illness wears it down.

In hospitals where leukaemic children die, the nurses say it is the parents who need most treatment, not the children.

Coomb and Suk-Yee lived together, but their only child was going to die and he wouldn't give her another. They lived together, but under constant, unrelieved strain. They lived together, shunning other people as if their sick child were a leper. Turned in upon each other, with the same thoughts recurring every day, they had begun to experience already that stale monotony, punctuated with episodes of frayed antagonism, which seems the destiny of nearly every marriage. So far, they'd endured; they'd even dissembled what they'd felt. But each was secretly relieved that Coomb had accepted Maguire's invitation. They hadn't made love for months. In bed, he lay awake and thought of his work; she lay awake and pictured her childless future. Sometimes she thought of the Chinese proverb about marriage, *Same bed, different dreams.*

Chapter Twelve

Moscow, Monday, 9 August 1971

Two days after Coomb walked moodily down the steps of the London underground, academician Valentski climbed wearily up the steps of the Moscow underground. He was going to visit his daughter, wife of Major Igor Smetanka, staff officer (signals) in the Russian military headquarters. It was hot. Sweat stained the armpits of his open-necked shirt. He carried a small parcel – a tin of Jakobs Kaffee, bought at great expense on the black market in East Berlin, where he had been lecturing a few weeks ago. Weeks that seemed now to belong to a time as distant and carefree as his childhood.

He looked worn. Age had suddenly declared itself in the haggard creases of his face. He'd hardly slept at all since the British agent's approach. He lay awake each night beside his fat, snoring wife, panic thudding through his veins, tumultuous thoughts charging through his mind. Turning from one frantic scheme for his salvation to another, he counted the dwindling hours by his wife's gurgling snores and the harsh, remorseless tick of the old alarm clock on the cluttered bedside table.

He thought of going to the KGB and telling them what had happened. But he was afraid of what Feodorev might have said about him, or, rather, of what the British might say he'd said. True or false, he would be suspected; innocent or guilty, he would disappear into the interrogation cells. He knew just enough about them to be terrified. He thought of defecting to the West, but knew he couldn't leave the country on any pretext except an officially approved visit. And it would take far too long to arrange a visit like that – it had taken three months to get his recent visit to East Germany approved. He even thought of suicide, but he was too timid. And anyway, he reminded himself silently, there was still some hope. The British agent had promised they'd leave him alone if only he could get them what they wanted. Suicide was for when the last hope failed. And, though he was in the trap now, there was still that last hope that the door might open and let him out again. His thoughts eddied and swirled, but the current carried him indifferently along.

So he was going to visit his daughter. They hadn't seen much of each other for months. He'd never liked his son-in-law, anyway – he was pushy and conceited. Recently, Valentski had begun to wonder whether he even liked his daughter, Lydia. She seemed to ape her husband's manners and mouth his shallow opinions too often. Her two children seemed to be going the same way as well. Valentski hadn't quite admitted this to himself, but really they were spoiled, insolent young boors. Still, he was going to visit them. He didn't tell his wife; he had no definite intention yet of carrying out the British agent's instructions, yet that was what he was going to do in the end. That was why he'd slipped the matchbox the agent had given him into his pocket. He was caught and, search as he might, there was no other way. A rat scurries all round its trap at first, sniffing for a way out. It is only later that it lies down and dies.

The Smetankas' apartment was at the top of a new block in a fashionable suburb. The two children were watching television when he arrived and briefly acknowledged him. Lydia had her hair in curlers. She didn't seem pleased to see him, but kissed him perfunctorily, nevertheless.

'I've got ten more minutes under the dryer,' she led him into the little bedroom, gesturing him to sit on the bed. 'Mind that magazine.' The springs creaked as he sat down. He slid the open magazine towards the foot of the bed. Lydia sat under the hair dryer in the corner and pulled the hood over her head. 'We're going out tonight. Regimental party.'

'Ah.' Valentski nodded absently, glancing round the

room. The curtain rail was coming out of the wall, hanging askew on two loose screws. New Russian buildings always seemed like that – finished cheaply, as though the workers had lost interest. He noticed Igor's uniform hanging on the door. The sight of it made his stomach churn.

'I've brought you some coffee.'

'Uh?' she cupped her ears.

'Coffee!' He held it out to her, raising his voice.

'Coffee? Oh, we've got plenty.'

'It's West German.'

'Uh?'

'West German!'

'Oh.' Her eyebrows lifted and she pursed her lips appreciatively. 'Put it in the kitchen, will you?' She was growing fat like her mother, and only just thirty. The line of her double chin was already clearly marked.

He put the coffee in the kitchen, looked out at the concrete walls of another, half-finished, apartment block and, with a sudden rush of panic, thought of opening the window and leaning out until he fell. He breathed in deeply and closed his eyes, then went back to Lydia. She was looking through the magazine and laid it down reluctantly when he came in.

He smiled weakly, self-pityingly. 'Go on, we can't talk – '

'Uh?'

'Go on reading! We can't talk while you've got that thing on your head!'

So she went on flicking the pages. For some reason, the way she licked her thumb before turning each page made her seem cheap, coarse and, worst of all, unapproachable. He watched her hopelessly, hands clasped between his knees, palms moist, tremors quaking silently through his stomach.

Later on, she made them both a pot of coffee in the kitchen.

'My, I wish Igor could get a posting to Germany,' she pouted discontentedly when she had finished her cup. 'Want another one? No?' And she poured herself some more.

'Look, why don't you come round after your party,

91

Lydia?' he forced out suddenly. 'I've got a bottle of schnapps too. Come and have a night-cap, the two of you.'

Lydia frowned. 'It might be very late . . .'

'Never mind.'

'Well, if it doesn't get too late.' She wanted to show off her new dress to her mother.

Valentski was no more than a name to British intelligence at first. A name that happened to fall from Feodorev's lips. It was true, some things about the regime did worry him. He'd heard gossip like everyone else and even read a few *samizdat*, though not recently. He'd known for years, if only vaguely, of the labour camps which still flourished, of the people prosecuted on trumped-up charges, whose real crime was that they'd claimed their constitutional rights, of the torture chambers of the KGB.

Only a week or two ago people had been whispering about the physicist Girov, for instance, who'd suddenly disappeared. Well, he was Jewish and outspoken – it was clear what had happened to him. It was terrible, people had whispered. And Valentski had whispered with them. But he was not the stuff of martyrs. His sympathy for the dissidents had always been discreet. He'd merely passively hoped for better times. He was an ordinary, mild and timid man. That was why he had nearly gone to the KGB when the British first approached him. But he had been *too* timid. If he *had* gone, the KGB would have been delighted. They'd have used him to catch Coomb. But he was too afraid of them. His fear led him into the trap, and he slammed the door himself.

Chapter Thirteen

London, Tuesday, 10 August 1971

When Coomb met Brigadier Stuart for lunch in his club – about a quarter of a mile from where the Chinese agent had been killed five weeks before – he was introduced to a third man, Johnston. Johnston was a little younger than Coomb and not at all military in appearance. The son of a Lithuanian Jewish refugee, a graduate of the School of Slavonic Studies at London University, he had been recruited into the intelligence service twelve years before. He had applied for the Foreign Service, failed at the final interview and a fortnight later received an enigmatic invitation to consider government service of a slightly different type from the diplomatic corps. Now he was in charge of intelligence operations in Russia. He would be responsible for Coomb's activities while he was in Moscow.

Stuart introduced Johnston as Coomb's 'manager', who was going to give him his instructions. Coomb didn't like the thought of getting instructions from a younger man, even such a quiet and unassuming one as Johnston seemed to be. He listened a little sourly when the coffee came, his fingers toying with the spoon on his saucer, while Stuart watched him through the blue haze of smoke from his pipe. In four days time, Coomb would be in Russia; Stuart was wondering whether it had been right to recruit him.

Everything had been made as simple as possible. Coomb was not to approach Valentski, but to wait for Valentski to approach him. If no approach was made, he was on no account to invite one. Valentski would know when it was safe to approach him and would do so only if he had some information to pass. Whatever information Coomb was given, he must pass it on to the British embassy as soon as possible. All he had to do was go to the consular section and ask if he needed a visa for a forty-eight-hour visit to Japan.

'Japan?' Coomb was surprised. He'd arranged his itinerary with Intourist three months ago, intending then to travel back to Hong Kong through Siberia and Japan. But now he'd expected he'd have to change his route and return immediately by the shortest way to London, where he'd be needed to work on the code. The Siberian route would take more than two weeks.

'Do you think you can just go and buy a ticket, laddie?' Stuart asked mockingly. Johnston explained that it would be impossible to change the route approved by Intourist without official sanction, and it was essential not to draw any attention to himself by asking for it now. Besides, the fact that his journey through Siberia had been approved meant that the Russians could not be intending any action for some time yet.

'That would be a fortnight's work lost on the code,' Coomb pointed out. 'At least a fortnight.'

'We don't know yet whether we'll have any code to work on,' Stuart reminded him. 'That depends on what Valentski's got to tell us – if he's got anything. If by some chance it's the key to the code, anyone can carry on from there, once you've passed it to the embassy. But if it's only some sort of vague clue – well, better to have the clue and the Russians suspect nothing than to arouse any kind of suspicion by having you change your plans. The last thing we want is Intourist referring you to the KGB for a security check. You're more useful to us getting a slight bit of information than doing anything else, you know . . .' He knocked his pipe out against the glass ash-tray. 'It's not as though you're the only cryptoanalyst in the country, after all. So don't be getting too big for your boots, will you?'

'Hmph.' Coomb leaned back in his chair. 'Thank God

you've put that stinking pipe thing out. I was nearly suffocating.'

He would be asked for his passport at the embassy, Johnston continued, and then called in to the vice-consul's office. There he could pass over his information and be given any further instructions that were necessary. If everything went smoothly, he'd be arriving in Yokohama on thirty-first August, at about midday. He should take a taxi to the British embassy in Tokyo ten miles away and again ask the same question at the consular section. There he would be briefed again.

'But I know I don't need a visa,' Coomb said. 'Besides, the Japanese immigration people would have told me when I arrived.'

'That's neither here nor there,' Stuart was stuffing tobacco into the bowl of his pipe again. 'Most people ask idiotic questions at consular offices.'

'Are you going to light that thing up again?'

'Not if you can repeat everything you've just been told.'

To his surprise, Coomb found he couldn't. He needed three attempts before he got everything right. Still, Stuart didn't light his pipe until he'd signed the bill and stood up to go. 'We'll leave first,' he said, gripping the stem between his strong but yellowing teeth. 'You leave in ten minutes or so. A silly, routine precaution, but we stick to the rules.'

A few hours after Coomb's lunch in Stuart's club, Chairman Mao Tse-Tung signed a paper authorizing Lin Piao, his 'close comrade in arms' to organize a special security force in Peking. The group's function was to ensure the safety of the Chairman himself and of any other senior members of the party designated by the chairman or Lin Piao. The force was to be detached from the normal military command structure and to be directly responsible to the chairman and Lin Piao. It was to consist of ten thousand men with tanks, helicopters, light artillery and a flight of planes, amongst which was a Trident jetliner recently purchased from Britain and fitted out to function as an airborne headquarters for Chairman

Mao. The force was formed swiftly. Lin Piao had already collected a nucleus of staff and men in anticipation of the chairman's authorization. The command of this little army was given to a protégé of Lin's named Hung, who came, like Lin, from Hupeh. Hung had served under Lin in his famous campaign in Manchuria and later commanded a force of 'people's volunteers' in Korea.

There was another force in Peking – apart from the normal military garrison. That was the 8341 Legion, the corps of bodyguards responsible directly to Mao and no one else, commanded by the fiercely loyal Wang Tung-Hsing. While the memo authorizing the formation of the new combined-operations group instructed its commander to work closely with the commander of the 8341 Legion, the precise definition of roles and duties was left to a later time. Hung pointed this out to Tiger Cat Lin at the very first of the many meetings they held to plan the organization, equipment and training of the new force.

'If there is any conflict of orders,' Lin answered mildly, 'you will refer the matter to me as defence minister for a decision.'

'But if there isn't time?'

'There will be time. You will be linked to me by phone at all times, day and night.' Lin coughed and went on patiently. 'An attempt could be made any day. You will never be more than two seconds away from me.'

Hung had served all his life under Lin, ever since the day he'd joined the Eighth Route Army as a barefoot peasant in 1935. For him, Lin had always been imperturbable, in victory and in defeat. He'd helped him chase the Nationalists out of China; he'd helped him retrain the whole army after the carnage of Korea. He owed each step of his career to Tiger Cat Lin. And now his career had been crowned with the most important command of all. He worked hard and meticulously to show himself worthy of Lin's trust.

But he wasn't the only soldier owing all he was to Lin. Lin had been teacher and model to a whole generation of commanders, who in turn had become teachers and models to a second generation. It was natural that their careers should have advanced more rapidly than others' since Lin's appointment, first as defence minister, then as Chairman Mao's successor. It was natural that this all-important new unit should be staffed and manned by those who depended upon Lin and upon whom Lin depended. It was natural, too, that those who were excluded because their careers owed nothing to Lin, who had already felt the twinge of envy, should feel it more sharply now.

Chapter Fourteen

Oxford, Wednesday, 11 August 1971

The day faded slowly, the dusk rising from the east and washing minute by minute across the dimming sky. At Coomb's feet, the river murmuring and rippling. Beyond, the dimming fields, the dimming shapes of cows, the darker dimness of hedges and cottages. A swan gliding past, graceful malevolence; the slow chiming of Great Tom's bell in Christ Church; a crow cawing in the beeches behind him; leaves rustling in the rising breeze; the breeze stirring the reeds at the river bank, too, feathering the surface of the darkening grey water. Coomb listened to the distant hum of traffic and the long chimes of Great Tom still throbbing, fading slowly with the day. He was remembering a woman, not Suk-Yee.

When was it he'd stood with her here, at this very spot? Fifteen years ago? The past closed round him like the evening with its grey, folded wings. Coomb's eyes let go their usual antagonistic flare and softened, grew empty, lost their focus. Here, against this tree, they'd leaned, only it was winter then, and watched the sky coldly darken. She had a black shawl round her head, her hands in the pockets of her coat. Watching the last light ebbing from the sky, she'd said something about English water colourists – only water colours could do justice to the tender, muted, English light – something like that. And then, in her room, overlooking the canal, they'd listened to the trains clanking along Port Meadow while she warmed sausages over a little paraffin heater that dried the air and stank of oil. She dressed in scarves and shawls and long, swinging woollen skirts, and it still stirred him to think of her. There was something about her, or perhaps it was just because she was the first woman he'd known, that made him give her the warmest, deepest place in his memory. Three months after she left him, he had met Suk-Yee in America and married her.

There is an age when the end of one love is so unbearable that a new one has to begin at once. Even Coomb, cold and spiky Coomb, had passed through that age.

He blinked and shrugged, looking outward again, at the last, wan light of the sky. In the softly sloping hills, hazy and grey, occasional lights shone comfortingly. *Electric lights,* he thought. *A hundred years before, they would have been gas-light or oil. A hundred years before that, candles. And a hundred years from now? Would there be any lights at all?*

But even Coomb's schooled and resourceful imagination couldn't envision that. The effort needed to detach himself from the clinging present was too immense. In the same way, he could never seriously contemplate the certainty of his own death. He raised his hand and looked at it in the fading light. Pores, fine dark hairs, veins like cords beneath the skin, strong and healthy. How could he take the thought of his own death seriously? Even for Sarah, whose body death had already laid claim to – he couldn't imagine now what it would really be like when the hour and moment of possession came. He liked to think he'd prepared himself, but in fact, the present held him captive. Even the most certain future takes us unaware.

He looked at his watch. Quarter past. He shrugged again and walked away towards Magdalen College, kicking a loose, smooth pebble in front of him. Perhaps the thought of his upcoming visit to Russia was working on his mind. He was normally of a morose, rather than a melancholy, character.

'Why, Mr Coomb, isn't it?' the porter peered out at him from the lodge. 'Long time no see.'

'It depends on your time scale,' Coomb replied brusquely. 'Three and a half years to be exact.'

'Well, well, as long as that, is it?'

'Mr Cramley still in his old rooms?'

'Yes sir. I didn't think it was as long as that.' He scratched his chin. 'Didn't you come to the college weekend a couple of years ago?'

'I've never been to a college weekend. And never will.'

'Oh.'

'Place looks much the same.' Coomb relented at the sight of the porter's crestfallen face. A lack of college spirit actually wounded the man's feelings, he remembered.

'They washed the walls last year,' he recovered slowly, speaking a little warily now.

'Did they? About time, too.'

'Terrible mess it made.'

'Ah.' Coomb nodded a little less curtly than before. He crossed the quad, passed the chapel and climbed Cramley's narrow staircase. The outer door was locked, but a light gleamed along the wide uneven crack at the bottom of the door. Coomb rapped imperiously.

No answer.

He rapped again.

Still no answer.

This time he hammered on it with both fists, paused, then hammered again. 'Come on Cramley, I know you're there!'

At last the inner door opened.

'Yes? Who is it?' Cramley's voice called out petulantly.

'Me! Open up, I've been knocking for half an hour.'

'Is that you, John?' His voice expressed resignation rather than welcome.

'Yes, it bloody well is. Open up, can't you?'

'Just a minute.'

'What's the matter, have you got an orgy going on in there? Didn't you get my letter?'

'What letter? From Hong Kong?'

'Where else?'

'You didn't say you were going to call on me without warning in the dead of night on the eleventh of August.'

'In the first place it's not the dead of night, and in the second

100

place I wasn't sure when I'd be free to come up to Oxford.'
Up to Oxford, he thought. *Up. Why do we always describe going to Oxford as though it were some kind of ascension?*
'Do I have to make an appointment to see you now?'

At last the door opened. Cramley stood there without his spectacles, tieless and with rumpled hair, which Coomb immediately noticed was turning grey.

'You look as though you've just got out of bed.'

'What?' He invited Coomb sheepishly into the room. 'We were listening to some music.'

'We?'

Then Coomb saw a tall girl sitting on the couch, slipping one bare foot into a sandal. The other foot was still bare. Her hair, which was long and fair, was as tousled as Cramley's. She looked up at Coomb uncomfortably, searching with one hand under the couch for the missing sandal, while she zipped the back of her dress up with the other.

'We were just listening to a record,' Cramley said again, tonelessly.

'Ah.'

'Er, Madeleine, this is John Coomb.'

'How d'you do?' Coomb gave a distant nod.

'He used to be a fellow at the college.'

The girl smiled, nodded, looked away, went on feeling under the couch. 'We were just listening to some music,' she parroted Cramley.

'I'm sorry I disturbed you then.' Coomb looked round the room for the record player. There was none. 'What were you listening to?'

'Bach,' said Madeleine. 'Mozart,' said Cramley.

'Ah,' said Coomb. 'Simultaneously, or one after the other?'

He smiled maliciously as the girl blushed. 'And is the . . . performance over now?'

Neither answered. Cramley walked across to the open bedroom door, went inside, came out carrying Madeleine's sandal. He closed the door carefully behind him, walked stiffly across to the couch, dropped the sandal at her feet and hooked the top of her dress together.

101

'Well, I'd better be going.' Madeleine stood up, slipping her foot into the sandal. Her confidence seemed to return now that she was properly shod and dressed. She held out her hand and smiled challengingly into Coomb's eyes. 'Goodbye Mr . . .'

'Coomb.' Her hand felt moist in his.

Cramley opened the door and went out with her. Coomb slumped down on the couch. 'I take it your record player is in the bedroom?' Coomb inquired pleasantly when Cramley returned. 'You're beginning to go grey.'

'On the spur of the moment I didn't think it was a bad cover-up.' Cramley relaxed suddenly and giggled, smoothing down his hair. 'You don't look any younger yourself. You could've been a bit more co-operative, though, asking what record it was, like that . . .' His eyes were weak and watery without his glasses.

'For God's sake, get your glasses on,' Coomb jerked his head towards the bedroom door. 'You look indecently exposed like that.' Then, as Cramley moved obediently towards the bedroom, 'What on earth do undergraduates see in an ageing philanderer like you anyway?'

'She's not an undergraduate,' Cramley called out. She's a graduate student.'

'Well, what does a graduate student see?'

'And I'm not ageing.' He returned, settling his glasses on his nose with a carefully assumed dignity. 'I suppose you do still drink, or have you given up all the vices?'

'Whisky, please.' He opened the Chippendale sideboard.

'I suppose Madeleine is a good name for the mistress of a fellow of Magdalen. Is it your rotten little novels she admires or your phallic assiduity?'

'Both.' He turned round with a large whisky in one hand and a martini in the other. His eyes twinkled roguishly behind the defences of his glasses now and he smiled contentedly. His cheeks were rosy and cherubic, although their colour owed nothing to innocence. 'And why are you in England? Alone, I presume? Not being unfaithful to your wife at last?'

102

Coomb took his whisky, drank some and lay back again on the couch, gazing round the room. There was a sensuous elegance about it which spoke of both the connoisseur and the libertine. 'I've never seen your bedroom,' he reflected aloud.

Cramley's eyebrows lifted mockingly. 'Have you acquired the one vice I lack?'

'I was merely thinking what a soft-living hedonist you are.'

'I try.' He sipped his martini and asked again. 'What brings you here this time? Your letter was, as usual, enigmatic.'

'Can you fix me up with a room in the college?'

'I expect so. It's vacation after all.'

'Then let's go out and eat something, after another whisky or so.'

'What are you doing in England?'

'How many women have you had since we last met?'

Cramley shrugged modestly.

'Doesn't the prospect of ending up as a dirty old man appall you?'

'That's why I try to fit as much as I can in now, my dear chap.' He laughed, the easy laugh of a man at peace with himself and the world.

'Why aren't you ever serious?'

'What is there to be serious about?' He laughed again. 'Oh, I know you've got your troubles. But I can't make them better by looking glum. Nor can you. How is Sarah, by the way?'

'Surprised you can remember her name.'

'Would you be surprised to learn that I tried my luck with Suk-Yee once?'

'I'd be surprised to learn you succeeded.'

'Well, you're right, I didn't.'

'As it happens, gigolos don't interest her. You're really just disgusting, you know.'

'No moralizing, please. No priggish sermons.'

'She's in remission, as they call it, now. Sarah.'

'Ah. I was thinking of sending her something for her birthday. In remission. It sounds like being on parole from prison.'

'It's more like a stay of execution. Do you know when her birthday is?'

'Sometime next month.'

'Mm. Well she's got everything she doesn't need already and what she does need you can't give her.'

Cramley sighed, drank, sighed again. 'Really, I don't know why I put up with you. You're as coarse and ungracious as ever.'

But Coomb ignored him, frowning down into his nearly empty tumbler. 'In remission means that the white count is down to a tolerable level while the cancer cells group for the next attack. When they attack, the white count goes up and we move on to another drug. If we're lucky – or unlucky, I don't know which – we get another remission for a few months, or even a year or two. Then they regroup and attack again. Then another drug and another remission. Until the last drug's been used. And then the cancer cells charge through her veins like the Mongols and slaughter every living cell. His fist tightened round his glass. 'Sometimes I can't remember how she used to look. And yet she was beautiful, wasn't she? I mean her bones were well formed, her body was firm and fresh, wasn't it?'

Cramley surveyed him thoughtfully. 'I hope she goes peacefully in the end. Yes, she was very pretty.'

'Mm?' Coomb looked up. A muscle twitched in his cheek and he rubbed it with his finger, as if he could wipe the spasm away. 'It's difficult to go peacefully with this particular disease. It makes a horror of the body as it goes along.'

'Has she had radiotherapy?'

'Yes. All her hair's gone. It'll come back,' his grip tightened round the glass again. 'It'll come back this time. It's just the effect of the radiotherapy. One day it'll be the effect of the cancer – it'll all fall out very quickly near the end. But now it's just the radiotherapy.' He smiled grimly. 'A sort of undress rehearsal for the final show. Did you ever read about the survivors of Hiroshima?'

Cramley nodded and shrugged, disclaiming either interest or recollection – it wasn't clear which.

104

'She's like them really. Another casualty.' He finished his glass at one go. 'And when the next nuclear war happens, about half the survivors will have her disease. The ones that get killed will be the lucky ones.'

The bitterness in his voice was so forbidding that even Cramley chose not to speak for some time. Coomb looked past him through the open window. A bat was flitting and wheeling just outside, shrieking its shrill inhuman cries.

At last Cramley spoke. 'The *next* nuclear war? We haven't had the first yet.'

'You forget that the Second World War ended as a nuclear war. You wouldn't have forgotten if you were Japanese.'

'Still,' Cramley got up and took Coomb's empty glass. 'I suppose there's a good chance that was the last one, though?'

'There's very little chance of that at all. The probability of nuclear weapons being used in some war somewhere before the end of the century is about eighty to ninety per cent.'

'Oh come now. You talk like a book. And a bad one at that.'

'The only question is whether it'll be soon or very soon. As food and resources get scarcer, people will be driven to it.'

'Well, drink this and be merry,' Cramley handed him another whisky. 'And for the last time, what are you doing in England?'

'I'm on my way to a logic conference in Russia.'

'I thought you'd given up logic?'

'They invited me. I accepted.'

'Are you giving a paper?'

'Yes.'

'What about?'

'You wouldn't understand.'

Once more Cramley sighed, drank, sighed again. He shook his head. 'You *are* difficult,' he said resignedly. 'You know I voted against you when you got your fellowship – I was quite sure you were mad.'

'At least I'm not a myopic sybarite like you.'

'Not everyone has my gifts, certainly,' Cramley bowed his head ironically. 'How's that far-sighted doomsday book of yours coming along, by the way? What is the latest date for the extinction of civilization?'

'My God, you're so flippant.'

Cramley chuckled. 'Because I'm more pessimistic than you are. You have grand designs for saving mankind; I don't think most of them are worth lifting a finger for. So I take pleasure in the present and let the future be what it will.'

'Is that out of your next novel? Why do people read such trash?'

'It's not elegant enough for any novel of mine. And anyway, the idea is trite. Which doesn't mean it isn't true.'

Coomb shrugged this off irritably and swallowed some more whisky. It burned his tongue. 'Sarah used to go to violin lessons,' he said suddenly, musingly. 'Before it got to be too much for her . . .'

Cramley cocked his head, listening. He had been fond of Sarah when she was two or three.

'The man who taught her was a refugee from China. He couldn't fit into the new system, so he ran away and swam across Deep Bay with a life belt.'

'Deep Bay?'

'It's about four miles across. It's the usual escape route, even though it has sharks, which mangle quite a few of them.'

'Ugh.'

'Anyway, he was very poor, by your standards. One tiny room in a slum tenement five floors up. Rats on the stairs, an open sewer in the street, brothels, pimps, opium dens, gambling joints all round. It wasn't an atmosphere conducive to music, but he was a good teacher. Anyway, the place smelled of generations of dirt and rottenness and squalor and hopelessness. I see you're wrinkling your nose?'

'No. Did he have a family?'

'Oh yes.'

'Where were they?'

'There.'

'Where?'

'There in that room with him. Six people in one room a

quarter the size of this one. Well you *are* wrinkling your nose now, anyway. Sitting here on your comfortable fat arse, you can't imagine surviving, can you, in circumstances like that?'

Cramley shrugged again, holding his glass up to the light. 'Frankly, no.'

'Well, the point of this little story is that that man was *not* poor. He wasn't really poor at all. He had more or less enough to eat, more or less a place to live; he even had electricity and a few possessions. Compared with three-quarters of the world, he was rich. Think of that.'

Thinking of it, or not thinking of it, Cramley sipped his martini, rolled it round his mouth and swallowed. 'And?' he asked at last.

'And? In thirty years' time, unless we blow ourselves up . . . which is more than likely, incidentally – some people in Oxford will probably be living like that violinist. In another thirty, they might be starving. Like twenty million people are starving now.'

The phone rang. It was on a little rosewood table by the window. Cramley went to answer it, glanced at Coomb and turned away, speaking softly into the receiver. His free hand caressed the cable. Coomb gazed past him out at the dark. The bat was still flitting about and shrieking. The room, he thought as he looked round it, was too comfortable for him. It oozed comfort.

'She's the daughter of a bishop.' Cramley announced as he returned to his chair. 'Madeleine.'

'I don't care if she's the daughter of the pope.'

'If you took a greater interest in women, you'd be less obsessed by the exaggeratedly depressing vision of the future you wallow in. A future which you won't even be alive to see, after all. I'm beginning to think you ought to see a psychiatrist.'

Coomb frowned down at his tumbler, turning it slowly in his large hands. 'The world as we now know it is about to end,' his voice rose harsh and distinct. 'I present this fact to you. And you tell me I ought to see a psychiatrist. I ask you, which of us is mad?'

Cramley yawned, covering his mouth with his hand. 'Excuse me – it's not that you're boring me – or not only that, anyway. It's also tiredness. Post-coital fatigue, you know.' He finished his drink. 'Do you want another one? No? I may be passing through Hong Kong, by the way, next summer.'

'Oh?'

'I'm teaching in California next year. I thought I might fly back by way of Japan and Hong Kong, rather than across the monotonous wastes of America. That is, if they'll pay the extra costs.'

'Hmph.'

'It doesn't sound as though you're going to ask me to stay with you.'

'Sometimes I go into her bedroom and look round it and I think this will all be different when she's gone.' Coomb seemed not to have heard Cramley. 'Her toys and things, they'll all be there, but they won't ever be looked at or handled in the same way again. They'll just be things, stiff and dead, like Sarah will be. They'll be unchanged really, and yet something will be missing. A way of looking at them, caring about them. Strange, isn't it?' He pursed his lips. 'Because I don't really enjoy bringing up children. Even before she was ill, the whole business of child-care made me impatient and irritable. But still, I keep having this thought of how different her room will look.'

Cramley took out a cigarette. The orange flare of his lighter lit up for a moment the lines in his shrewd sensitive face. His eyes puckered at the corners slightly as he drew on the cigarette, still gazing at Coomb.

At last he shrugged and got up. 'Let's go and eat.'

But Coomb lay there on the couch, not stirring. 'I've walked through all my old haunts in Oxford today. I've been to all my old, favourite places. It's like having the past flash before your eyes when you're drowning.'

'Do you always get drunk so easily?' Cramley went to the phone again. 'I'll see about a room for you, then we can go and eat.'

* * *

At seven the next morning, Coomb climbed over the college wall at a place long known to undergraduates, strolled through the deer park, where the dew lay glistening on the grass, walked once more through all the familiar back-streets to the station and caught the first train to London. He watched from the window as first the grey slate roofs and then the tall spires and towers of Oxford, gleaming in the morning sunlight, slowly receded. Then he went to the restaurant car and ordered some coffee.

Cramley slept peacefully until half-past nine, when Madeleine phoned again.

Chapter Fifteen

In August 1969, a second secretary at the Russian embassy in Washington invited an American specialist in Sino-Soviet affairs to lunch. The second secretary had been cultivating the American for some time, for the Russians knew that, although he wasn't a member of the administration, he was often consulted by the State Department. During the lunch, the second secretary mentioned that the clashes along the banks of the Amur and Issuri Rivers were inducing some people in the Kremlin to consider a pre-emptive strike with nuclear weapons against China. What did the American think the United States government's reaction would be if that actually happened?

The Russian knew the American would relay this question to the State Department. It came very quickly before Nixon and Kissinger. Between them, they decided that no hint whatever should be given of what the American reaction might be. If America indicated it would be neutral, that might encourage the Russians to attack; if it indicated it would support China, that would jeopardize the détente America hoped to achieve with Russia; and if it indicated any kind of support for Russia, that would imperil the new policy of rapprochment towards China. The best was therefore to leave the Russians guessing.

At their next meeting, also a lunch, the American was able to say only that the United States' response to a pre-emptive strike or any other attack on China was quite unpredictable. The American knew the second secretary, who was also an officer of the KGB, would relay this answer to Moscow.

The Russians decided against a pre-emptive strike for the time being and began planning another way of dealing with China. This plan was ready to be implemented in 1971. The Americans would have called it destabilization. It was like the plan the CIA would devise in 1973 for making Chile more responsive to American desires. Only for Russia the stakes were higher.

Oreanda, near Yalta, Thursday, 12 August 1971
One after another the shiny black Zil sedans drew up outside the villa. The guards saluted as the grey-haired men got out, straightened themselves, looked round and were conducted up the steps. Some were tall, some thin, some stooping, some pudgy, some neither one nor the other. Most wore grey or black suits. In the front of each car sat a bodyguard. The cars rolled away to the courtyard at the back, where palm trees held their elegant heads up high and plainclothes sentries inconspicuously strolled along the walls beneath their shade. On top of the villa, a tall white flagpole rose, but no flag hung from it in the humid air. The gentle waves of the Black Sea broke quietly on the empty shore a hundred yards away. The mid-morning sun glinted on the water and bleached the sand. This was the villa in which the West German Chancellor Willy Brandt would be entertained by the Soviet leaders when he visited Russia the following month. Today it served a different purpose.

The men were ushered into the conference room and took their places at the oval table. Some were amiable and talkative, some taciturn and tense, some neither one nor the other. What they all had in common was power. Glasses of the best vodka were placed on little Caucasian mats before each place. Business did not begin until the doors had been closed. Only one secretary was present, dressed in a white blouse and sitting unobtrusively at a desk in the corner. She had been told not to take notes of the discussion, but to keep a record only of what was decided.

Outside the door stood two KGB officers in plain clothes. The villa had been scoured for electronic listening devices

111

during the past twelve hours. The KGB technicians had had to work through the night – as a security precaution, the decision to hold the meeting in this villa had not been taken until two days ago. The purpose of the meeting was to decide whether or not to implement the plan known by its code name as Engineering Project 571.

The author of the plan was a colonel in the First Chief Directorate of the KGB, but that would become known only if the plan failed. If it was successful, the chairman of the KGB would ensure that the credit went to him. He was aiming at a seat in the Politburo. The last security chief to attain that honour was Lavrenti Beria, one of Stalin's closest confidants; Krushchev shot him in 1953. The present chief hoped for better luck.

Engineering Project 571 was a plan for the overthrow of Chairman Mao Tse-Tung and the establishment of a government in Peking which would be more accommodating to Russia. The overthrow was to be accomplished by means which would make Russia appear innocent of any complicity in the plot. The new government would not at first indicate any change of policy towards Russia, but the way would gradually be prepared by a cooling of China's attitude towards America through the cancellation of Nixon's visit to Peking. Later on, Russia would offer concessions in the border negotiations with China, and China would gradually edge itself back into the 'international socialist camp'. Within a few years, technical, commercial and military agreements between the two countries would inaugurate a new era of harmony and co-operation.

The leaders of the plot in China were not mere opportunists; their motives were at least partly impersonal. They knew that Russia and China must come to terms some day and they believed that day should be sooner rather than later. At the same time, they saw nothing but danger in a flirtation with America, the chief of the 'imperialist' powers. That would only postpone the inevitable settlement that must be made with Russia while gaining nothing substantial in return. They distrusted both Mao's doctrine of self-reliance and Chou's policy of détente with America.

As for the Russians, they were anxious to buy peace with China now, before the balance of military power tilted against them. They had assured the Chinese leaders whom they were secretly dealing with that they would offer considerable concessions in return for peace along the border and the quiet dropping of the truculent accusations of 'revisionism' hurled against them every day.

But there were risks. If the plot miscarried and the Russian involvement in it was revealed, the Chinese response might be violent. Secrecy, for want of which most plots in recorded history have been bungled and botched, was absolutely essential. And just in case the plot did fail, Russian forces must be ready to meet some vengeful stroke from an enraged China – a stroke which might lead by remorseless, steady escalation to nuclear war.

Was it all worth while?

The meeting in Oreanda had been called to decide that question. Reports were given on military preparedness, communications with the plot leaders and the organization of the initial stages of the coup. Particular attention was paid to security, which was the province of the KGB. The whole operation had been devised in elaborate secrecy. The names of the plot leaders were never written down, and only a select group of people had ever heard them spoken. Military commanders in the field still didn't know exactly if, when or why they would be alerted, although they'd been training for months.

A special code had been designed for communication between the plotters and their supporters on both sides of the border. This code was not to be employed unless absolutely necessary, so that very few messages in it would be sent until just before the coup took place, when rapid communication over large areas would be essential. In that way, it was thought, there was no chance that the code would be broken and the plot uncovered before the operation began. Then, of course, there would have to be a great deal of radio traffic which would inevitably be picked up by the enemy. But no

113

code can be broken immediately, even when many messages are transmitted in it; and specialists who had produced this one were confident that, unless the enemy obtained the key, the coup would be over before they could break the code.

The code itself was quite simple. It had to be. Many of those using it would be inexperienced signallers. A more complex one would have been more secure, but operationally less efficient. The simplicity of this code, then, made it all the more important to preserve the security of the key. On that score, the KGB reported that the two leaks which had been discovered – one involving a Chinese double agent in London, the other a counter-revolutionary element in Russia itself – had been plugged before the security of the code could be endangered.

The grey-haired men argued for four hours. Some were for boldness, some for caution, some for a bit of both. Sandwiches and caviar were munched, light wines moderately consumed. In the end, the hawks prevailed and the decision was made. Engineering Project 571 would be implemented.

The Zil sedans drove up from the lengthening shadows of the car park, each with its bodyguard, and the men got in, sniffing the salty, humid air. They were driven to a military airport near by and flown away in different planes, some east, some west, some north. Their wives hardly knew they'd been away.

At the villa in Oreanda, workmen were sent to prepare the rooms for Chancellor Brandt. Many microphones were installed. The waves of the Black Sea lapped the shore in a gentle, peaceful rhythm.

The next morning, in Peking, the dour, stocky Korean embassy official had to collect some papers from the Russian consulate. Late in the afternoon, when the streets thronged again with workers going home on their heavy upright bikes, he let himself into the shaded courtyard of an old decaying house in a lane near the zoo. In an upstairs room, a man watched through the slats of the unpainted wooden shutter, then quickly pulled on a loose hooded robe that reached to his feet.

The stocky Korean was let into the room and said merely, 'They, too, are going ahead with Engineering Project 571. There are no more leaks in the pipes.'

The hooded man's head moved a fraction and his muffled voice said, 'Your wife will get the camera next week.'

On his way back to the embassy on the crowded number 60 bus, the Korean looked out at Tien An Men Square, where workmen had begun preparing for the National Day Parade on 1 October. Huge red banners had been erected and were already drooping in the damp and breathless air. *Long Live Our Great Helmsman Chairman Mao Tse-Tung and Comrade Lin Piao, His Close Comrade in Arms.*

His eyes wincing against the sloping sun, the Korean thought what a good picture the banners would make. His mind dwelled contentedly on the thought of the Minolta that would soon be his and of the Swiss record player and German television that already were.

Chapter Sixteen

Moscow, Saturday, 14 August 1971

Ordinary vodka bottles in Russia do not have corks or replaceable tops. When the metal foil seal is pulled off, there is no way of closing the bottle again to make it airtight. Whether as consequence or cause, Russians never leave a bottle unfinished. Académician Georgi Valentski and his son-in-law, Major Igor Smetanka, were half-way through their second bottle. At first they'd been drinking equal amounts, but gradually Valentski had slowed down. He was drinking one glass to every three or four of his son-in-law's. Igor Smetanka was displaying the exaggerated cocksure ebullience that alcohol usually induced in him. Previously, Valentski would have recoiled fastidiously from Smetanka's flushed face, his red-rimmed eyes and raucous, patronizing voice, but now he welcomed and encouraged them.

They were alone now. Lydia had gone to bed – vodka always made her peevish and sleepy. Valentski's wife was away, visiting her sister in Leningrad. Smetanka laughed coarsely at one of his own jokes, which was so involved that Valentski had scarcely been able to follow it. Still, Valentski forced a smile, feeling in his pocket for the matchbox the British agent had given him.

They were sitting in the Smetanka's living-room. Outside, the lights of Moscow glittered cheerfully. Valentski could see through the uncurtained window across to the megalith of Moscow University, where only two weeks ago he'd been an innocent and, it seemed now, a carefree man. Smetanka poured himself some more vodka, slopping some on the wooden table he'd smuggled in from Finland. He hadn't noticed that his father-in-law wasn't drinking any more. He reached inside his unbuttoned shirt and scratched his shaggy chest, repeating the last line of the joke and laughing his slobbery laugh again. Valentski smiled his tight, bleak smile and felt the hard edges of the matchbox pressing against his fingers.

'Tell me though, is it really so difficult to break a code?' he asked. It sounded quite natural, for the joke had been about a signals officer who sent letters in code to his commanding officer's wife.

'Right under his nose she promised to screw him,' Smetanka was still scratching and chuckling. 'Right under his nose. What?'

'Well, as a mathematician I would have thought it should be quite a simple matter, if you have enough data, I mean – '

'Balls!' Smetanka wagged his finger under Valentski's nose. 'You academics don't know a damned thing when it comes to the real world. I could give you a message now . . . I could give you a message now – ' He stopped and pushed himself up suddenly, swaying slightly against the table. 'Just got to deliver a different kind of message first. Won't take a minute . . .' He giggled and lurched unsteadily towards the bathroom, banging the doors open on his way.

Valentski heard him belching, sighing and staling like a horse, too drunk to shut the door. With a trembling hand he took the matchbox out of his pocket, emptied the tiny white tablets into his son-in-law's glass and filled it up with more vodka. He could hear Smetanka staling and sighing still. The tablets fizzed, sank, bubbled and dissolved. Valentski dropped the matchbox into the vulgar metal wastebasket under the table and gazed out of the window at the tower of the university.

It was after midnight. The moon was rising, in its first quarter. Valentski's hands were still trembling, his heart thudding in his chest. Smetanka tried twice to flush the toilet, cursed the plumbing and lumbered back into the room. Valentski was afraid he would wake up Lydia or the children, so he got

117

up, murmuring 'Getting chilly, isn't it?' and shut the door.

Smetanka eyed him blearily, grasping his glass in his heavy, hairy hand. 'Where were we, whaddid you say?'

Valentski watched him swallow some of the vodka, scarcely bothering to taste it first on his tongue. 'You said academics didn't know – '

'Right. You damned well don't.' Smetanka took another swallow of vodka and licked his lips. Apparently, the pills were tasteless – at least to a drunken palate. 'I could give you a message, give you a message it'd take you mathematicians a hundred years to break. Hundred years . . .'

'Really? But if there were a lot of other messages in the same code?'

'I don't care if you are an academ, academ, academician. Hundred years.' He nodded solemnly, 'Hundred years.'

'But surely – '

'I worked on the damn thing, I tell you. Tried it out. Top secret.'

Valentski refilled Smetanka's glass and poured a little into his own. Now, he thought with a quaking stomach, now he was actually committing treason. The die was cast. 'What's this so-called unbreakable code for?'

'So-called? So-called?' Smetanka leaned across the table, scratching his chest again. 'If anyone doesn't have the key, I tell you it would take him months to crack it. Months. Even with thousands of messages to analyse. So-called, indeed.'

'You said it would take a hundred years,' Valentski objected pedantically.

''Cos you're a bloody academic mathematician, never get your hands dirty. Signals branch,' he thumped his chest, 'signals branch, a couple of months. Mathematician like you – hundred years. Mos' important branch, signals. Specially now. Mos' important branch, by far.'

'And what's it all for, anyway?' Valentski's voice sounded small and distant to himself, as if it weren't really his at all.

'Listen,' Smetanka gulped some vodka and propped his head on his hands. 'Listen. Tell you something. Different kinds of codes, see? Field codes, intelligence codes, quick

codes, slow codes. Diff'rent kinds, see? This one, the one *I*,'
stabbing his chest with his forefinger, 'the one *I* helped
develop – did mos' of the work if you really want to
know . . .'

'Yes? Did you?' Valentski masked his nervousness with a
show of respect.

'This code, they tell us it's got to be quick, see? Got to be
easy to transmit, use in field, send by Morse code, very
secure, get on with it. So we got on with it. My brain-child.
Me. Major Igor Smetanka. Ought to be proud of me. Here,'
he slumped right across the table and beckoned Valentski to
lean forward. 'Know what letters are easiest to send?'

'What d'you mean?'

'Morse code. Easiest to send in Morse!' He leered, his
thick lips flecked with spittle. 'Got to be easy to transmit,
see? Firs' thing you do is work out a key with the easiest
letters. Get it?'

Valentski leaned back, deliberately looking puzzled.

Smetanka shook his head sadly. 'You may be all right in
Academy of Sciences, but you'd be a dead loss in signals.
Dead loss. Don't even know differen' between subshit,
shubshtitution key 'n' transhposhition key, do you? Eh? So
what use are you, old man, what use are you, eh?'

The pills Valentski slipped into Smetanka's vodka are known
as truth pills. Their effect is to lower a person's threshold of
discretion. Alcohol has the same effect on many people,
including Smetanka, but it is relatively crude in its operation
– inhibitions are relaxed, but so is clarity of mind. Truth pills
relax inhibitions better than even the largest tolerable doses
of alcohol, without producing the blurry incoherence that is
alcohol's drawback. Every intelligence service uses them.

Valentski made notes in the bathroom of what Smetanka's
loosened tongue had revealed, while Smetanka sprawled
across the table, snoring. It didn't make much sense to
Valentski and he was afraid it wouldn't satisfy the British.
Yet, sitting there on the wobbly lid of the toilet, he felt a
sense almost of elation in his weary body. So far, he'd got

119

away with it. Perhaps he'd get away with it completely. Perhaps . . .

Smetanka woke up and stumbled to bed at about four in the morning. Valentski slept on a chair in the living-room.

Lydia, cross-tempered, shook him awake at seven. He helped her make some coffee. Crapulous but unsuspecting, Igor joined them later in the kitchen, while the two boys squabbled in their tiny bedroom.

Chapter Seventeen

Peking, Monday, 16 August 1971
Peking stands in the north-east of China at about the place
the heart would occupy if the whole country were a human
body. Tien An Men Square is in the centre of Peking and the
Great Hall of the People is on the edge of Tien An Men
Square. Prime Minister Chou En-Lai stood by a pillar in the
Great Hall of the People, chatting in uncertain French with
the ambassador from Guinea-Bissau. So he stood just off the
centre of the heart of China. Beside Chou, Kang Sheng
listened with polite, owlish incomprehension, the tired skin
of his face wrinkled like a withered apricot, his eyes blinking
under the bright lights.

When the ambassador moved away, Chou turned to Kang
Sheng, raising his mai-tai in a half-ironic toast. 'Well, Old
Kang?' His thick grey eyebrows lifted inquiringly.

Old Kang peered across the vast room as if looking for
someone. 'Tiger Cat Lin's plan will give him the right to
carry the chairman off to his lair at any moment,' he said
ruminatively. 'Or even to create the moment.'

Chou's brows drew together slightly. He examined his
wine with an air of connoisseurship not quite consonant with
the image of robust, earthy communism the party liked to
promote. His blue-grey Mao jacket, too, was a shade too
delicate, fitted a shade too well. Old Kang had often hinted it
was unwise of Chou to dress more carefully than either Mao
or Lin. It would so easily remind people that he alone did not
come from the purest peasant stock. But there were some
things even Chou would not compromise on. He liked to

look dapper, and dapper he would look. He smoothed his sleek grey hair down and drank with thoughtful satisfaction.

Old Kang drank too, though he had little taste for the fiery stuff, and waited for Chou to speak.

'Your people must find out what the Russians are up to, then.' Chou said at last. It seemed irrelevant at first, but then he added. 'Perhaps you'd let me alone know what you find out.'

Old Kang rubbed his watery eyes behind his thick-lensed glasses. 'Someone's getting our agents,' he said ruefully. 'Someone who knows our intelligence service very well.'

Chou drank again, bowing and smiling to a passing African diplomat. Old Kang turned to leave, eyebrows raised in his habitual expression of mild surprise. 'Tiger Cat Lin is perhaps hunting for something,' he ventured. 'Or someone.'

'Everyone seems to be hunting for someone.' Chou was examining his wine critically again. Suddenly he tossed it off with obvious relish, throwing back his head. Old Kang waited a moment longer and his patience was rewarded. Chou smiled, either at the ambassador from Senegal, who was about to join him, or at Old Kang, who was about to leave. 'Still, when the tiger comes from the mountain,' he quoted softly, 'the dogs can bite.'

He gave a smile and a cordial diplomatic handshake to the Senegalese ambassador. The official photographers caught him with an abstracted look in his eyes, however, and that picture was discarded. He was wondering who his most dangerous enemy was – Chiang Ching, who had tried to bring him down during the cultural revolution, or Lin Piao, who had leap-frogged over him into second place. His practised conversation betrayed no sign of his preoccupation with other matters to the Senegalese ambassador, though, who came away believing Chou was as fascinated as he was by Chiang Ching's ideas about revolutionary opera and the proletarian spirit of the Yellow River Piano Concerto.

Chapter Eighteen

Leningrad, Tuesday, 17 August 1971
The black Intourist limousine swung away from the Neva down the dimly lit, but crowded, Nevsky Prospekt, towards the Moskovsky Station. Coomb was catching the overnight train to Moscow. He looked back at the wide, grey waters of the darkened river, glimpsing the three, tall floodlit funnels of *Aurora*, the cruiser that had bombarded the Winter Palace in October 1917 and lay now, a revolutionary shrine, moored to the bank of the Neva for ever. Then the arch of a wooden bridge blocked it from view and he turned back. The car passed a long queue of people at a bus stop.

He gazed past the brown-haired head of the stolid, wordless driver as the shops slid past in the lamplight on either side. 'The main shopping district in Leningrad,' the pleasantly evasive Intourist guide had called Nevsky Prospekt as they drove down it from the airport the day before. Later that day, Coomb had seen people patiently lining up outside the shops for a few baskets of unripe tomatoes, for undersized eggs, for limp, green vegetables, even for plain, wooden pencils. And behind the dilapidated but still imposing facades, he had found, as he strolled back to the Astoria – his Intourist hotel – smelly unpainted courtyards, boarded windows, unlit, crumbling stairways.

He fingered the briefcase on his knees. The driver, in a cheap blue suit, on the collar of which a light fall of dandruff had settled, slewed the car round insolently across the path of an oncoming crowded tram and stopped outside the station.

Coomb climbed out. The driver dropped his suitcase on the kerb and drove off sullenly without a word. It was Coomb's second day in Russia. He'd already grown used to the dour brusqueness of most officials except Intourist guides.

At the airport he'd felt his palms sweating while his passport and visa were examined. But as soon as he was passed on to the Intourist guide, he'd lost all his anxiety, as if the ease with which he'd come into the country was an omen of his future success. He'd wandered unhindered throughout the city, travelled on a bus, walked through the Impressionist gallery of the Hermitage Museum like any tourist and sat in the park opposite his hotel, watching children playing on a merry-go-round. He'd become almost unconcerned about meeting Valentski, as if that would take care of itself. He'd watched the children playing and thought of his daughter. He'd read through the paper he was to give at the conference.

'Mister Goum?'

Coomb turned. A young girl with an Intourist badge in the lapel of her shapeless brown raincoat stood peering at the label on his case.

'Coomb, *da*.' He answered in Russian, taking the case from her as she tried to lift it.

'You speak Russian?'

'A little.'

She seemed disturbed, rather than pleased. 'Your train is on Platform Three. Can I have your ticket?'

'What time does it leave?'

'Eleven o'clock. We must please hurry.'

It was five to eleven. Coomb followed her up the steps to the shabby, unpainted station. They pushed their way through a crowd of drably dressed soldiers, travellers, onlookers and furtive, slickly dressed men who looked like touts. All the passengers seemed to be carrying cardboard boxes tied up with string, or paper bags full of cooked potatoes and bread. The passengers were all hurrying, the others just standing and watching.

The Intourist girl kept dodging ahead of Coomb, then looking back anxiously for him. She was a dowdy girl, with lank, brown hair and colourless cheeks. Her legs were bare beneath her raincoat, her brown shoes worn and scuffed. She showed Coomb's ticket to an inspector at Platform Three. He shrugged and pointed. 'Platform Two,' she said nervously, hurrying on.

He had to take long strides to keep up with her, almost running through the crowds. As he did so, bumping his case against his legs, Coomb became suddenly aware of something. The place was silent. Of all these hundreds of people hurrying to and from trains like him or just patiently standing about, hardly any of them were talking. Nor were there any loudspeaker announcements of train departures. No porters shouting their way through the crowds. No sounds of music, no clatter of dishes from some station restaurant or café. Not even the shriek of a whistle. Nothing but the muffled scurrying of feet echoing off the colourless walls and cavernous roof, or the occasional blasts of steam from an engine.

The girl showed his ticket again, and this time they were waved ahead. They hurried down to the eleventh car. The conductor glanced at the ticket, glanced at Coomb and nodded to the open door. The train started moving as Coomb turned to thank the Intourist girl. But she was already walking away, her thin, young shoulders hunched with either care or dejection.

Russian trains, like Russian people, are divided into two classes, soft and hard. The soft – higher-ranking bureaucrats, officers and official visitors – travel soft. The hard – all the rest – travel hard. Coomb was travelling soft.

He walked down the corridor, its carpet protected by a strip of white canvas laid down by the conductor, until he found his compartment. There were two berths in it, already made up with fresh white sheets and a grey blanket. In the upper berth a grey-haired man lay sleeping, his brown trousers hanging down by the window, one bare foot protuding from the blanket over the side of the berth. The windows were shut and Coomb sniffed the air suspiciously. So far, it seemed fresh. He left his luggage under the lower berth and went out into the corridor again. All the doors to the other compartments were closed, the curtains drawn. He looked out of the window. Already they had left the city. The darkened countryside glided slowly past as the wheels clanked over the rails with gathering speed.

The train passed a little station with a wooden hut and a single light. A woman with a yellow scarf round her head held up a signal disc, gazing blankly at the lighted carriages. Then there were empty fields, silver birch woods, occasional lights glimmering in the darkness, muddy tracks following the rails for a time before they led away through sudden gaps in the woods. The clanking of the wheels grew faster. The carriage began to sway.

Coomb heard the door of the next compartment rumble open. The cheery confidence of American voices streamed out into the corridor.

'I've got the Maxwell House in here somewhere.'

'OK, Chuck. I'll get some water from the samovar.'

Coomb turned his head. A giant, blond young American was stepping over a shiny, bulging, leather portmanteau into the corridor, holding two glasses in metal stands. He nodded amiably to Coomb.

'Good evening,' said Coomb.

'Hey, you speak English?'

'I'm afraid I *am* English.'

'Tom Cooper,' the giant American held out his free hand. 'Southwestern Baptist College.'

'Coomb. John Coomb.'

'Glad to meet you, John. Chuck, we got company.'

'We have?'

Another blond giant stepped over the bulging portmanteau, a jar of Maxwell House coffee in his hand. 'Chuck Smithson,' he tossed the Maxwell House into his left hand and grasped Coomb's with his right. Coomb's bones crunched.

'Coomb,' said Coomb.

'John Coomb,' said Tom Cooper.

'Glad to know you, John,' said Chuck. 'You a tourist or . . . ?'

'No, I'm going to a conference in Moscow.'

'You don't say,' said Chuck or Tom – Coomb had already forgotten which. 'Not the mathematics and logics conference?'

'Yes it is, actually.'

'That's great!' said Tom or Chuck. 'So are we.'

'Really?'

'Hey what a coincidence! Are you reading a paper, John, or just listening?'

'Well, I am giving a paper, yes.'

'You are?' Their eyes widened slightly with respect. 'What about you?'

'Well, we offered, but . . .' began one of them.

'They just didn't have room on the programme, I guess,' finished the other. 'Er, say, would you care for some coffee, John?'

'No, thanks, I'll get some tea.'

'OK.' He nodded down the corridor. 'You know you can get it from the samovar down there.'

'Can I?'

'Sure. You just have to ask the conductor.' He strode back down the swaying corridor to where the conductor was checking a glistening chrome samovar. The other giant stood beside Coomb, looking out of the window. His large freckled knuckles gripped the rail as if he were going to crush it. 'Not much to see,' he nodded at the birch woods marching past. 'Have you been in Russia long?'

'This is my second day. And you?'

'Four days.' He pulled a tattered guidebook out of his pocket – *Europe on Five Dollars a Day*. 'Then we're doing the rest of Europe. After the conference.'

'Ah.' Coomb was watching a single yellow light twinkling far off in the immense blackness of the woods.

'Say, it's just struck me,' the American's voice was suddenly uncertain, 'You're not the Coomb of Coomb's

Paradox are you?'

'Yes, I'm afraid I am.'

'And you're reading a paper on Russell? Foundations of Russell's Mathematical Philosophy?' His voice was rising with growing excitement.

'Well, that's the title, but I may stray a bit.'

'Well, imagine that! I never thought I'd travel on a train with the author of Coomb's Paradox. Why that's one of the most fascinating – '

'Here you are, John,' the other giant interrupted. 'Got you some tea from the man.'

'Do you know John's the Coomb of Coomb's Paradox?'

'Coomb's Paradox? No? You don't say.'

Coomb sipped his tea. It burned his lip.

'I never thought I'd travel . . .'

'That's what I said.'

'And you're reading a paper on – ?'

'Russell, right.'

'It's a small world,' said Coomb, blinking.

'Say, I'd really like to talk with you about that paradox,' Chuck – or Tom – said, spooning coffee and milk powder into his glass of scalding water. 'I guess you don't have any time right now?'

'Well, I am a bit tired . . .'

'Sure. Maybe some time during the conference?'

'Yes.' Coomb sipped his tea again and burned his lip a second time. 'How did you like Leningrad?'

'Not much of a hotel.'

'No?'

'And the churches are all empty.'

Coomb didn't see the significance of this, so he ignored it. 'Architecturally it has the makings of a fine city, though. Or the endings.'

'The food's awful.'

'Hmm. The Hermitage collection is atrociously hung too, isn't it?' he remarked mischievously. 'And badly lit?'

'Hermitage?'

'In the Winter Palace.'

'Oh, right. The Winter Palace, right. We didn't get around to that.'

'Perhaps they're ashamed of it. Since none of the good paintings are later than 1917, I mean.'

'Yeah?' said Chuck or Tom. 'Nope,' said Tom or Chuck.

'And no reproductions of the good paintings either. Only the tedious Socialist-Realist ones.'

'Yeah?' said one. 'That's the way it goes,' said the other.

'Well . . .' Coomb turned towards his compartment.

'Say, John, would you care for a cookie?'

'Er, no, thank you. I think I'll get some sleep.'

'Sure thing.'

'Goodnight.'

''Night, John. 'Night.'

The Russian lay snoring above Coomb, one foot protruding from the blanket as before. The air was beginning to sour a little, so Coomb left the door ajar. He switched on the reading lamp and took out the paper he was going to read at the conference. But he didn't read it. He gazed through a chink in the curtains at the blank darkness outside and listened to the wheels beneath him. Their clanking had changed to a rapid, rhythmical chattering, swaying the carriage gently from side to side.

Gazing out at the empty darkness, Coomb tried to imagine what he foretold in his book – a world in which the machines stood broken and useless and men learned to scavenge for food in rotting cities scattered over a barren, poisoned land. And, as usual, he could not do it. Even his imagination was too weak. Only the image of his daughter came to him, bald, waxen-skinned, her body inexorably sagging and collapsing. He closed his eyes to squeeze the image out.

The Americans' voices sounded outside again. Glancing through the crack in the compartment doorway, he saw their reflections in the corridor window. They were kneeling together by the lower berth in their compartment, heads bowed, hands clasped in front of them. Now he understood why they had been disappointed by the empty churches. He slid the door a little further open and listened to the words of their prayer over the steady chatter of the wheels. They were saying the Lord's Prayer, but not with the reverential intonation Coomb associated with worship. It was with the same easy, confident familiarity they had adopted towards him. Evidently they were on first-name terms with God as well.

He slid the door closed again, until only a crack of light and a thin shaft of air came through. The Russian above him turned over and sighed.

Chapter Nineteen

An intelligence agent is normally trained for many months or even years before he is sent out. But only a week had elapsed between Stuart's meeting with Coomb in London and Coomb's arrival in Russia. Stuart thought the possible gains justified the enormous risk he was taking, but he couldn't be sure. There were two obvious dangers about Coomb. The first was simply that he was an amateur. To offset this, his job had been made as easy as possible, but there was always the chance that an amateur might choose to use his initiative. Coomb might, for instance, decide to ignore the instructions he'd been given and approach Valentski himself, or make it obvious that he was waiting for an approach from him. Either way, he would invite suspicion from the KGB, who kept all foreigners under some kind of surveillance.

The second danger was one that couldn't be provided against – the danger that the KGB knew of Coomb's services to British intelligence in the fifties and would suspect him of working for them now. Stuart thought that unlikely, however. There was no reason to think the Russians knew about Coomb's occasional work in the fifties, but, if they did, they would also know he hadn't been used for a long time. Certainly, they couldn't have known he was going to work for intelligence again when Valentski invited him to attend the conference, because the idea of approaching Coomb hadn't even occurred to Stuart until months later. On that score, then, Stuart's mind was fairly easy.

But there was one thing neither Stuart nor Johnston had thought of – the paper Coomb was to deliver at the conference. They had both assumed it would be some safe academic piece on logic and mathematics. In fact, it was nothing of the kind.

As soon as he got the invitation, Coomb had thought of using the conference as a forum where he could publicize his views on the impending ecological crisis. He intended to shock the delegates into an awareness of it, not merely by what he said, but also by the very fact that he said it at an international conference in Russia designed for a completely different purpose. That, he thought, would startle people into thinking about the global catastrophe threatening man's future. It was to be a demonstration, although a rational one. That was why he'd wanted to go to Moscow in the first place, why he'd found it easy to accept Stuart's offer later on.

He didn't stop to think what the KGB would think of his using a conference in Moscow as a platform for a demonstration of his morose predictions for the future of mankind. Being a naïve man, he didn't have any idea of the tortuous and concealed motives others might attribute to him. And being an arrogant one, he didn't really care.

Moscow, Friday, 20 August 1971

Coomb was to give his paper at three o'clock, in the main lecture hall of the Mathematics Institute. Apart from shaking hands with him at the inaugural cocktail party, Valentski hadn't once come near him. Coomb had met mathematicians from East Germany and logicians from Poland. He had, like most participants, listened to some papers with indifference and toured Moscow during others. He'd managed to avoid Chuck and Tom, who took earnest notes during every paper and studied the Bible in the intervals between them. He'd been greeted with surprise by several of his former colleagues from Europe and North America, who had heard of his changing interests and asked him what he was doing there. He evaded most of their questions by saying he was going to talk about Russell. The more persistent questioners he reprimanded with a basilisk stare.

He had dutifully attended the entertainments arranged for

132

foreign participants, had even gone to the ballet, which he detested, in order to make himself available to Valentski. But Valentski, who had also been present at every function, had never even looked his way. Watching him discreetly, Coomb noticed how much he had aged. (He noticed age in others but never considered whether it was noticeable in him.) He wondered whether Valentski really had anything to pass on to him at all. But that afternoon, Valentski was to act as Chairman when Coomb gave his paper; perhaps he planned to approach Coomb then. If not, he wouldn't have many more chances. The conference was ending and Coomb was leaving for Siberia on the midday train the next day.

Coomb entered the hall at five to three. It was nearly full. He sat down on the dais and took his paper out of his briefcase. Valentski was not there yet. Coomb crossed his legs, folded his arms and glanced through his opening sentences. His heart was beating a little faster. He felt this was the most important paper he would ever give. His role as an agent seemed at this moment far less important – as did even the possibility of a Sino-Russian war, which he thought could be no more than an early local episode in a drama of which the dénouement would be global disaster. It was the dénouement he was concerned with, not the episodes that might lead up to it.

Just before three o'clock, academician Valentski came in accompanied by three Russian professors. He left them in the front row, climbed laboriously up the steps to the dais, gave Coomb a brief, wan smile, asked in passable English if he was ready and stood up to introduce him.

Coomb gathered his papers together and took his place at the lectern. A few people were still coming into the hall. He waited for the shuffling and banging of seats to die away, looking out at the faces raised expectantly towards him under the neon lights which hung down from the high ceiling. Amongst the faces he noticed Tom's and Chuck's. They were sitting together, their pencils earnestly poised. He pulled the microphone closer to his mouth and tapped it authoritatively, as a conductor taps the rostrum with his baton. Still he

133

waited until the last whispering and murmuring had faded and they were all watching him. He realized how much he enjoyed having an audience. At last he began.

'The title of my paper has been announced as "Russell's Contribution to the Foundations of Mathematics". But as I have changed my mind about Russell's importance, I am not going to speak on that topic today. Indeed, I no longer find it worth while to make the kind of remarks which that title implies. However, what I do want to say is not disconnected with Russell. Not the Russell of mathematical philosophy, but the Russell who was imprisoned for pacifism in the First World War, who warned of the rise of totalitarian tyranny before the Second World War and who predicted the extinction of life on earth if ever the third, nuclear, war broke out – as it may yet, and sooner than we think.' (Coomb had pencilled in this last phrase in London, after he'd talked with Stuart. It was the only change he'd made to his typescript.)

'Mathematical philosophy is important, but, as Russell often insisted, the survival of civilized man is more important. And that is what I am going to talk about today. I shall place before you an array of facts, most of which perhaps we already understand in isolation, but which we never consider in their interconnected totality. In this totality, they suggest consequences which may be fatal to mankind, and I shall spell out what these consequences are. Then I shall delineate the means by which man could still avoid, or at least mitigate, them. Finally, I shall try to estimate what likelihood there is that man will adopt, or even try to adopt, those means. I think you will agree with me, when I have finished, that these things are infinitely more important now than the seductive, but non-urgent problems of mathematical philosophy.'

He looked up. Every face was turned to him and he could see puzzlement or incredulity on each one. His heart thudded as he went on.

'What then are the facts? They are of three kinds: ecological, socio-economic, military-political. First, then, the

134

ecological facts. They can be summed up in this statement: In a period equivalent to two days in the life of a fifty-year-old man, the human race has increased its population and industrial activity to a point at which the earth can simply no longer sustain them . . .'

He spoke for nearly an hour, instead of the advertised thirty minutes. He'd spent several weeks preparing the paper and it was clearly and simply argued, with only glimmers here and there of the doomsday rhetoric that pervaded the typescript of his book. The style was plain and academic, eloquence sacrificed to precision.

He argued from simple facts to simple conclusions – the earth's resources were running out, they couldn't support unlimited economic growth and a vastly increasing population. There was no substitute in sight for our dwindling food and energy reserves. Shortages would lead to unrest and war unless governments acted now to curtail both economic production and population growth. They would also have to redistribute wealth and resources more evenly – to save some from starvation, others must give up their abundance.

But governments by their nature were incapable of taking these steps, or even considering them. So, unless enormous efforts were made by those who understood the need for political, social and economic change, the world would simply slide down to catastrophe. If anything would convince a group of rational impartial men, he'd thought, this would.

But after only ten minutes, he knew it wouldn't. Already, he was losing his audience. They were the wrong people in the wrong place at the wrong time. Some resented the unannounced change of subject, some discounted what he said because of the rumours they'd heard that he was a crank; some were bored by anything except theorems. Feet began to shuffle, chairs squeaked, whispering gradually rose to a constant murmur.

'Most of the people that have ever starved are starving now . . .' Coomb tried to hold them with a few striking images, by raising his voice or lowering it, by glaring at them, by speaking faster or slower. But he sensed with growing hopelessness that it was of no use.

After half an hour, the first person edged out of his seat on the aisle and walked stealthily out. By the time he'd reached the last paragraph, the hall was more than half empty. He became conscious only of his voice, instead of what he was saying. He stumbled over words and lost his place. He had to stop and clench his fists before he could go on. He closed his eyes a moment and the image of Sarah's wide-eyed, ravaged face floated across his mind. Again he lost his place, and there was an embarrassed, whisper-filled hush until he found it. He glanced up at the audience again. Most of them weren't even looking at him. They were gazing blankly past him, shifting uncomfortably in their seats, whispering openly to each other, sometimes three or four together.

He read the final sentences at last in a voice that was hollow and had lost all its defiant conviction. He felt he no longer believed what he was saying himself, but somehow he had to go through with it. 'I've tried to describe the probable future of the human race in the next hundred years. Even if the best happens, it is going to be bad. Probably it is going to be very bad. Starvation, poverty and unrest can only increase. I hope I have aroused in you an awareness of the dangers which threaten civilization. If we do not become aware of them and act immediately to avert them, I do not see how we can survive. If I have succeeded in that, there is at least some hope.'

His paper ended there, but he spoke one more broken sentence.

'Only I am afraid I have not succeeded.'

He sat down in silence, feeling suddenly limp and tired. There was not even a perfunctory clap from the audience. He didn't care now whether the faces looking up at him were perplexed, embarrassed or scornful. He didn't dare look at them. He merely noticed out of the corner of his downcast eye that a light at the back of the hall was flickering and wondered numbly why nobody had switched it off.

Valentski went to the lectern, brushing past him without a

word. Coomb sipped from a tumbler of water that had been placed on the desk in front of him. His hand was trembling. Valentski spoke one or two short, unsteady sentences through the microphone. He thanked the speaker for a very unusual paper, hummed uncertainly, glanced at his watch and regretted that, as it was now time for tea, there would be no opportunity for discussion. Seats flipped up, murmuring and coughing began again and they all shuffled out, subdued at first, then gradually louder and more talkative. Coomb heard chuckles here and there, and knew they were chuckling at him.

He looked up at last, at their backs filing through the doors, absently noting Chuck's and Tom's among them. In the silent emptiness of the hall, he too was silent and hollow. His belligerent spirit had drained right out of him. He wanted to slink away and hide. The image of Sarah's face floated suddenly across the blankness of his mind again, framed by her dark straight hair as it used to be. He saw the beauty of her large brown eyes, not quite slanting, neither Asian nor European. They seemed to reproach him for making a fool of himself.

A voice roused him.

'You left your paper on the lectern.'

Valentski was holding the typescript out to him. His hand was shaking slightly, but Coomb didn't notice that then.

'Oh. Thank you.' He took the sheaf of pages listlessly.

Valentski nodded coolly and left him. At the foot of the dais, the same three Russian professors were waiting. Valentski walked out between them. They were muttering and shaking their heads as they left the hall together.

Coomb opened his briefcase. He was about to drop the dog-eared pages inside when he noticed another page slipped between them with Russian words typed on it. He glimpsed the word 'code' by the margin. His pulse started suddenly, but his mind stayed blank for two or three seconds. He watched his hand letting the typescript go and closing the briefcase. So Valentski had passed him something after all. He got up slowly, trying to think, his mind exhausted. He had meant to go straight to his hotel, feeling too depressed to join the others at tea. But, now that Valentski had passed him something, he ought to be more careful. He had conscientiously attended all the other functions and, he recognized reluctantly, he mustn't invite suspicion by behaving any differently now. He walked slowly down to the tea room, feeling absurdly that his briefcase had suddenly become large and conspicuous.

He sat at a slightly grubby plastic table by himself, sipping hot tea from a glass. Several people looked at him curiously. He sensed that others were talking about him behind their hands. He sat still, closing his mind to them, noticing only that Valentski was at the other end of the room surrounded by several Russians and East Europeans.

Then he felt a hand drop on his shoulder. He jumped.

'Say, that was a really interesting paper, John.' It was only Chuck – or Tom – Coomb still didn't know which.

Coomb sighed with relief and steadied his voice before he spoke. 'You must be the only person to think so.'

'Do you have a spare copy? We'd like to read it through if you have.'

Coomb smiled weakly and gave him the only carbon.

'Thanks a lot, John.' He was about to sit down when someone called to him from across the room. He hesitated a second, then turned away, tucking the carbon into his bulky folder. Probably they'd both got copies of every paper they'd heard. 'Enjoyed it very much, John,' he smiled as he left, 'Very interesting. We must talk about your paradox some-time, too.'

Coomb sat there doggedly with his briefcase on his lap. The room gradually emptied as people returned to the hall to hear the final paper of the conference.

'. . . Hope this one'll be more interesting,' Coomb heard an English voice saying from the door. He got up, went down the stairs, out into the August sunshine, and walked with assumed casualness back to his hotel. He felt exposed and vulnerable – the shirt-sleeved Russians in the streets all seemed to be eyeing his briefcase suspiciously. But he forced himself not to hurry. His hotel was the National, near the Kremlin, where the *Guardian*'s correspondent had been approached a few weeks ago. He climbed slowly up the thickly carpeted stairs to the third floor and nodded to the stern-faced concierge, who silently handed him his key. He opened the door and 'locked it behind him.

The sunlight was beaming through the windows. He drew the curtains, sat down on the bed and opened his briefcase. His pulse began to quicken. It was not one, but two sheets that had been slipped between his own pages. One fell out from the middle and another from near the bottom. They were thick, coarse-grained sheets, a slightly different size from his own, with a few loosely typed paragraphs on each. He looked at them with both excitement and distaste. Instead of a prophet, he had become a mere spy.

After some seconds, though, his excitement overcame his distaste. He read through the paragraphs quickly. At first he was disappointed. The first page consisted of almost random notes of a conversation the author, presumably Valentski, had had with 'A'. They dealt with matters that Coomb thought irrelevant – when A had been ordered to work on a new code, how many were in his team, where the different members came from, by what date the code had to be operational. In fact, this information was exactly what an intelligence analyst would have wanted – he then would have been able to construct a hypothesis about the purpose and scope of the Russian code by interpreting the clues which it offered. But Coomb was not an intelligence analyst. His flair was merely for cryptoanalysis. So it was not until he read the second page that his attention was captured. And then he experienced a thrill of discovery such as mathematicians feel when the solution of a problem suddenly occurs to them. His self-recriminating depression fell away. If what he read was true, it gave him the key to the new Russian code.

He read it through several times. A feeling of elation and buoyancy swept over him, as sudden and overwhelming as the dejection he'd felt before. He entirely forgot his paper and the issues it dealt with. It was as though he'd never given it, never written it, even.

It was half-past five. The embassy would be shut. He'd have to wait until tomorrow. He could phone now, but that would be dangerous. All calls would surely be monitored. Partly in a sudden rush of zeal, and partly because now he had time to waste, he decided to transfer the important information from Valentski's pages to something safer and less noticeable. He went into the bathroom and looked round. The cardboard carton containing his new tube of toothpaste was open on the washbasin, the tube beside it. He pulled the bottom flaps of the carton out and carefully unsealed the long flap along the side. Then he sat down on the edge of the bath, resting the flattened carton on a rickety stool, translated and transcribed Valentski's two pages of notes into tiny letters on the inside of the cardboard. He tucked the flaps in again, put the toothpaste tube back inside, tore up Valentski's pages and flushed them down the lavatory.

It was half-past seven when he'd finished. He went down to the restaurant for dinner, feeling both exhilarated and tense. As he'd already learned to expect after his first day in Russia, it took an hour for the simple meal he ordered to appear, although there were only about a dozen diners in the room. He nibbled thick-sliced Russian bread while he waited and drank from a bottle of sweet port wine. His thoughts circled round the letters he had copied onto the toothpaste carton, only occasionally swerving into recollection of the fiasco of his paper. After all, he told himself then, people would react differently when his book was published. Already that episode belonged to the past, was shrouded in the unreality of time.

When he'd finished eating, he went back to his room, packed his case, cleaned his teeth, examined the carton again and went to bed early.

Chapter Twenty

The most important place in an Intourist hotel is the counter where Russian officials regulate the lives of foreign visitors. Smiling or bleak, but always indifferent, they issue tickets in exchange for travel vouchers, arrange transport to and from stations or airports, hand out meal coupons (to be paid for in hard currency) and check that no one deviates from the approved itinerary.

Coomb went to the Intourist counter of the National at nine-thirty. He intended to go to the British embassy when it opened at ten, before catching his train at midday. In his briefcase were his passport, his conference paper, a volume of Chekhov's short stories, his shaving things, his toothbrush. And his toothpaste in its cardboard carton.

The girl at the counter was tall, buxom and young, with upswept, bleached blonde hair and bored, brown eyes. She glanced up at him and then went on filling in some official form.

'*Dobroe utro*,' Coomb said after some time.

'Good morning,' she muttered in English and finished writing, clipping the form to another, before she looked up at him again. 'Mr Coomb?' she asked.

'Yes. I've come for my ticket.'

'Come this way.' She opened the counter for him and led him to a glass-panelled door behind her. She opened that too and closed it as he went in.

A man of about forty with dark hair and a baggy grey suit sat behind a desk with a closed file in front of him. Another

141

younger man sat in an armchair in the corner, flipping through the pages of a magazine.

'Sit down, Mr Coomb,' the man at the desk spoke in American-accented English.

'I've come for my train ticket.' Coomb sat down opposite the desk with a vague but growing sense of apprehension. He placed his briefcase on the floor beside him.

'How have you enjoyed your stay in Moscow?' the man asked pleasantly.

'Very interesting.'

'Very interesting?' The man's eyebrows rose slightly.

Coomb reached down to open his briefcase. 'Do you need my passport?' he asked, a little too co-operatively.

'We also found your speech yesterday very . . . interesting.'

Coomb glanced up, passport in hand, stomach suddenly uneasy. 'Oh?' He was looking at the man behind the desk, but at the same time he was aware that the other had stopped leafing through his magazine and was watching him appraisingly. He straightened up slowly, holding his passport on his knees. 'Oh?' he said again.

'According to our present view, you have violated article one ninety stroke one of the Soviet criminal law. Possibly article seventy also.' The Russian took Coomb's passport and laid it on the desk.

'One ninety one?' Coomb asked woodenly.

'One ninety *stroke* one. Circulation of fabrications known to be false which defame the Soviet state and social system.' His voice was gradually becoming harsher. 'Maximum punishment, three years' deprivation of freedom.'

'I don't understand, I – '

'Don't understand?' He leaned forward to stare at Coomb intimidatingly, then opened the file in front of him. He turned the pages slowly, frowning, licking his finger before turning each page, then paused. *The main political ideologies are all fraudulent*, he read out loud. 'That is a defamation of the Soviet system.'

'I didn't say that.'

'Yes.'

'I did not. I said the ideology of unlimited economic growth was fraudulent. I can show you the words in the typescript.'

'It is unnecessary. Your words were recorded.'

'That is not what I said.'

The man shrugged and started turning the pages again, licking his finger each time. In the corner, the man in the armchair lit a cigarette.

The man behind the desk glanced up at Coomb again then read out slowly, *Governments are unable to contemplate any future beyond their present five-year plan.* He pursed his lips. 'Defamation of the Soviet social system. Who has instructed you to slander the Soviet government like this?'

Before Coomb could answer, the phone rang. The man picked it up, said, 'Smolnov' and listened, nodding and murmuring '*Da*' or '*Niet*' occasionally. Coomb tried to clear his mind and think, while his heart beat unsteadily in his chest. But the Russian's words kept running through his head, knocking other thoughts aside before he could gather them. *Article one ninety stroke one . . . we also found your speech very interesting . . . three years' deprivation of freedom.* . . . Still, one hope seemed to glimmer. They seemed to be interested only in his speech, there had been no mention yet of Valentski. Didn't they know, or were they going to come out with it in a minute? He willed himself to think what he should say if they brought up Valentski, but only *one ninety stroke one* came into his head – that and the image of his toothpaste carton idiotically prominent in his briefcase.

The man behind the desk put the phone down, glanced round at the other and nodded. The other got up, dropped his magazine on the chair and left the room.

'I demand to see the British consul,' Coomb blurted out in a tone that he tried to make sound indignant.

The Russian ignored him, frowning down at the page he was reading, while he reached in his breast pocket for a crumpled pack of Russian cigarettes. He lit one, flicked a flake of tobacco off his lower lip, turned the page, turned back, turned it again. 'Article seventy,' he murmured thoughtfully, 'Anti-Soviet agitation and propaganda. Maximum penalty, ten years' deprivation of freedom. Who has been putting you up to this, Mr Coomb?' His voice had softened again. He sounded merely concerned for Coomb's welfare now, anxious to help him shift the blame onto the proper shoulders.

'No one's put me up to anything. I haven't said anything against the Soviet Union – you can read the whole paper.'

The man lifted his hand, letting the blue-grey cigarette smoke curl lazily up over his face and eyes, which he half closed. 'Why did you not speak about the, er, the subject you were invited to speak about? Why did you suddenly give this other speech? What was the point of your deception?'

'Because I . . . well, I knew the organizers wouldn't accept a paper on the subject I wanted to speak about . . .' Coomb ran dry. 'I wanted to get people to listen,' he went on lamely. 'And I assure you there was nothing anti-Soviet in anything I said. You can read it for yourself.'

The Russian grunted, still frowning down at the file. Coomb wondered whether he'd been listening. But after some moments, he looked up again. 'Give me the text of your paper.' Then, as Coomb took the paper out of the briefcase, 'Show me that book, too. Empty your briefcase.'

Coomb opened the case wide. The toothpaste carton lay on top, but he took his shaving things out first. He undid the sponge bag and laid his razor, his spare blades, his soap on the desk. He paused. 'I have a right to see the British consul – '

'Hurry up. What else is in there?'

Coomb took out the toothpaste carton and laid his tooth brush on top of it. 'That's all.'

'Now your pockets.'

'What?'

'Pockets.'

Coomb's wallet, notebook, pen, cash, his crumpled handkerchief all joined the neat row on the desk. As each thing went, he felt more naked, more vulnerable, more humiliated, more frightened.

The Russian got up, put his cigarette in the corner of his mouth, frisked Coomb carefully, then grunted. 'All right, sit down.' He went back to his own seat.

Coomb glanced at his watch. Five to ten. It would take twenty minutes at least to get to the embassy. If they didn't look inside the toothpaste carton and let him go, he might still make it. Unless they were playing with him. Unless they already knew about Valentski. Unless they hadn't been bluffing when they talked about the Soviet criminal law. He swallowed down a mounting wave of fear and tried to bluster. 'I warn you I shall protest to my embassy at once, as soon as I leave this room.'

The Russian ignored him. The silence made his voice sound small and lost. The Russian took up the typescript of his paper and leafed through it, then stowed it tidily at the back of the file. 'Is this the only copy?'

Coomb thought of Chuck and Tom. 'Yes,' he lied.

'Hmm.' Half an inch of ash dropped off his cigarette onto the desk. He blew it away. The grey dust settled on Coomb's knees. The Russian's hand reached out over Coomb's things while he read from the file. Coomb watched it hover over the toothpaste, then, as the Russian looked up, settle on Chekhov. The Russian flipped through the pages. First from back to front, then from front to back. He had squarish fingers with well-kept nails. The tips of the first two fingers were yellowed with nicotine. He took Coomb's briefcase, looked inside, ran his fingers along the seams of the pockets, then dropped the book back into it. Next the sponge bag. His hand explored the inside, tested the plastic lining, turned it inside out. Slowly, deliberately, he picked up the razor, the soap, the blades. One by one, he weighed them in his hand, then packed them neatly back into the bag and gave it to Coomb. 'Put it away.'

Coomb watched him take the wallet, turn it over, slip his fingers into the pockets. After his passport, the coins and his handkerchief, it would be his notebook and then the toothpaste carton at the end of the row. The Russian was frowning down at the wallet, running his thumbnail along the seams. Coomb unbuttoned the sponge bag, picked up the toothbrush and put it inside. He picked up the toothpaste carton.

'Not those,' said the Russian. Leave them there.'

Coomb's finger tightened for a second around the cardboard, then he shrugged ostentatiously, as if it didn't matter to him, whatever the Russian wanted to see. He put the toothpaste carton down and laid the toothbrush back on top of it. His heart was thumping. He forced his hand to remain steady as he pressed the stud on the sponge bag and placed it beside the Chekhov in his case. 'I've got a train to catch, you know,' he started to protest again.

'Who is this?' The Russian held up the creased, faded snapshot of Suk-Yee and Sarah that Coomb had carried in his wallet for years. Sarah looked quite healthy in it, blinking in the sun and wearing her own hair then, not a wig.

'My wife and daughter.'

'Hm.' He slid it back into the wallet. 'Why did you marry a Chinese? Aren't your own women good enough for you?'

Coomb's lips pressed together. He said nothing. Suk-Yee looked younger in the snapshot too. Less careworn. He watched the Russian examine his bank notes, rubbing each one separately between his finger and thumb. Two pound notes, a red hundred-dollar bill from Hong Kong, some roubles. The Russian peered at the watermarks, snapped the bills taut, folded them carefully together and slipped them back into the wallet. Then the Russian currency exchange voucher and his Hong Kong driving licence.

'So you are a colonialist, Mr Coomb?'

'No.'

'You live in Hong Kong? That is a British colony, isn't it?' He compared the details on the licence with the first page of his passport.

'It doesn't follow that I'm a colonialist. Any more than if I live in Russia it follows that I'm a communist.'

The Russian's eyelids flickered, and he surveyed Coomb stiffly for several seconds. Then he passed the wallet silently over the desk. He nudged the coins across without a glance and picked up the notebook. It was half-full of jottings that Coomb made whenever they occurred to him, to use at some later time for his books and articles. Now there were only the passport, the handkerchief and the toothpaste left.

'What is this?' The Russian tapped the notebook with his forefinger.

'A commonplace book.'

'What?'

'A commonplace book.'

'What is that?'

'I write notes in it.'

The Russian frowned over Coomb's almost illegible scrawl, turned a page or two, then gave up. He slipped the book into the back of the file, on top of Coomb's paper.

Coomb watched his hand move towards the handkerchief, fastidiously wave it away, then take up the toothpaste carton. Coomb's mouth went dry.

The Russian picked at the flap of the carton and hinged it open. The tube fell out, squeezed flat at the bottom. The Russian weighed it in his hand, then looked up as the door opened behind Coomb.

The other Russian had come back. He muttered something in his colleague's ear. Coomb gazed helplessly at the toothpaste carton lying open-flapped in his interrogator's palm. The interrogator nodded, looked down at the file, glanced at his watch and pushed back his chair. He drummed with his fingertips on the hollow carton. 'Your paper contains slander against the Soviet system,' he spoke with casual, arrogant contempt. 'We shall confiscate it. You can go.'

'Go?'

'Yes. Catch your train.' He tossed the toothpaste carton onto the desk and pushed across Coomb's passport.

Coomb forced himself to pocket his handkerchief first, before he slipped the toothpaste back into the carton. 'What, what about my commonplace book?'

'What book?'

'My notebook.' He placed the carton in his briefcase,

glancing at his watch. Twenty past ten. There was still time. 'Can I have it back, please?' He took his passport.

'It will be returned to you later.'

'So I can go now?' Coomb stood up, still not quite certain.

'Your ticket is outside. You will be taken to the station.'

'I . . .' Coomb hesitated, then chanced it. 'I want to go to the British embassy first and report this whole incident.'

'There is no time.'

'My train doesn't leave until twelve.'

'Mr Coomb, do what you like when you are outside Russia. While you are here, you do what we tell you.'

Coomb gave in. He followed the second Russian out of the room, collected his ticket from the buxom, off-hand Intourist blonde and went upstairs for his case. There he saw why there wasn't time for him to go to the embassy. His case was empty, its contents scattered over the bed and floor. He looked round at the Russian, who was lounging, arms folded, against the door.

'You must pack your things quickly.' The Russian tapped his watch and gazed back at him stolidly.

Twenty minutes later, Coomb was put into an Intourist sedan by the Russian, who got in beside him. It took half an hour to reach the station. A man wearing an Intourist badge in his lapel met them there and led them silently to the train. It was very long and very crowded. Coomb got in. The Russians watched him through the window. Exactly at midday the train pulled away from the platform. It would be ten days before he could reach the British embassy in Tokyo. The code lay safe but useless in his briefcase.

The KGB wasn't really interested in Coomb at all. He had been watched briefly in Leningrad and on the way to Moscow, but they didn't know then that he'd previously worked for British Intelligence. And nobody saw Valentski slip his two sheets of paper into Coomb's text. However, the professors who appeared as Valentski's acolytes were, unlike Valentski, party members. They were expected to relay anything unusual to the KGB, as a reward for which they might count eventually on becoming academicians themselves.

148

And Coomb's speech was certainly unusual. It had been reported to a Captain Smolnov of the Moscow KGB, who had had the recording of it transcribed the same evening. Captain Smolnov was in the Second Chief Directorate of the KGB, the functions of which include the surveillance and investigation of foreigners inside the Soviet Union. Coomb's file was checked. There was almost nothing in it – a few details of his passport, his residence and publications, a note that he had not behaved suspiciously while he was being watched in Leningrad.

Captain Smolnov guessed that Coomb was probably some sort of crank – by no means a security threat. The only trouble he foresaw was that the man might make a nuisance of himself by trying to distribute copies of his paper to Russian academics. He wrote a memo recommending a 'scare' interview and routine surveillance, then took the file to his immediate superior, Major Krylenko, who glanced through it, yawned and initialled the recommendation. It was late in the evening.

Smolnov carried out the interrogation himself – he liked to show off his English. When he was satisfied that Coomb carried no inflammatory material in his luggage, he ended the interview. The meticulousness of his search through Coomb's briefcase was mere intimidation – he'd never expected to find anything. He intended all along to let Coomb catch his train. However, a junior official in the Ministry of Production discovered at the railway station that his berth on the trans-Siberian express to Khabarovsk had been commandeered 'for government service'. He would not, after all, be able to make the visit to his parents that he'd been planning for six months. He wrote a letter promising to come next year and spent his leave in Moscow instead. His berth was taken by a grey-haired KGB officer who had never risen above the ordinary chores of eavesdropping in restaurants, tailing suspects and searching rooms in their occupants' absence. He would have no trouble recognizing Coomb. He had watched him before, when he travelled in the berth above him on the overnight train from Leningrad to Moscow.

Chapter Twenty-one

Two hours after Coomb's train left Moscow, Stuart read a freshly decoded cable from the British embassy which told him Coomb had made no contact and was presumed to have left on the train according to schedule. Then another followed with a report of Coomb's speech, which the second secretary had heard of by chance from a friend who was attending the conference. Stuart's lips tightened and he drummed on his desk with his fingers for a few seconds, then shrugged. Apparently, he'd backed a loser. Valentski couldn't have given Coomb any information, Coomb would be out of reach for nearly two weeks and Russian intentions were just as obscure as before. He conferred with the Russian and China departments. They agreed with him that nothing would be lost by giving their information to the Chinese.

He requested an interview with the prime minister and foreign secretary the next morning. They agreed that the meagre information they possessed should be passed to the Chinese chargé d'affaires.

Maguire was there when the foreign secretary received the chargé d'affaires. The spruce little Chinese perched on the edge of a chair designed for greater girths than his and listened silently while the angular Briton told him of the coded message found on the corpse in Soho and dropped on the floor of a Moscow hotel. His head jerked birdlike to one side in cautious acknowledgement as he took the copies of the message and folded them without a glance at their contents.

'The Chinese government would have preferred to be informed earlier of this,' he said precisely.

'The British government was not sure at the time whom Mr . . . ah . . .'

'Chan,' prompted Maguire.

'Chan, yes, whom Mr Chan was spying on,' observed the foreign secretary with a courteous smile. 'Or whom he was spying for.'

The chargé d'affaires slipped the messages into the breast pocket of his Mao jacket and buttoned the flap. Maguire thought he evinced as little interest in them as he would have done in a cocktail invitation.

'The Chinese government will . . .' he paused, hunting for a word that would not imply a sense of obligation or gratitude, 'will *welcome* the information the British government has now provided. However, we have no knowledge of any spies of any kind in this country.'

'Ah,' breathed the foreign secretary affably. 'Quite so, quite so.'

Five hours later, Old Kang was wakened from his sleep by a cable from London. He fumbled for his glasses, blinking weakly and watery-eyed in the sudden harshness of the electric light, and peered perplexedly at the paper in his hands. He looked more bemused than enlightened as he read it through, first quickly, then slowly, then quickly again. He ran his fingers through his scant, ruffled hair, frowned and rubbed his chin. At last, swallowing the stale sleep in his mouth, he put a call through to his office, dressed and made himself some green tea.

Trans-Siberian Railway, Monday, 23 August 1971
By the evening of the third day, Coomb had got used to it. He had grown used to the filthy, pungent-smelling toilets at the end of the carriage, to the scummy basins without plugs, to the crowded, cluttered restaurant car with its stained and littered tablecloths and its crates of food and drink stacked under every chair. He had got used to the smell of over-ripe

151

food seeping into the corridors from the 'hard' compartments, to the cold, boiled potatoes squashed on the floors and the string bags bulging with beets wrapped in newspapers. He had got used to the sour smell of unwashed, sweaty clothes, to the stolid, bovine men in vests, who played cards in the corridors or read old magazines, who shaved, smoked, ate and drank, or simply gazed out dull-eyed through the windows. He had got used to their women gossiping, feeding children or placidly sleeping in the crowded compartments like cows in a byre. He was used to the sun's ruthless heat burning through the open windows in the afternoon and to the sudden, foreshadowing chill which came at night. He had got used to the birch woods and the empty, endless fields, to the log houses and broken fences scattered along the track, to the lulling, hypnotic rhythm of the train's swaying, clattering movement. The stout, pompous conductress in the 'soft' carriage, strictly prohibiting all 'hard'-class Russians from even walking along the corridor – he had got used to her too, and to the man with grey hair in a brown suit who passed by his compartment every hour or so and hung about by the door whenever the train halted. He had got used to it all.

And he hadn't looked once at the inside of his toothpaste carton. It lay wrapped up in his sponge bag now, untouched except when he brushed his teeth. Morning and evening, he went to the toilet, locked the door, took the half-squashed tube out of the carton, squeezed it, scrubbed his teeth and replaced it, all with the most deliberate casualness. He'd guessed the grey-haired Russian was watching him, but he didn't know whether there was also some hidden camera tracking his movements even in the toilet. So he tried to behave normally at all times. He schooled himself to forget about the carton, first by finishing his Chekhov, then by gazing broodingly out at the vast countryside that swung slowly past his window.

A feeling of fatalistic lethargy stole over him, beginning with the enforced inactivity of his body. For the present, he was helpless; there was nothing he could do but wait. So long

152

as he was in Russian hands, he must wait. He was like an ant in a bear's paw – at any moment he might be crushed. But if he kept still, the paw might relax and let him crawl away to freedom.

If the KGB didn't arrest him on the train, he could still be caught by the customs men at Nakhodka, where he was scheduled to embark on a Russian boat. Then there would be the two-day voyage to Yokohama. The great paw could close tight at any time. Perhaps the bear knew all about Valentski. Perhaps it was only waiting to see if he was going to lead it unsuspectingly to another contact in Russia. Or perhaps it was merely suspicious, watching slyly for some self-incriminating word or gesture. Perhaps it had lost interest in him altogether, its paw loosely holding him out of heavy inertia. He had no way of telling. There was nothing he could do but wait. Wait. He didn't even feel afraid. There was no need yet.

He stood in a patient, glazed-eyed line for forty minutes and bought the last but one bottle of vodka in the restaurant car. He gazed out of the window. He thought of the fiasco his paper had been, of the man who had interrogated him, of Stuart waiting helplessly for news. He thought of his daughter and of Suk-Yee. He tried not to look at his briefcase where the sponge bag innocently lay within handy reach on top.

The trans-Siberian express is more like a medieval caravan than a train. People live on it for ten days, travelling from Europe to Asia with their food, their families and their belongings. Many get drunk, some quarrel, a few conceive. Some are born on it and some die. Pickpockets make a living from it: prostitutes try. The stations are like oases; peasant women with scarves on their heads put up stalls to sell bread, fruit, vegetables and sour cream. The caravan stops for fifteen or twenty minutes; the travellers bargain and buy. Sometimes police board the train and hustle someone off, sometimes stretcher-bearers carry a motionless, battered body away. Then the caravan's wheels begin to turn again. The oasis station slides slowly back, the obligatory statue of

Lenin thrusting his goatee belligerently towards the east, and the peasant women fold up their stalls. The caravan rolls on. It is six or eight hours until the next oasis.

The travellers gaze out at the land they pass through and live off but which is not theirs. They are strangers in a strange land. They don't even share the same time. The railway runs on Moscow time, regardless of the eleven different time zones it passes through. At ten in the evening Moscow time, the sweaty, hairy-legged waitresses close the exhausted restaurant car, although it may be eleven in the morning by the sun. But half-way across the continent, food supplies will have nearly run out anyway. Not even the watery soup with greasy balls of mutton in it is served any more. By then it makes little difference that there is a restaurant car at all, let alone what hours it keeps.

Coomb munched bread dipped in a jar of preserved fruits, which he had bought at a station oasis while the grey-haired Russian loitered behind him. He licked a jar of sour cream, bought at the same stall; he drank tea or vodka. His lethargy grew heavier as his mind absorbed his isolation and his helplessness. He was suspended in a travelling cocoon, unable to act or move, from which he would eventually emerge into a different state.

Drugged by the rocking of the carriage on its clattering wheels, he gazed dimly out at the birch forests covering the hills and valleys, at the rolling meadows, at the unknown rivers and streams that foamed through rocky beds or glided, smooth and swelling, between broad, grassy banks.

Occasionally he saw peasants sleeping in a clearing where they were scything the grass, their faces unburned and sweaty, their heads pillowed on their arms. He felt like them, not capable of thought or action, but only of the passive absorption of elemental things – earth and sky, woods and grass, rivers and hills. The low wooden farms and villages, scattered here and there beside the railway, passed like puffs of cloud in a limitless blue sky, mutely emphasizing the vast vacancy in which they stood. During the nights, Coomb saw nothing for hour after hour but the blurred shapes of nearby

154

trees and, beyond them, the outer darkness – not one light, not one movement, not one sound of human life. The land was as unpeopled as the sky.

Somewhere beyond the dark rim of the hills, perhaps there were nuclear missiles being readied, aimed at Peking or Canton, or nuclear bombers being fuelled, but Coomb realized with a slow surprise that now, at this moment, he didn't care. Powerless to act upon the world, he gave up caring for it too. All that seemed to matter was this smooth swaying motion, this hypnotic rhythm of metal wheels on metal rails, this green land undisturbed by man. The thought of the war, famine and disease which he'd previously believed menaced mankind brought no emotion with it now, no conviction. Even Sarah's drawn face and smooth, pale skull became a thing detached, a thing that had no claim on him, smooth and remote like another planet in another universe. If he were dying, he thought dreamily, he might feel no differently.

In the mornings, he rolled up his blankets and leaned back against them, watching the train's shadow slipping over the long, dewy grass outside the window. In the evenings he leaned there still as the sun set, watching the light trembling and dying in its last struggle against the dark. At night, he unrolled the blankets and lay huddled beneath them, watching the stars and the darkened earth while the curtains flapped in the chilly wind and the train wheels clattered evenly beneath him.

Chapter Twenty-two

There were two kinds of enemy anxious to get rid of Mao Tse-Tung. The first was the Nationalists. During the civil war, they had set a price on his head, but had succeeded only in catching his second wife, whom they promptly shot. After their retreat to Taiwan, they had doubled the price. Several times they had infiltrated agents through the nets of the communist border guards, making clumsy attempts to bomb, shoot or poison him. But always they had failed.

The second kind of enemy was the party members who had personal or political reasons for wanting Mao out of the way. These were the more dangerous enemies because their enmity was secret. Old Kang was far more worried about them than about the Nationalists.

The last attempt on Mao had been made only a few months ago. While its failure had been a result of the routine precautions which all Chinese leaders took, Old Kang had been dissatisfied that his counter-espionage department hadn't uncovered the plot beforehand.

A bomb had been planted on the train by which Mao was expected to travel from Shanghai to Peking. Instead, he travelled by plane – a last-minute change of plans which was often made to mislead would-be assassins. Mao had escaped, but the bomb hadn't been discovered on the normal checking of the train and might have killed him if he'd been travelling on it. And there was no clue to the identity of the saboteurs.

Such miscarriages and uncertainties nagged Old Kang. His puzzled frown grew more perplexed. He assigned more agents to the case. They sought information not only in China, but also in Europe and America. One of the agents was Chan, the man who was stabbed to death in Soho on the twenty-ninth of June. He'd been one of Kang's most valuable men. Ostensibly the operator of a travel agency in Soho, he was in fact a double agent working for both Russia and China. For the Chinese, he gathered real information which often provided China with a foreknowledge of Russian intentions.

Instructed to glean information about any Russian scheme to assassinate Mao, Chan had stumbled on something quite by chance. It was a coded message lying on the desk of the KGB officer to whom he regularly reported in a 'safe' house in Bayswater. The KGB officer, whom he knew only as Ivan, told him the message concerned an important new operation in China. The phone rang next door and Ivan went to answer it, rashly leaving the message on his desk. Chan at once started copying it down, but Ivan came back before he could finish.

Ivan saw Chan hastily pocketing a piece of paper and, immediately suspicious, demanded to see it. Chan dashed out of the room, down the stairs and into the street. The KGB officer fired one shot at him and, when he saw Chan had escaped, phoned the Russian embassy. His words sounded innocent to the British monitoring the embassy's calls, but the message contained double-talk words which signalled to the KGB officers in the embassy that a serious security leak had occurred. Within an hour, fifty people were searching for Chan. (At that time the embassy had over a hundred KGB officers working from it.)

Then Chan made the mistake that killed him. Assuming the Russians would expect him to head for the Chinese legation offices at once and would try to intercept him on the way, he decided to hide until later that night, hoping they'd think he'd slipped through their hands and give up. In fact, the confusion and alarm at the Russian embassy in the first half-hour or so after his escape probably provided the only chance he ever had of reaching the Chinese legation safely.

After that, the Russians were well organized, and they didn't give up.

Chan was seen cautiously approaching the legation soon after midnight. He escaped again and fled in panic towards Gerrard Street, where the Chinese colony contained many who would protect him – but also many who would not. A number of Chinese 'triad' secret society gangsters in Soho were in Russian pay. The Russians had alerted them, and it was the members of a triad gang who caught Chan, knifed him and went through his pockets. Interrupted by the chance appearance of a prowling police car, they left a fragment of the message behind. Otherwise, Chan's death might have looked like an ordinary robbery or gangland killing.

Until the British revealed what they knew, Old Kang couldn't be sure why Chan had been killed. Now he understood. He arranged a secret meeting with Chou.

Peking, Monday, 23 August 1971
Chou sat in his stiff-backed chair, hands resting on its arms, head tilted slightly back, scrutinizing Old Kang through half-closed lids. Suspended on the wall behind Old Kang's head, the obligatory portrait of the Chairman smiled impenetrably down at them. On the bamboo table between them stood a pot of green tea and two rice-pattern cups. Chou's cup was half-empty, Old Kang's untouched. If the press had taken a photograph of them then, it would have looked as if Chou hadn't a care in the world, while Kang had all of them.

When Old Kang had finished, Chou's head came forward a little and his slim fingers spread out over the arms of his chair, but his expression was unchanged.

'Whom do you suspect?' he asked at last.

'The same person you suspect.' Old Kang sipped from his cup and then frowned down at the pale, warm tea as though searching even there for some clue to the mystery.

The corner of Chou's mouth suggested a smile. 'And we have no evidence?'

'What's worse, if we're right, he may have most of the

army with him already. I've been watching his appointments with some care.' Old Kang's glasses twitched as his mournful frown deepened. 'He's been pushing his own men for years. And this new force of his – '

'We must have evidence.' The fluid muscles in Chou's cheeks set almost imperceptibly, yet enough to give his face a rigid, stony look. 'What about these messages?'

Old Kang's frown deepened so much it became downright comical, and Chou's mouth twitched into a momentary smile again at the sight of it.

'If the British can't break them, we certainly can't. They have much more experience with codes like this.'

'Without evidence, we can't act.' Chou took out a cigarette and tapped it on the glass table top.

'Shall we go to Mao?'

Chou shook his head decisively, glancing up at the Chairman's picture behind Kang's head. 'Without evidence? How can we?' He felt the shadow of violent death stretching out towards him and with it the ruin of all the policies he had so painfully coaxed a reluctant Mao to accept. But still, no photograph would have detected any hint of that in his calm and almost smiling expression.

'Mao might think we were trying to get rid of Lin for our own reasons.' It was the first time Chou had named the man they both suspected, and he acknowledged it with a lift of his bristling brows, then named him again, as if some taboo had been removed. 'Mao didn't find it any easier than Lin did to accept the Americans or to invite Nixon. We must find out how much support Lin has in the army.'

'He's the chosen heir. How can he fail to have support?' Old Kang blinked at him in watery reproach. 'Besides, I've found out already. If the red sun were to set tomorrow, nothing could stop the Tiger Cat's star from rising.'

Chou sat still for some seconds, lighting his cigarette. The matches were damp and he needed three. 'Your metaphors are not always well chosen,' he remarked absently. Then, 'I don't think Chiang Ching would like that prediction. He spoke warily. It was Old Kang who had introduced Chiang

159

Ching to Mao at Yenan in 1938. 'She too perhaps has aspirations?'

Old Kang's eyes dropped. 'She's being watched. On the Chairman's orders. She has faults, but she isn't plotting. At least, not yet.'

'Ah.' Chou got up, his body spare and sprightly still. 'Keep watching Lin's friends. I think I'll have a talk with the British chargé d'affaires. We've let things go too far.'

Chou's calm demeanour was no symptom of either apathy or resignation. The next day he set up a special unit to collaborate with the most reliable of Old Kang's intelligence agents. He discreetly alerted his many friends in the party and those in the army who were jealous of Lin. He arranged through the British chargé d'affaires (who had to refer to London to find out what it was all about) a degree of co-operation between the Chinese and British intelligence services that made them temporary allies. In 1967, the embassy building had been burnt down by a mob of howling Red Guards, who kicked, abused and spat upon the retreating staff, mainly women, as they filed nervously out through the smoking compound. The new chargé d'affaires sat in his new building and wondered if that too would be burned down if his government backed the eventual losers.

The theory of espionage has a long history in China, going back two thousand five hundred years to the writings of Sun Tzu. Chou was perhaps as worthy of the tradition as Old Kang. In 1931, a leading spy of the communists changed sides in Shanghai and became a double agent for the Nationalists. When he was uncovered, the leader of the communist underground movement, Wu Hao, is said to have ordered the execution of the spy's entire family. Wife, children, brother-in-law, sister-in-law, parents-in-law – no one was spared. Eight people were killed in all, as a warning to would-be traitors. 'Wu Hao' was an alias of Chou En-Lai.

Such ruthlessness was not uncommon, either in Shanghai in the thirties or in the long tradition of Chinese espionage. Sun Tzu, for instance, wrote, 'If a piece of secret news is divulged by a spy before the time is ripe, he must be put to

death, together with the man to whom the secret was told.'
And Wu Hao's counterpart in the Nationalist party in
Shanghai, 'Butcher' Tai Li, is said to have got rid of
suspected communists by roasting them alive in the fireboxes
of railway engines – thereby saving fuel as well as purging
society of its grossest impurities.

Chapter Twenty-three

Trans-Siberian Railway, Wednesday, 25 August 1971
Coomb woke gently, like a swimmer rising from the sea, the heavy waters of sleep washing softly off his body. At first he lay there only half-awake, while a vague, uncertain dream melted away behind his still-closed lids. Then a shapeless feeling of unease replaced the evanescent images. Something was wrong. He opened his eyes and realized what it was. The train had stopped.

He peered at his watch, still set on Moscow time. The hands pointed to twelve-fifteen, but the day was just dawning outside. It was cold. He sat up, wrapping his blanket round him. The train was perched on a steep embankment in the middle of a large, marshy plain. A soft, white dew-mist lay over the ground, and the train seemed to be floating in it like a ship becalmed. The tips of birch and fir trees poked through the mist like lonely scattered islands. Further away, the shapes of dark grey hills began to show, their crevices and valleys filled with the softness of the mist. Gradually the sky paled with light.

Then, as he watched, there came the remote clanking of wheels over points, the owl-like hoot of a whistle and a steady vibration rising up from the embankment through the carriage. The ground trembled in anticipation, then with a whoosh that shook the whole compartment, a train rushed past the window. The blurred, black carriages flashed past Coomb's eyes one after another while between them he caught glimpses of the undisturbed mist clinging to the hills, lying still and heavy over the plain. It was a passenger train, but all its windows were sealed with metal covers and there were no lights. It clattered past, seemingly endless, carriage after darkened carriage, like some fuming dragon with armour-plated scales.

And as he watched, Coomb's mind was dragged back to the world he'd forgotten. The train was going east, as they were. It must contain troops or military supplies – something that had to travel concealed and found no place on official railway schedules. Was it part of the Russian build-up for an attack on China? For the first time after many days, he felt a sense of guilt. If he hadn't made his futile demonstration at the conference, he would have been able to pass Valentski's information on to the British embassy in Moscow. Would it be too late by the time he reached Tokyo – if he ever did reach it? The metal carriages clattered grimly past.

Then suddenly the train had gone, one red light smouldering on the back of the last carriage. The air grew calm again. Coomb stood up and leaned by the window. A breeze was just rising. The sun beyond the hills was warming the sky, and the mist was slowly melting. Slate-grey water gleamed here and there in marshy pools. There was no sound at all now, except the breeze singing through the telephone wires.

With a groaning shudder, the train started again. It had just entered the Soviet region of Amur, along the south of which the Amur River runs, the border with China.

Chapter Twenty-four

He was officially designated Mao's successor, but Tiger Cat Lin never felt certain he would actually succeed him. First, there was his very eminence. As crown prince to Mao's monarch, his position was as precarious as it was prominent. The suspicion of his superior frowned down on him from above; the envy of his rivals scowled upwards from below. A crown prince is appointed to ensure a smooth succession, but the reigning monarch may understandably regard him rather as someone with an interest in his early death. So, at least, it seemed with Mao. Lin had sometimes felt Mao's heavy, moonlike face contemplating him with a guarded, calculating reflectiveness that was less than frank and less than friendly.

But if that was the danger from above, the dangers from below were hardly less menacing. Lin needed the fingers of both hands to count the rivals, each with his own faction, whom he believed to covet his place. And that didn't include Chou, whose apparent indifference to the supreme position might be merely a mask beneath which worked a sly ambition disclaimed in public.

Then there were the ideological and policy differences. Lin was too radical for some moderates, too moderate for some radicals, too much a soldier for some party men, too much a party man for some soldiers. Mao stood for grand self-reliance, Chou for an arrangement with America, Lin for a settlement with Russia. Mao wanted the party to control the gun, Chou wanted the bureaucrats to manage the party, Lin wanted the soldiers to command the bureaucrats.

Besides, there was the matter of Lin's fragile health. Mao

was older, but he seemed more robust than Lin. If nature ran its course, Mao might outlast him. No man likes to think he is heir to something he may not live to inherit. And if he is ambitious, the thought breeds not only dislike but also impatience. And Lin certainly had ambition; as long as his wife, Yeh-Chun, was there to nourish it, so people said, his ambition wouldn't flag. But even if it should, there was always the spur of fear. Were his rivals, or Mao himself, already plotting to destroy him? If so, he had to forestall them.

All these threads were spun in the intricate web of Tiger Cat Lin's motives. The spider of his will hung from one of these threads, but Lin couldn't have said himself which one it was.

Peking, Thursday, 26 August 1971
Sometimes the enormity of what they were planning over-whelmed Lin with a sudden, breath-catching fear that made his fingers tighten. It happened again that night as he looked up from the file on his table to the photograph of the Chairman pinned on the plain white wall opposite him. There was something immovably solid about that face. Lin's fingers curled and his stomach moved uneasily. For a few scared moments he wished he could back out and run home like a frightened child, but where was home if not here? His guards were patrolling outside. Yeh-Chun was next door, helping to clear away the dishes from the evening meal. There was nowhere to run to – and no need to run. But still the childish dread lurked there in the shadows of his mind. For a few seconds he crumbled inwardly, but outwardly he merely frowned, as if puzzled by some recalcitrant logistic problem.

Then his fingers slowly loosened. He breathed deeply and stretched. He let his fingertips drum idly on the stiff cover of the file, headed simply, *Engineering Project 571*, while he looked calmly now through his glasses into the dark, smiling eyes of the Chairman's photo. Beside it was a green metal bookcase, its top shelf filled with the works of Mao. On the shelf below, forlorn and insignificant, stood the few pamphlets he had written himself: *How to Train Soldiers*, *Important Principles of Command* and – the one he was proudest of – *Long Live the Victory of People's Wars*. Insignificant though they looked compared with the massed volumes on the shelf above, he reminded himself reassuringly that a million soldiers of the PLA studied them each week and the pamphlets, if not philosophically profound, were practical and true. 'Practical', he whispered, 'True'.

He looked away to his plain, wooden bed with its cotton blanket neatly folded on the kapok-filled mattress at its foot. He was still a soldier, after all, and he clung to the unvarnished but secure austerity of a soldier's life. It strengthened him to think he hadn't been corrupted. No one could accuse *him* of yearning for the prerequisites of power. The rumours about Chiang Ching filtered through his mind, rumours of a luxurious bedroom on her personal Boeing, of villas with imported furniture. At least no one could accuse him of *that*.

Opposite the table stood two cheap, wooden stools. The rest of the room was bare, the walls whitewashed and without adornment. There wasn't even a desk lamp. The only lighting came from the solitary bulb which hung down from the ceiling, spreading a dim, yellowish light over the table. It wasn't really strong enough for his tired eyes. When he looked up at the bulb he saw a dull glare with a hazed halo round it, like a weak moon on a misty night. Never mind; nobody could accuse *him* of enjoying privilege or luxury. He undid another button of his tunic. The summer air was still and sticky in the little room, even in the evenings, and his vest felt sweaty. He fingered the scar which the Japanese bullet had left in 1937. That, too, seemed to reassure him.

'Yeh-Chun,' he called quietly and coughed. Almost at once the door opened. 'Have we any beans left?' He glanced up at his wife's face over the rims of his glasses. They were a poor fit, always slipping down his curved, thin nose.

'Yes.' Then, as she turned to go, 'Wu is here.'

'Already?'

'I just heard him.'

'Ah.' Lin glanced at his watch, then got up as Wu Fa-Hsien came in. 'Would you like some fried beans?'

Wu's nose wrinkled slightly. 'No, thanks. Have you got a cold again?'

'It's coming.'

Wu grunted and sat down on one of the stools. He was too big for it and bulged over it uncomfortably. He glanced round the room fastidiously as if to say, *Can't you do better than this?* But Lin had opened the file and was reading it intently.

'You promised me an answer,' Lin reminded Wu in his reedy voice at last, looking up inquiringly over his glasses. 'About the air force.'

Wu nodded. 'It all depends on the first step.' His voice was as large as Lin's was small. 'If he' – nodding at the photograph on the wall – 'isn't taken care of at the beginning, and if the radio station doesn't start broadcasting our story at once, I can't guarantee what the local commanders will do. Or rather, I can guarantee. They'll wait and see.'

'Mm.'

'But if it's done quickly and convincingly, they'll all follow my lead. Most of them, anyway.'

'Mm.' Lin was peering down through his glasses at the map on page thirteen of the file.

'What about the Russians?' Wu asked brusquely.

'The Russians? They won't move unless they're attacked.'

'I meant sanctuary. If we fail.'

'Ah,' Lin looked up again mildly. 'If we can get there, of course they'll look after us. What do you think – if the first stroke fails, what are our chances of escape? By plane?'

'I'll have one standing by, but . . .'

Wu lifted his heavy hands and let them fall expressively as Yeh-Chun came in with a steaming bowl of fried, yellow beans. 'I've warmed these up,' she explained almost apologetically. 'From supper.' And she was gone again.

Lin picked up a single bean delicately with his chopsticks. 'Won't you have some?'

Wu shook his head, wrinkling his nose again.

Lin ate carefully, picking up each bean individually and chewing with his head cocked to one side. He swallowed and paused. 'If we fail, people will think we only acted for personal gain, for ambition.'

'That won't matter to us then,' Wu shrugged.

'But it does now,' Lin munched thoughtfully. 'I would like people to know it wasn't just to climb the mountain top but . . .' he pressed his lips together a moment, then licked them with the pale tip of his tongue, 'to put China back on its old course. The one *he*' – Lin glanced sharply at the silent, watching photograph of the Chairman – 'used to want as well.'

'Better make sure the first stroke succeeds, then,' Wu said curtly, indifferent to the delicacy of Lin's conscience.

Lin pushed the bowl aside and pored over the map in front of him. Wu's brusqueness, his loudness, his assumption of equality gnawed quietly but persistently at his mind. While he traced the route his soldiers would have to go to reach the radio station, he half-sensed, half-refused to sense that when the coup was over, he might have to reckon with Wu. And that reckoning might lead to another and that to yet another. . . . He glimpsed the entrance to a long, dark tunnel, which would grow longer and darker the further he went in. Blinking and frowning, Lin forced his mind back to the present. 'Let's go over it again,' he shifted his bamboo chair a little so that Wu could join him at the table.

'How is Tou-Tou? Haven't seen her for a long time.' Wu dragged his stool along the floor so that the leg squeaked jarringly.

Lin brushed back his wiry, grey brows with the knuckle of his forefinger. 'Very well. A good daughter. Here,' he pointed to the line of arrows on the map. 'I don't think we've allowed enough time for the radio station to be surrounded if the signal's given at one-fifteen. This detachment has got to move from the barracks at one o'clock at the latest. Everything depends on precise timing.'

As they bent over the file together, Lin began to feel that this was an ordinary operation after all, no different from any

168

of the others he'd planned. His eyes widened slightly as he recalled his first victory against the Japanese at Pinghsingkuan in 1937, when his men had suddenly charged through the bronzed September cornfields upon the astounded enemy. *September*, he thought, *a lucky month for me.*

Wu was tapping the map with his little finger, its nail a shade longer than the others, as if he had vestigial longings to be a mandarin. 'It will take the helicopters ten minutes from the airfield to this point.'

'But they mustn't move until they hear the signal that we've got the radio station.'

'In clear or in code?'

'Everything must be sent in code until the whole operation is finished.'

Yeh-Chun came softly in and sat beside them on the remaining stool. They discussed the plan until one in the morning.

It was a simple plan. Lin would order the new special security force to storm the Chairman's residence at Chungnanhai in the Imperial City, on the pretext that the 8341 Legion had mutinied and was holding him prisoner. The 8341 Legion, also known as the imperial guard, was in fact composed of loyal veterans, most of whom had served Mao for fifteen or twenty years. They would never mutiny – nor would they surrender. Chan Tung-Hsing, their commander, had been with Mao from the beginning of the revolution, when he used to sleep across Mao's doorway with a loaded rifle. Now he slept in his own bed, but still it was never far from Mao's. People said Chan chose only orphaned soldiers for the imperial guard – they must have only one loyalty.

The legion would resist fiercely, but their communications with the rest of the country would be cut off and they would be overwhelmed in the end by Lin's far stronger force. In the confusion of the attack, Lin would ensure that Mao, Chan and those around them were all killed. At the same time, Chou would be arrested together with his most prominent supporters and accused of suborning the 8341 Legion and

169

planning a *coup d'état*. Control of the radio station and the press, which would be seized in the first moment, would guarantee that only the news Lin had prefabricated for them would be fed to the stunned millions of China. With Mao and Chou out of the way, Lin would have enough support in the Politburo and the army to ensure that, as Mao's designated heir, he would in fact succeed him.

A simple plan, and a daring one. It would involve a great deal of blood-letting, but Tiger Cat Lin could accept that, had accepted worse in the past. He had watched his army in Korea surging bravely forward in human waves – waves that broke into the red spray of a myriad corpses on the jagged, booming rocks of the concentrated fire that met them. The blood that flowed in Chungnanhai would be a mere trickle compared with that.

Wu insisted on one change in the plan – they must make certain that Chiang Ching was killed as well. She might not be in Peking when the signal was given – her movements were often unpredictable – but wherever she was, they must send people to kill her. Lin was for dealing with her later, but Wu was adamant, and in the end Lin deferred to his vengefulness. Chiang Ching had had Wu accused of bourgeois tendencies during the cultural revolution and he had eventually lost his post as commander of the air force. It had taken him six months to get reinstated. That was a humiliation he would never forgive.

Chapter Twenty-five

Trans-Siberian Railway, Saturday, 28 August 1971
Coomb had had to change trains at Khabarovsk, twenty miles from the Chinese border. He'd been led off the old train by an unsmiling Intourist girl and told he would have to wait one hour for the next one. Clasping his briefcase tightly, he'd strolled in the barnlike ticket hall under the curious, vacant gaze of peasant women and bored soldiers. He'd walked round the grassy park outside the station, where, for a change, not a dynamic stone Lenin, but the grey figure of the city's founder, the cossack Khabarovsk himself, confronted the indifferent citizens.

From time to time Coomb had noticed the grey-haired Russian in the brown suit hovering behind him. At last he'd been put onto a special train reserved strictly for foreigners and Soviet diplomats leaving Russia. It was an old train, recalling Czarist splendours, with walnut panelling, ornate mirrors in brass frames, private showers for each compartment and a restaurant car with pure white tablecloths and starched napkins, where smart, efficient waitresses served appetizing food.

Except for the waitresses, conductors, cleaners and a few diplomats, there were no Russians on the train. Coomb's travelling companions, all of whom he avoided, were tourists or businessmen from Japan, Australia or America. Except, of course, the grey-haired Russian in the brown suit, who continued to pass Coomb's compartment regularly, casting furtive, flinty glances through the window.

The train left Khabarovsk in the evening, for the track

passed several Russian military installations, and the journey was always timed to blindfold prying eyes with darkness. Coomb sat in the corner of his compartment, a tasselled reading lamp at his shoulder, gazing at his face reflected on the passing night outside the window. Several times they stopped, while trains of black, covered trucks and sealed carriages clanked slowly past, monstrous and sinister in their dark, ponderous motion.

Late at night, Coomb brushed his teeth in his private shower, but still did not unfold his toothpaste carton. Then he wrapped himself in his blankets and tried to sleep. Tomorrow the train would reach Nakhodka, the Russian port. He would emerge from his travelling cocoon.

Would the bear's paw let him go or close round him at the last moment? Would they search him as thoroughly at customs as the KGB man had in Moscow? There he'd been saved by the purest luck. Tomorrow, if they really searched – in a sudden rush of panic he felt certain they would. He could see them opening the toothpaste carton, gathering round him, leading him away. . . .

He ought to destroy the carton, throw it out of the window; no one would blame him for saving himself. Stuart had no right to use him like this anyway. He sat up, paused, forced himself to sit still and think. Slowly he realized he wasn't going to throw the carton away; he was going to take his chance and go through with it. He sat there the rest of the night shivering in his blanket, wondering dully what stupidity of pride or foolhardiness it was that had mastered his animal, self-preserving fear.

Three or four times an hour, sealed trains went clanking past the window, each carriage like a coffin, blind and menacing.

During Coomb's restless night, Academician Valentski in Moscow had panicked too. His nerves, taut for weeks, suddenly snapped. Ever since he'd slipped the two sheets of paper into Coomb's typescript, he'd been fearfully expecting a dawn knock at the door, a tap on the shoulder in a crowded street, some unannounced caller at his office. He saw questioning expressions in his colleagues' eyes, felt he was being followed, suspected his secretary of going through his desk. He dared not sleep, couldn't eat, snapped at the persistent solicitude of his uncomprehending wife. He avoided his son-in-law as assiduously as he'd cultivated him before, and his daughter's consequent coolness he interpreted as suspicion.

One day, on the bus to the university, he looked up from his damp, nervously clasped hands and met the eyes of the man opposite him, a burly middle-aged man in a dark suit. He looked away, glanced up again and found the man's eyes still gazing at him unblinkingly. He shuddered inwardly. With trembling legs, he stood up and got off at the next stop. the man got off too and walked across the road, pausing at the window of a food store. Valentski's legs nearly buckled under him as he walked quickly away, down a side street, then down another. He jumped on another bus, walked half a mile, approached the British embassy. The entrance was shut.

He walked past, his knees wobbling, crossed the road, paced up and down, his heart racing with fear. At last with a desperate lurch he launched himself across the road. His legs carried him to the entrance. He pressed the bell. He was going to beg for asylum, to defect to the west, to inquire simply if he could visit Britain – he was too muddled by fear to know which. Then, as his finger released the bell, he realized with sickening clarity that he was acting suicidally, that he was only inviting suspicion, that the British would disown him, that he must endure and hope that his fears of the KGB were groundless. He turned to run away.

A car crawled along the curb behind him. The rear door opened. 'Tovarich,' a voice called quietly.

He faltered, pretended not to hear, hurried on.

The car drew even with him. 'Tovarich!' the voice called again, authoritatively.

He stopped and turned, trembling. 'Yes?' he answered meekly.

The summons had come. He had brought it on himself.

When the British embassy official opened the door, there was no one there. Only a black Zil saloon car driving slowly away down the road.

Chapter Twenty-six

The special security force had finished its first exercise at dawn. Both Lin Piao and Hung had been up all night. Lin looked tired and haggard, Hung fresh and vital. They sat in Lin's office in the Defence Ministry wearing their olive green, baggy uniforms, sipping their tea and waiting.

Lin edged back his cuff to look at his watch. Ten past nine. How like Chan to be deliberately late. He noticed how frail his wrist looked in his capacious sleeve and let the cuff drop. The two men's eyes met. They looked away and sipped their tea again. Lin caught himself gazing at the Chairman's photograph on the wall, at those bland, impervious, measuring eyes.

A few minutes later, the orderly knocked. Before he could be announced, Chan Tung-Hsing marched in, small but sturdy-looking in his uniform. 'Sorry I'm late,' he said curtly to Lin. His eyes coldly acknowledged, without welcoming, Hung's presence.

Tiger Cat Lin had risen courteously. Hung reluctantly rose too. 'Thank you for coming,' Lin said.

'What's the trouble?' Chan eyed Hung impersonally in a critical survey of the room. Hung might just as well have been a hatstand.

They sat down as the orderly brought Chan some tea. He sucked it up and smacked his lips. 'Well?'

Lin glanced at his round face, thick, strong neck and barrel chest. The sight of such crude good health triggered a twinge of envy in him. His own chest was beginning to ache. Soon

175

the cough would start. 'The special security force has just finished its first exercise,' he began noncommittally.

Chan nodded casually, 'Any good?'

'Everything went according to plan except for one thing,' Hung started, then hesitated, waiting for Lin.

'Which was?' Chan didn't even glance at Hung.

Hung's face flushed at Chan's insolence, but Lin was as usual unperturbed. 'To put it simply,' he spoke almost regretfully, 'your people refused to co-operate despite my explicit instructions.'

'Ah.' Chan sucked up some more tea and gulped. 'Your people wanted to enter Chungnanhai. My orders are not to let anyone in without a pass. I can't let just anyone running around in uniform into the Chairman's compound, at midnight, can I?'

'Those troops are special security force troops carrying my orders countersigned by the defence minister,' Hung's eyes glared at him, his voice rising. 'As you very well know.'

'But they didn't have a pass, did they?' Chan asked bluffly. 'As you very well know.'

'They had the defence minister's signature on their orders! Chairman Mao's close comrade in arms!' Hung leant forward. 'My job is to protect the Chairman. How can I do it if I can't get near him? Are you saying you won't obey the defence minister's orders?'

'I obey the Chairman's orders,' Chan flicked an imaginary speck of dust off his spotless uniform. 'And as for protecting the Chairman, I was doing that before your special force had ever been organized. I obey the Chairman's orders,' he repeated truculently and stood up. 'Is there anything else to discuss?'

The cough was at its worst as Lin drove with Hung back to headquarters at midday. It was a dry hacking cough that went on for half a minute at a time, leaving him gasping for breath. Hung sat beside him, glaring rigidly at the back of the driver's head as if it were Chan's and he wanted to blow it off.

They were passing Tien An Men Square when Lin had got

176

enough breath back to speak calmly. 'I will raise it with the Chairman after the next Politburo meeting,' he said. 'But if it happens again, you have my authority to do whatever is necessary to carry out my orders.'

'Chan thinks he owns Peking,' Hung nodded grimly at a group of soldiers from the 8341 Legion. 'Look how they strut about. Just look at them!'

They could be a menace if they got out of hand,' Lin suggested pointedly. 'If people put ideas into their heads . . .'

Hung glanced round at him quickly. But the tiger cat didn't follow up his hint. He'd dropped the seed; that was enough. Better to let it grow quietly in Hung's receptive mind.

He gazed out at the Tien An Men balcony, from where he would review the National Day Parade on October the first. Banners and streamers covered it already. 'It is an imposing sight,' he murmured. He could see his seat and the place from which he would address the nation. He imagined the square filled with soldiers, row after row of them, and himself stepping up to the rostrum for his first speech as chairman.

'Yes, an imposing sight,' he murmured again. Then, louder, 'This afternoon we'll go through the details of the Chungnanhai defences again.'

Chapter Twenty-seven

Nakhodka, Sunday, 29 August 1971

Intourist buses met the train to ferry the passengers to the quayside. Coomb sat with his briefcase on his knees and saw the sea, the white stack of the boat, the soldiers and police milling about as the bus lurched and jolted over the unmade road. Beside him sat a Japanese businessman. Behind him, the grey-haired Russian in the brown suit. Coomb's fingers curled and uncurled round the worn, leather handle of his briefcase. He kept licking his dry lips. His stomach turned slowly, insistently.

'Don't drink the water,' smiled the Japanese businessman. His mouth was full of gold fillings.

'What!'

'On the boat. Don't drink the water.'

'Oh. Thank you.'

The coach stopped by a long, low wooden building.

'Customs,' smiled the Japanese. 'Passports.'

'Are they very strict?' Coomb tried to sound casual.

'They open everything.'

The Japanese stood in front of him, the Russian behind. There seemed to be more officials than passengers. The Japanese showed his passport and went through to the customs counter. Coomb showed his passport. The Russian slipped round the counter, touched the official's arm, and motioned him out of earshot. Coomb watched them whispering, glancing back at him. The official came back, consulted a black book on his desk, checked Coomb's passport again and passed it back.

'Customs,' he said, jerking his head. 'Number six.'

Coomb swallowed and went through.

Number six was a fat woman in a grey uniform. Coomb opened his suitcase, handed her his passport. The Russian in the brown suit approached her. She glanced back at Coomb, nodded, went to her desk and returned with the common-place book they'd taken off him in Moscow. He slipped it into his pocket.

'Russian currency?' she asked him as she groped inside his suitcase.

'All gone.'

He watched her turn to his briefcase. She opened the sponge bag, took out the toothpaste carton, shook it, put it back, took it out again and examined it intently.

'What is this?'

Coomb's pulse raced. 'What?' he said weakly.

'This?' She tapped the carton with her fat forefinger, holding it under his nose. 'This word?'

'Word?' repeated Coomb stupidly. He leaned forward. 'Fluoride.'

'Uh?'

'Flu-or-ide.'

'Ah. Fluoride.' She bared her teeth and made vigorous brushing motions with her finger. 'Fluoride?'

'Yes.'

'Fluoride. Tooth. Good, good.' She put the carton back, nodding and smiling approvingly as she probed further inside the suitcase. 'Good, good.'

Coomb felt his nerves slowly slackening. His pulse slowed. He tried to look unconcerned.

After riffling the pages of the Chekhov, the customs inspector gave his passport back and waved him on. He walked out of the building, across to the gangway, showed his ticket and went on board. He turned to look back at the quayside, still breathing unsteadily. The Russian in the brown suit had disappeared.

An hour later, the boat cast off and Coomb's last lingering

179

fears slipped away. Now he must certainly be safe. They couldn't have suspected him after all. As the dark, mauve hills round the port began to dim and merge with the dark, mauve sky, he grew lightheaded and impatient to work again. He knew he mustn't take any chances, even at this late stage, so he wouldn't let himself examine the toothpaste carton. But he carried it on deck with him in his briefcase and his mind kept circling round it, eager now to get at it as soon as he could.

They passed the harbour breakwater. The pilot was leaving. Coomb watched him clamber down the companion-way, jump aboard the dirty grey pilot launch and lift a heavy hand in parting. The launch cut away, back towards Russia. The wind freshened and the ship began to lift.

A loudspeaker spluttered somewhere behind him, summoning the passengers in Russian, Japanese and finally English to the first sitting of dinner. He gazed down into the green, swirling sea a few minutes longer, then went to the restaurant. He was sharing a table with the gold-toothed Japanese businessman, who again warned him not to drink the water. Coomb smiled almost genially, resting his hand protectively on the briefcase beside him. 'I shall drink nothing but wine,' he said.

The ship was called *Felix Dzerzinsky*. Coomb had little use for history, regarding it as a rag-bag of enlightening tales; but if he'd read enough to know whom the ship was named after, he might have sensed the presence of an omen. Felix Dzerzinsky was the founder of the Cheka – the first communist secret police – in 1917. It was from the Cheka that, through many metamorphoses, the present KGB emerged. A portrait of Dzerzinsky hangs in the office of the chairman of the KGB at 2 Dzerzinsky Square, Moscow, next to the Lubyanka prison.

180

Chapter Twenty-eight

At first the KGB officers who took Valentski in for questioning expected it to be a routine affair – some unbalanced intellectual, acting on his own, who imagined he'd be able to whine and snivel on the British ambassador's shoulder. But when they discovered he wasn't an unknown, self-styled poet or painter, but a member of the Soviet Academy, they began to take him more seriously.

Academicians are no laughing matter. His interrogation was taken over by more sophisticated officers, and he was spared the casual beating which might otherwise have been given him as a matter of course. To his new interrogators, he was at first a mystifying case. He gave absurd reasons for his behaviour outside the British embassy and, when their absurdity was exposed, fabricated equally absurd ones to replace them. He protested his innocence, demanded his rights and pleaded for mercy, all in one breath.

Clearly he was frightened out of his wits, but what was it all about? They'd been questioning him for several hours before they got a clue. In one of his panicky protestations, he mentioned his son-in-law, a major in the army, as a guarantor of his own political reliability. A check of Smetanka's file turned up information about his present posting. The interrogation became more pointed, Valentski more frantic. Reports were passed up to higher officials. Smetanka was pulled in, bellowing his innocence. He kept on bellowing it through his subsequent pain.

It was clear that the truth, whatever it was, would have to come from Valentski. Academicians are rarely beaten, though that is not an indication of respect for learning. More exquisite methods of questioning are employed, methods which break the mind while leaving the body unmarked. As academicians often appear in public and receive attention from the foreign press, it's better if their bodies are unbruised, their limbs unbroken.

Lubyanka Prison, Moscow, Monday Morning,
30 August 1971
The bare, brilliant light had kept Valentski awake despite his exhaustion, greater now even than his fear. So he'd lain with his head turned to the wall, covering his sore lids with his arm. Occasionally he'd slipped into a merciful, black unconsciousness for a moment, only to be awoken almost at once, starting at some real or imagined noise. He felt the coarse cloth of his jacket sleeve rough against his skin and smelled its warm woollen smell. Somehow it comforted him, reminding him of the home and the life he'd lost, the life outside those walls. But then he heard the guards coming again, heard their metal heels ringing on the stone floor, heard the key turning in the lock. He cringed.

'On your feet then! Come on!'

But he couldn't stand. So they dragged him out into the corridor like a sack of straw, neither brutally nor kindly – simply indifferently. His legs trailed, hobbled unsteadily beneath the sack of his body, stumbled and trailed again. His heart thudded sickeningly in his chest and his arms trembled weakly. A wordless moaning came from his mouth.

They took him past the usual room. His stomach lurched with panic. Were they going to shoot him now? He raised his head imploringly and tried to hang back, but they jerked him forward like a dog. His false teeth were gone, he had no shoelaces or tie, his belt was gone and his trousers hung down by his hips. He could see his corpse already, slumped in a cellar with a hole in the back of the head, shrunken, stiffening, pathetic in its half-dressed shabbiness. He wanted to scream, but only the wordless moaning came. They dragged him on. He sobbed in childlike humiliation as he felt himself soiling his trousers. Still they dragged him on.

Into another room, and he was suddenly overwhelmed with tearful relief to see the same two interrogators there. He would never know their names, but their presence reassured him somehow. They weren't going to shoot him, then, not yet. They sat behind a long desk, chatting and smoking. Against the wall there was an iron hospital bed with a man in a white coat standing beside it. A doctor. Were they going to care for him, be kind to him after all? He tried to smile his gratitude, but they weren't looking. Then, as they dropped him into the chair in front of the desk, he noticed the KGB uniform under the doctor's white coat. The sight crushed his meek, uncertain hopes, and a new terror quaked through his body.

The guards turned to go, but the chief interrogator held them back. They stood behind Valentski expectantly. He felt even more vulnerable with the door open like that behind him. The chief interrogator breathed a curl of cigarette smoke out of his mouth, up over his face, frowning slightly as it passed over his eyes. He opened the file on the desk, slowly flicking the pages over. The other swallowed some tea, gazing at Valentski with casual, hard blue eyes.

Valentski licked his lips. He would tell them everything, whatever they wanted to know. He couldn't take any more.

'Georgi,' the chief interrogator began familiarly, not troubling to look up, 'We've established certain facts, so you needn't trouble to deny them any longer.'

Valentski nodded meekly, abjectly. He only wanted to please them now. He'd keep nothing back. So long as they'd leave him alone afterwards, let him sleep.

'The facts are connected with your son-in-law, Major Smetanka. He's confessed that he gave you secret information . . .' Now he looked up, inquiringly.

They were bluffing. Smetanka had told them little – he didn't know himself what Valentski had extracted from him on that drugged and drunken night – but they wanted to test their suspicions by observing Valentski's reaction to this false bit of information.

Valentski swallowed and nodded abjectly again. 'It wasn't his fault,' he mumbled, feebly anxious to spare his unloved, selfish daughter and her vulgar, stupid family. 'He couldn't help it.'

The two interrogators glanced at each other briefly. The chief interrogator looked down again. He reached for the phone, and spoke quietly into it. 'Maxim? Send him out now.' Putting the phone down again, he leant back to consider Valentski. 'Naturally, you've passed this information on to a foreign agent. The penalty is death. However, if you make a full confession . . .'

He ended on a rising note, holding out a trembling, shimmering hope. Before Valentski could answer, though, he heard someone being dragged down the corridor, moaning with pain.

'Turn him round.'

The guards lifted Valentski's chair and dumped it facing the door. He realized now why it hadn't been shut. It had been left open deliberately. He wanted to close his eyes, but a fascinated terror forced him to look. The footsteps came nearer, the moaning was low and wordless. Two guards passed, dragging Smetanka. His feet trailed behind him and his head fell loosely forward between them. His face was grey and corpse-like. Blood ran down from a welt on his cheek. The last time Valentski had seen him, those cheeks had been flushed with life and alcohol.

'Major Smetanka's been having a hard time of it,' the chief interrogator remarked pleasantly behind Valentski. 'But he's being very co-operative now. Turn him round again.'

Valentski was lifted and dumped again. He heard the door close behind him.

'We want a full confession from you, my friend. That's your only hope. And just to make sure you tell the truth, we're going to give you a little medicine.'

'I'll tell the truth, don't,' he protested, 'I'll tell the truth.' The words slithered through the gaps in his gums where his false teeth had been.

'Put him on the bed.'

184

The guards lifted him, sobbing and pleading, and sat him on the bed.

'Please, I'll tell you everything.' He felt giddy and faint.

'Lay him down. No, the other way.' It was the doctor who spoke now.

His eyes were going grey, his breath came in unsteady gasps, his heart thudding in his chest, his pulse echoing through his body. The doctor took his wrist, placed two fingers on it, listened and frowned.

'Can't take much.'

'Never mind. His sort don't need much.'

The doctor shrugged. 'Roll up his sleeve.'

Valentski watched them helplessly now, through a wavy mist of fear and nausea. They were trying to push his jacket sleeve up, but it was too tight.

'Never mind, in the arse.'

They tugged his trousers down, rolled him onto his side towards the wall and pulled up his shirt.

'Pooh, couldn't you have cleaned him up?' the doctor's voice complained. 'Hold him like that.'

There came the clink of metal instruments. Valentski's panic became a frenzy. He tried desperately to protect himself, but they knocked his arms away effortlessly and gripped him tighter. A needle jabbed into him with a prick and a long dull ache and then was slowly withdrawn. They let him roll over onto his back again. He saw their faces floating above him. The chief interrogator had his cigarette in his mouth. How strong and clean they seemed, their uniforms so spruce, their hair so clipped and brushed, their chins so firm and smooth.

Suddenly he felt his breath going. His lungs no longer worked properly and he had to suck the air in. It got worse. He was suffocating. He couldn't breathe. He gasped and heaved for air but none came. His arms flapped and jerked; he tried to call out, to implore them, but no sound came, only the frantic gasping and jerking while they looked down at him like anglers at a drying fish. His head was bursting, his eyes starting out of their sockets, his hands flapping, his

185

breath going, and the terrible certainty of death making him writhe in helpless panic.

They watched with a detached yet riveted interest for several minutes while the frenzied spasms grew wilder and wilder, then suddenly ceased. His body collapsed into stillness.

The doctor lifted his limp arm and felt for his pulse.

'Is that all?' asked the chief interrogator, a shade disappointed.

'They say it's like dying without death,' the doctor replied.

'It only took a few minutes.'

The doctor shrugged, disdaining to explain the mysteries of his art. 'I think you'll be satisfied.'

When Valentski's eyes opened, he was shuddering, covered in a cold sweat, saliva dribbling from his mouth. His eyes wandered crazily, without expression. He didn't seem to recognize his tormentors at first, but as the chief interrogator leaned over him, his pupils dilated wildly and terror gleamed in them again.

'That was a small dose, Georgi. We can give you a bigger dose, we can keep on doing it twenty times a day, seven days a week. It doesn't cost us a thing, we don't even have to exert ourselves. Do you understand?'

Valentski nodded feebly, staring up at him while pressing weakly back onto the bed away from them all.

'Right. Well, all we want from you is a full, detailed confession. No holding back, no little lapses of memory, no covering up, otnerwise another jab, all right? And it'll be a bigger dose next time.'

Valentski was still staring at him wild-eyed. As he nodded again, the imploring look came back into his cringing face. 'Not again,' his voice whimpered. 'Please, not again.'

The interrogator patted his shoulder soothingly. 'You play it straight with us, we'll play it straight with you. But remember – ,' and he lifted the syringe off the table by the bed, waving the sleek, shiny needle over Valentski's face. A drop of its poison gathered at the aperture and hung there, shivering. 'Remember, if you try any tricks, you get more of this. All right?'

Valentski shut his eyes as he nodded. Tears squeezed out of their corners and trickled down his face. The doctor frowned as he took the syringe from the interrogator's hand and put it back on the table. He didn't like laymen handling his instruments.

The chief interrogator, oblivious, patted Valentski's shoulder again. 'All right then, Georgi, what about some tea, then, eh?'

The drug they gave Valentski is called succinylcholine. It is occasionally used during surgery, when the patient is already unconscious from a general anaesthetic and it is necessary to relax his muscles. In a conscious patient, it produces muscular convulsions, inability to breathe, agonizing pain and, eventually, paralysis, until the effect wears off. Hence, if doctors suspect a patient was not fully unconscious when succinylcholine was administered, it is a standard precaution to inject another drug, scopolamine, at once, which erases all memory traces for several hours back. It is not known exactly how succinylcholine works or what it is like to experience it. Those who have been administered the drug while conscious have not been able to describe their experiences coherently.

Valentski told them everything. The report was read at once by the alarmed chairman of the KGB, who brought it immediately to the Soviet leaders. At the same time, a message was flashed to the master of *Felix Dzerzinsky*, ordering him to reduce speed and set a secret watch on Coomb without arousing his suspicion. The master handed the responsibility for Coomb's surveillance over to the supernumerary radio officer who'd brought him the message and was, in fact, a KGB official.

When Coomb awoke the next morning, the coast of Japan, which should have been in sight, was nowhere to be seen. The ship rolled gently on the smooth, waveless sea, as if it were becalmed.

Chapter Twenty-nine

The meeting was hastily convened and lasted just under two hours. Now that the security of the code was uncertain, the whole operation was jeopardized and the apprehensive doves wanted to abandon it. But some of the hawks argued that the British agent was still in their hands and couldn't have passed on his information yet. Why not deliver him to the KGB's department of 'wet affairs' (as the liquidation section had been dubbed by some grim humorist) and carry on with the operation as agreed? The trouble with that, the ruffled doves replied, was that nobody could be sure the British agent hadn't passed his information on already. The KGB's surveillance of him had been perfunctory, some added with a trace of sourness, and there was simply no way of telling now whether or not he'd communicated with other agents.

At this point the KGB was able to spread its wings. Ignoring the implied charge of incompetence, the KGB chairman said that the security leak could easily be turned to their advantage. Let the British have the code and allow them to intercept messages in it. The messages would be deliberately invented to mislead them. At the same time, a small adjustment to the original code could be made to render the key the British possessed useless. There was time for all concerned to learn the adjusted code before it was necessary to implement it.

The British would be lulled into believing they knew the Russian intentions. And what they were allowed to 'discover' would divert their attention from China. Then, when the operation was mounted, the new code would baffle the British until it was too late. They would be unable to warn either China or America in time to influence the outcome.

And the traitor Valentski? His distracted wife, who had reported his disappearance to the police, would be told that her husband had been found wandering the streets and taken to a psychiatric hospital, where he was too ill to be seen. So if the British had agents who had noted his disappearance, their suspicions could be allayed with this story. Which, as a matter of fact, was largely true. Valentski was indeed now in a psychiatric hospital, in the maximum-security wing controlled by the KGB.

Encouraged by this, the hawks grew stronger. A fluttering dove or two changed sides. The same white-bloused secretary typed the decision – to follow the KGB plan.

The conference room emptied. Stale cigarette smoke hung over the table in heavy layers. The solid, vacant chairs stood untidily, where their occupants had pushed them back and left them. Downstairs, the Zil limousines were summoned one by one into the courtyard and bore their passengers away, in strict order of precedence. It was after six and the light was going. Soon the summer would be over.

One hour later, bells rang on the bridge of *Felix Dzerzinsky* and in the sweating engine room. The ship quivered slightly, as if tensing itself, then eased forward, its engines throbbing. Looking innocently down from the main deck, Coomb saw the bow wave curl up high and glanced at his watch.

Before long, the coast of Japan appeared like a long, low bank of cloud on the horizon.

Chapter Thirty

It was late in the evening when the ship entered the roads. Coomb leaned over the side by a lifeboat, sniffing the sulphurous industrial air and gazing out at the heavy pall of smog which hung over the flat, monotonous city. His nerves began to tense again. In half an hour the gangway would be down. Surely he was safe now; the Russians wouldn't have let him get this far if they'd suspected him. Yet now that the final test had come, he felt his pulse quickening with fear. Heavy hands might still clamp down on his shoulders as he approached the gangway. Half-seriously, he wondered whether to stand on the lower deck, so that he could jump overboard if necessary. But he told himself not to be ridiculous and merely opened his briefcase to check that everything was there.

It all went quite smoothly. He joined the line at the gangway, showed his landing card, walked across the quay into the customs hall and in a few minutes stood in another line for taxis. The passengers shuffled forward, pairing off with the snorting diesels as if in some mechanical dance. *How easy it all is*, Coomb thought, as, looking back through the taxi window, he saw the white bows of *Felix Dzerzinsky* for the last time.

The road to Tokyo cut through the middle of Yokohama, following looping underpasses with factories lining them on each side. The taxi stopped at a toll gate. The driver paid, a bell rang and Coomb saw a sign in English – Tokyo. The toll road was an expressway on concrete stilts, stalking over shanty towns of little wooden houses, past vast, steel-framed factories and huge, gleaming metal tanks of gas and oil. Here and there, patches of grass grew between the shadows of the concrete stilts, lifeless in the glare of the street-lamps. Lorries, buses and tankers drove past Coomb in the other lane, their lights flashing one after the other over his eyes. Here was the paradigm of industrial man, whose decay and collapse he foretold in his book. But he did not think of that now. He nursed his briefcase on his lap and thought impatiently of the Russian code.

The expressway ended, easing itself down into the outskirts of Tokyo. Coomb saw the Tokyo Tower ahead. At ten past ten he got out at the British embassy and pushed the bell on the side of the heavy, locked gates.

The car which had parked on the other side of the road half an hour before drove away as he was let in.

They were waiting for him. An official led him along a corridor, up a flight of stairs, into a small study. Two men were there, Coomb's 'manager', Johnston, and a tall, bald man whose name Coomb didn't catch.

'You're late,' Johnston said. 'Was the boat delayed?'

'I've got the key to the code.' Coomb opened his briefcase.

'Coffee or tea, or something stronger?' Johnston asked. 'What happened in Moscow? Why didn't you call at the embassy if you had the key?'

'First things first. Look at this.' He unfolded the carton at last. 'What about some whisky? Look at this. I bloody near died getting this out of Russia.'

It was the other man who studied it, putting on his glasses, while Johnston poured Coomb a whisky.

'Have there been any more messages?' Coomb looked over the tall man's shoulder.

'No, but we can try it out on what we've got.' He sniffed. 'I see, this is the substitution key, is it? And this is the transposition key? Presumably they change the transposition key every twenty-four hours or so . . .' He spoke as flatly as if he were studying a grocer's bill.

'Presumably, but once they start sending a lot of messages out in it, it'll be easy to –'

'Yes.' He sniffed again. 'Very neat, isn't it? Easy to send. Obviously meant for use in the field.'

'Mm. Have you got those messages here?' Coomb hadn't touched his whisky yet. 'Let's try it out on them.'

The tall man glanced at Johnston.

'Let Brian have a go at it first,' Johnston said. 'I've got to debrief you.'

'Debrief me?' Coomb was beginning to feel light-headed. 'Isn't that what they do in prep schools?'

'Not exactly.'

'It's not really necessary, is it?'

'Yes, I'm afraid it is.'

'Well, how long will it take?'

'Two or three hours, at least.'

'Can't it wait till the morning? I'd like to work on this code first.'

Johnston was unexpectedly firm. 'I'm afraid it has to be done straight off.'

Coomb sat down, pursing his lips, and then swallowed some whisky. 'Well, let's get on with it then.'

The tall man left with the code. Coomb looked up at Johnston, who was plugging in a tape recorder.

'Are you going to tape me?'

'Afraid so. Do you mind?'

Coomb shrugged. 'Any mail for me, by the way?'

'Er . . .' he was adjusting the microphone. 'No, I don't think so. Now, let's start with the main things first. How did you get this information? Why didn't you call at the embassy?'

The debriefing lasted for more than four hours. Coomb's manager asked question after question, the significance of which Coomb was often quite unable to measure. The reaction to his speech and the details of his interrogation by the KGB had to be dragged out of his memory almost word by word – that he had expected. But the behaviour of hotel staff and train conductors, the routes taken by Intourist guides, the dates and times at which he visited different places in

192

Leningrad or Moscow, whether it was dark or light when the trans-Siberian express passed through Perm or Irkutsk, what the Japanese businessman had said to him on the boat – all these details seemed absurdly unnecessary. Yet they interested Johnston as much as the circumstances of Coomb's startling speech at the conference and how Valentski slipped him the two pages of information.

Part of this questioning was intended to test Coomb's veracity, although that was not seriously in doubt. The rest was meant to discover whether the Russians knew of or suspected Coomb's relationship with Valentski. For British Intelligence was as alive as the KGB was to the opportunity that a known enemy agent unwittingly presents for feeding the other side a controlled diet of false information.

At half-past three in the morning, Johnston switched off the tape recorder. He was satisfied that the Russians didn't suspect Coomb, although a final assessment wouldn't be made until after his conference with Stuart.

'Well?' Coomb had drunk half a bottle of whisky. His eyes were tired and sore. 'Well?'

'We won't know for sure until we've gone over all this in London.'

'Won't know what for sure?' Coomb stood up and stretched.

'Oh, what to make of it all . . .'

'Is that Brian what's-his-name working on the code now?'

'It will have been flashed to London by now. He's probably having a go at it himself, though.'

'Who is he exactly? Seemed to know what he was talking about.'

Johnston didn't answer. He was gazing down at the tape recorder, drumming on the plastic buttons with his fingertips.

'Who is he?'

Still he didn't answer. Instead, he glanced up at Coomb, then took a small buff envelope out of his pocket. He handed it to Coomb almost shamefacedly. 'This came for you yesterday.'

'What?' Coomb looked down at it, puzzled. 'For me?'

193

'I'm sorry I couldn't give it to you as soon as you arrived. I had to debrief you first. I had no choice, I had to.'

'What?' Coomb heard himself ask stupidly again. He watched his hands drawing a cable out of the unsealed envelope. When he saw what it was, he knew already what the message would be and his fingers unfolded it reluctantly. The world seemed to hold still for a moment as he read.

COME AT ONCE STOP SARAH SINKING STOP SUK-YEE

'I'm sorry,' he heard Johnston's voice saying.

He read it again, then heard himself asking unevenly, 'When did you say it came?' His hands felt as though they were trembling, although they looked perfectly still.

'Yesterday morning. We've got you booked on the first plane to Hong Kong in the morning.'

'The first plane in the morning?' Coomb folded the cable along the same creases, then opened it again as if to make sure. Months afterwards Johnston remembered seeing Coomb's face sag and grow old before his eyes.

'What time will that be?' Coomb asked at last.

'Seven o'clock. I'm very sorry. I'm sorry I couldn't – '

'Seven o'clock,' Coomb nodded and sat down, still gazing at the cable. His voice sounded hollow and lifeless. 'Would you send a wire that I'm coming, please.' Resting his chin on his hands, he stared empty-eyed across the room.

Johnston left him. Minutes or hours later, someone came in, then went out again. Coomb only sat and stared, seeing Sarah's face where the wall should have been. Her expression seemed to keep changing, except for her eyes, which gazed at him in fearful, uncomprehending reproach.

Before Coomb boarded his Cathay Pacific plane at Haneda airport, British cryptoanalysts in London had decoded the two messages that had come into their hands nearly two months before. The first, a mere fragment, was in Russian; the other in a Russianized version of Chinese. The Chinese one referred tersely to preparations being made in all units for Engineering Project 571. In the Russian one, the same words 'Engineering Project 571' appeared. It was a member of the China department who noticed that the Chinese numerals 571 could also be pronounced to mean 'armed uprising'.

Chapter Thirty-one

Peking, Tuesday, 31 August 1971
Peking slept. Soldiers of the 8341 Legion patrolled the grounds of Chungnanhai, manned the machine-gun nests and guarded the doors to the Chairman's house. Trip wires zigzagged invisibly through the darkness, concealed bunkers controlled the approaches, lookouts watched from the roof. The Chairman had been guarded like this round the clock for twenty-two years. He would be guarded like this until the day he died. Peking slept, the imperial guard watched and Mao Tse-Tung listened in his study as Chan Tung-Hsing upbraided him.

'There's no excuse for this force! You were wrong to approve it, but if it exists, at least let me command it.'

Mao's face was slack and heavy as he listened to Chan's blunt scolding. No one else would have dared to speak to him like that, but Mao allowed, even encouraged, Chan to do so. He needed someone round him who never troubled to conceal his thoughts. So he lolled back in his cushioned, creaking chair, his tunic half-undone, and heard Chan out. His eyes were tired, almost lost in the full-moon face that was beginning to crumple with age, and his mouth sagged. He wasn't the serene, benevolent Mao of the photograph on Tien An Men Square. Or the watchful chairman of the Politburo. He was just a tired old man.

At last he lifted his hand, and that too seemed heavy and tired. 'The decision has been taken. This force has a purpose, and your people must co-operate with it.'

'And who gives the orders?'

'Lin Piao and myself.'

Chan's neck swelled. 'You trust Lin Piao more than me?'

'No.' Mao's lids drooped, his eyes sank into the wrinkled skin. He seemed to have fallen asleep. But then he breathed in heavily and sighed.

'There's no one I trust more than you,' he conceded slowly, almost dragging the words out, 'But Lin is going to succeed me. I must build him up. He doesn't think like me, but he thinks more like me than the others do. At least he'll keep some of what I've done. . . . At least he'll do that . . .'

His eyes opened and he looked round the book-lined walls as if they formed the limit of what he'd done – the only walls in China, perhaps, that had no portrait of himself upon them. 'There's nobody else.' He thought of his son An-Ying in his Korean grave. An-Ying would have been forty-six now. 'There's nobody else,' he repeated.

Chan snorted and slapped his thigh impatiently, but Mao shook his head. 'It's no good. It's got to be Lin. Get used to it. There's no one else.' His voice hardened as he spoke and some of the granite authority that had crumbled from his face returned.

Chan compressed his lips, sighed and stared sullenly down at the floor.

Mao's face slowly crumbled again. The harshness gradually went out of it. He was thinking of An-Ying once more, who might have done great things. Somewhere in the villages of China, the children borne Mao by his third wife, Ho Tzu-Chen, might still survive, but he would never know. On the Long March they'd simply had to abandon them, let them go without trace. No, he'd never find them again. And if he did, they'd be strangers to him now. If only An-Ying had lived, though. He remembered the comment of the Han historian, *A death can be heavier than a mountain.*

Chan glanced up at him with sudden, puzzled concern. The Chairman hadn't realized he'd spoken those last brooding words aloud.

Chapter Thirty-two

On Monday and Thursday mornings, after their rounds, the doctors at the hospital gather in a consulting room and confer about each patient. They drink tea or coffee, examine the charts, scrutinize the X-rays, the blood counts and the bone marrow tests and consider what more can be done. If there seems no more hope, they cut off all medicines except pain-killers and let death at last take its prey.

A patient is a little cosmos of nerves and cells, and the doctors are the gods of this little cosmos, dispassionate arbiters of life and death.

So they had opened Sarah's file while Suk-Yee waited in the room next door and Coomb – Coomb still gazed impatiently over the rails of *Felix Dzerzinsky* at the placid waters of the Sea of Japan. Blood counts, drug doses, bone marrow tests. . . . They looked and shrugged. There was really nothing to discuss. The consultant wrote with his gold-nibbed pen – *No further medication except morphine* – and scribbled his initials with a flourish beneath. He went to tell her mother.

The end with leukaemia is sudden and foul. The body collapses inside and out. The nose bleeds, the mouth bleeds, the stomach bleeds – watery, pink stuff, not good, red blood. Sores break out all over. Any remaining hair falls out. Mercifully, the patient sinks into a coma. It's harder on those who watch, particularly if what they are watching is their own child.

Suk-Yee knew at once when she saw the solemn consultant coming towards her, clipping his fountain pen back into his pocket. But still she had to be told.

Hong Kong, Wednesday, 1 September 1971

They'd put him in the first-class section. He didn't know how he'd got his ticket, how he'd been eased past the customs and immigration counters, how he'd come to be sitting there with his seat-belt fastened while the music oozed through the cabin and the stewardess smiled her synthetic solicitude. But as the plane took off he noticed he was in the first-class section.

The hours passed. His limbs were heavy, his eyes still and empty. He took coffee and refused food. The captain came and asked if he was enjoying his trip. He answered yes and closed his eyes. The stewardess offered him drinks. He took coffee again. The hours passed. Soft, indifferent clouds. Calm, indifferent sky. Still, indifferent sea.

The plane slanted downwards and his fear lurched higher, the fear of facing at last that concluding reality which he'd so long deceived himself he was ready to accept. He saw Sarah's face as it looked when she used to play the violin, chin down on the rest, eyes on the music, hair falling over her shoulder. He screwed his eyes shut, but the image would not be squeezed away.

Closer the soft clouds, further the calm sky, nearer and nearer the unruffled sea. The plane sank down, bumped, landed. Coomb tried to nerve himself. He didn't want the flight to be over. He didn't want to get out. But through the window he could see the terminal building growing remorselessly clearer, the landing steps already snaking out towards him.

People were standing up, yawning and talking. He sat hunched and still. The music droned on. The stewardess adjusted her hat, pouting into the mirror.

A voice said, 'Mr Coomb?'

'Yes?'

It had begun. The last act.

'This way, Mr Coomb.' A man in a neat, grey suit with a club tie of some sort led him ahead of all the passengers, down the steps, across the scorching runway, into the empty VIP room.

199

'What about immigration and . . . ?' Coomb asked unnecessarily.

'I'll look after that Mr Coomb. If you'll just let me have your passport? Thanks.' And, discreetly, he was gone.

'Er – I want to phone. Is there – ?' And then Coomb saw Suk-Yee and knew. She was sitting on the edge of an armchair behind a little table, an untouched cup of coffee before her.

She didn't move when she saw him. He walked towards her. She looked stiff and fragile. Her cheeks were pale and taut, her lips colourless, the skin round her shadowed eyes taut. She was gazing at him blankly. And that heavy blankness told him everything.

But still he wanted not to know. He sat down opposite her silently, clutching even now the childish, futile hope that magically, if he didn't speak, what hadn't yet been said could still become, by not being said, not true.

'You weren't here,' she said flatly.

His self-deception deserted him. He felt himself sliding down through its wreckage into a pit of darkness. 'They didn't give me your cable.'

'What?' She seemed not to understand.

He shook his head, meaning *it doesn't matter*. 'How – where is she?' he forced out.

She stared at him, her eyes filling. 'She's gone.'

'Gone?' So he knew with finality now that he wouldn't have to watch her die. He was spared that, and he felt shame at the relief it brought.

'Last night.' Her lips trembled. She gazed away across the vacant, heartless room.

'What . . . How did it . . . What happened?' The questions fell from his mouth like dry little sticks.

She shook her head heavily. 'It began a week ago. Over a week. Just a little infection, that's all, but . . .'

'What?'

'She didn't have any resistance left, they said. She had no immunity against it. They couldn't do any more, they said, they could only make it easier – ' Her voice quavered as she

200

went on in a rush. 'She kept asking for you.'

'Oh my God.'

'She kept asking for you, John. She kept asking for you.'

'All right.'

'She kept asking for you. Why did you go away? Why didn't you come back? Why?' Her face suddenly broke. The tears brimmed over and trickled down her cheeks. Her mouth twisted and quivered.

'All right, Suk-Yee.' He took her hand.

'She kept asking. Right up to the end. She kept asking. She couldn't understand why you didn't come.'

He stared down at the cold coffee between them, at her hand loosely clasped in his. He saw Sarah's face again as it used to be. She would have looked like Suk-Yee.

Suk-Yee's shoulders were shaking. 'She just couldn't understand why you never came.'

'They didn't tell me,' he said bitterly.

'What?'

'In Tokyo. And the boat was late. But I was too late anyway, far too late.' He spoke jerkily, unsteadily. 'When did . . .'

'What?'

'Last night. What time?'

'Last night? Eleven o'clock, I think. About eleven.'

'About eleven?' He looked away, numbly, blankly, towards the door. The discreet man was coming back, Coomb's passport in his hand. 'Eleven,' Coomb repeated dully. At eleven Johnston had been asking him his meaningless questions, Suk-Yee's cable snugly hidden in his pocket.

'We've got a helicopter waiting for you,' the man said, handing Coomb his passport. 'We can go now. Let me take that case for you.'

He steered them out into the brightly throbbing sunlight towards the helipad. The burnished, silvery helicopter stood ready, its rotor arms smoothly spinning. A yellow-gowned, smiling stewardess greeted them in the gale from the clattering blades, holding her pill-box cap down with one hand and her long slit skirt with the other.

Chapter Thirty-three

There are two operations commonly performed in devising a code – substitution and transposition. In the first operation, letters of the alphabet are substituted for the letters of the message that is to be coded. That by itself provides little security; it is the second operation that makes the cryptoanalyst's job difficult. In this second operation, the substituted letters are scrambled into a different order. To break the code, a cryptoanalyst must work out the transposition key before he can begin to think about the substitution key.

Valentski's information, although incomplete, provided the British cryptoanalysts with the means to reconstruct the principles of both the transposition and the substitution keys for the Russian code.

The idea was simple, and Smetanka, Valentski's hapless son-in-law, was right to be proud of it. He'd taken the eight Russian letters which are easiest to send in Morse code and made a grid of them, with eight columns and four rows (see opposite).

There are thirty-two spaces on the grid and thirty-one letters in the Russian alphabet. So he next filled in the grid with the thirty-one letters of the alphabet, placed at random, leaving one space on the grid empty. (This empty space, or dummy, could be used to deceive enemy crytoanalysts.) The grid was the substitution key. Suppose that the word ЛЭHHH (Lenin) is to be encoded (the letters are already on the grid). Reading from left to right first, then top to bottom, ЛЭHHH becomes AA, ДД, ГН, НФ, ГН. Each letter of the original word has been replaced by two letters;

	А	Д	Г	Н	О	Р	Т	Ф
А	Л							
Д		Э						
Г				N				
Н								Н

(The horizontal letters correspond to the Roman letters A, D, G, N, O, R, T, F. The vertical letters are the same as the first four horizontal ones.)

this makes it longer to send, but that is offset by the fact that the grid consists of the eight letters which are easiest to send by Morse.

The next stage was transposition. Smetanka wrote down the numbers from 1 to 10 horizontally, in jumbled order. Messages which had already passed through the substitution process were then to be written under the numbers, from left to right. Thus ЛЭНН, which would have already become АА, ДД, ГН, НФ, ГН, would be written under the numbers like this:

2   4   5   1   3   9   7   6   8   10
АА   ДД   ГН   НФ   ГН

And the message would be sent in the sequence 1 2 3 4 5 as
НФ   АА   ГН   ДД   ГН.

Both the arrangement of the letters on the grid (the substitution key) and the order of the numbers (the transposition key) could be changed as often as desired. (In fact, they were changed every twenty-four hours.) That would delay attempts to break the code, but if the principles were known and enough messages intercepted, any competent cryptoanalytic team would be able to work out the new keys. Valentski's information gave the British team the principles. By a lucky chance, the two messages they had to work on were encoded on the same day, with the same keys – that made their job easier.

Until they discovered Valentski's treason, the Russians had used the new code sparingly – and never in radio transmissions. But two days after Coomb's arrival in Japan, messages in the code were sent over the air. Unlike cables, radio messages are public, in that anyone listening on the right frequency can read them. That was what the Russians now wanted. They fully intended their messages to be read and deciphered. And so they were.

The traffic was all between stations near the Iranian border and the headquarters of the Russian Military Region at Ashkhabad. Although the substitution and transposition keys were changed daily, the Russians made sure enough messages were sent for the British to be able to decode them promptly. It appeared from them that the Russians were going to hold large-scale manoeuvres near the Iranian border. And indeed a number of under-trained Russian units were ordered without warning to move from their base camps to forward positions, where they were uncomfortable, poorly supplied and bewildered.

The British ambassador in Teheran sent cables to London expressing his disquiet over these moves, but Stuart wasn't in the least deceived by the Russian feint. The two earlier messages, which the Russians didn't know had been intercepted, quite clearly pointed to an operation against China. And the lack of massive preparations along the Chinese border supported the view, discreetly hinted at by the spruce little Chinese chargé d'affaires, that the Russians were planning to support a *coup d'état* rather than to mount a full military attack.

But why did the Russians bother to lay a false scent? One

of Stuart's foibles was to hang photographs of the other side's intelligence chiefs on the wall of his office. He gazed into the eyes of the KGB chairman, who stared back unblinkingly at him through slightly crooked glasses, his left eye apparently wider than his right. The obvious hypothesis, despite Johnston's contrary report, was that the Russians knew Coomb had got their code and were using it now to plant misleading clues about their real intentions. A circumspect inquiry by the British cultural *attaché* in Moscow as to whether Academician Valentski would be able to meet some visiting British academicians the next month elicited the regretful response that he was in hospital. This confirmed Stuart's hypothesis. The code they'd got now was useless. He warned his cryptoanalysts to prepare for a new code and asked Coomb urgently to return to London.

Coomb had just seen his daughter's body cremated. He refused.

In Peking, Old Kang's tired frown grew more and more worried, Chou's icy calm more and more frigid. They suspected Tiger Cat Lin, but had no evidence. If he were plotting, they didn't know who was in it with him, how he would strike, or when. All Kang's efforts to trip Lin up had come to nothing. They approached Chan Tung-Hsing, who told them crossly that the Chairman would hear no ill of Lin. All they could do, then, was set their traps and spread their nets, uncertain whether their quarry was before, behind or all round them.

On the fifth of September, the special security force held another exercise under the direction of Lin Piao and Hung. This time Chan Tung-Hsing grudgingly had to allow Hung's men into the Chairman's compound at Chungnanhai. Hung let fall some slighting remarks about the siting of the defences.

Chapter Thirty-four

Peking, Tuesday, 6 September 1971

On his way to the Russian embassy in the morning, the stocky Korean stopped his official car on Fuwai Street and sent the driver back for some documents he'd left behind. When the car had gone, he walked quickly across Yuehtan Park, down a little lane with an unmade road and into an old, decaying house with a shady courtyard. There, behind a loose stone in the wall, he found a slip of paper with rows of letters on it. He returned to Fuwai Street and waited under the shade of a tree, while schoolchildren marched and drilled behind him, extolling in piping voices their great helmsman Mao Tse-Tung.

When the driver returned with the documents, the Korean slipped the paper under the third sheet and delivered them to the Russian embassy. He had to wait. The slip of paper contained a message in the new code, and the KGB cipher specialist was busy with a message that had just come in from Moscow. Decoded, the Korean's message gave the exact timetable of Engineering Project 571 and urgently requested the Russians to avoid any activity on the border which might appear provocative at the time of the coup. Otherwise, Chinese commanders innocent of the plot might assume that Mao's death heralded a Russian invasion and start an unnecessary and dangerous war.

At last the Russian official handed back the documents, asking him to have the details on sheet twenty-two verified by his ambassador. That was a coded instruction for the Korean to take a message to another house at ten o'clock that evening. The Korean assented ungraciously. He didn't like late nights.

The message was the one that had just come in from Moscow. It said that in order to ensure instant communication over wide areas, all future messages concerning Engineering Project 571 should be sent, in code, by radio only.

The Korean did his sluggish stint at the embassy and at half-past nine went out for a walk. He wandered down several lanes until he came to a large, ugly, modern building, just off the broad road laid where the walls used to run between the Inner City and the Chinese City. He entered the building, climbed some unlit concrete stairs, knocked on a door and was let in.

This time there were two other men as well as the familiar hooded figure. The other men were dressed in ordinary blue overalls and wore no hoods. He glanced briefly at them and laid his message in front of the hooded man. One of the others picked it up and started decoding it.

'It's late,' the Korean said in his imperfect Mandarin. 'I don't like doing this at night.'

'Five thousand American dollars have been paid into your account,' said the hooded man in his muffled, reedy voice.

The Korean shrugged. That didn't make it any earlier.

It was hot in the room, airless. The window was shut and covered with a cloth. The naked light bulb glared into their eyes from the middle of the ceiling. They waited while the man decoded the message letter by letter. The hooded figure coughed suddenly, a long, dry, rasping cough. The Korean wiped the sweat off his forehead with the back of his hand. The other man stood, arms folded, against the door. The hooded man was still coughing. The Korean noticed a cockroach crawling across the rough cement floor near his shoe. He lifted his foot to stamp on it, but it scuttled away out of reach.

At last the man had finished. He laid the message before the hooded man, whose coughing fit was only just subsiding, and stood back respectfully. The hooded man had to bend his head to read it. He nodded as he understood, then glanced up at the Korean. 'We may not need you for some time. If we do, we'll let you know.'

'I've been told my replacement at the embassy comes next month.'

The hooded figure nodded again. 'We won't want you to stay here after then.'

The Korean stood up.

'Show him the way,' said the muffled reedy voice.

'I can find my own way.'

'We want you to go out a different way.'

The man who had stood by the door accompanied him down the stairs.

'This is the same way, isn't it?' muttered the Korean peevishly.

'Not at the bottom.'

They passed the first landing. It was dark.

'Mind your step,' warned the man. 'Know who you've been working for?'

'Do you?'

'Of course I do.'

'Well so do I,' lied the Korean carelessly. He wasn't going to lose face in front of a mere bodyguard, especially a Chinese.

'Do you? How did you find out?'

'By his voice,' he guessed rashly. 'I've heard it often enough on the radio.'

The man let him go ahead at the next landing. He walked silently behind the Korean for a time and then started whistling loudly.

'You don't have to let the whole of Peking know we're here, do you?' the Korean complained irritably.

'Turn right at the bottom.'

The Korean turned right. It was darker this way. 'I can't see a thing,' he complained.

He didn't see the hands that suddenly grabbed him and covered his mouth. He didn't see the men who hustled him away. He didn't see the tub of water they shoved his head in.

208

He opened his mouth to scream, but that only sucked the water deeper into his lungs. Desperately he held what was left of his breath and tried to fight them off. But it was no use. His frantic kicking and struggling grew feebler and feebler. Then suddenly he realized why they were killing him. It was because they'd believed his boast, because they thought he knew who the hooded man was, because they were afraid he'd talk and give him away. He must tell them it was a mistake, an empty lie; he didn't know, he couldn't betray him, he couldn't. . . .

But his words were only gasps of bubbling water; his head was bursting and the pounding in his ears was getting louder and louder. And then the men holding him relaxed their grip as his body ceased even to squirm and went still and limp at last.

Later that night they dropped his body into the Golden Water River, where it was found floating face down the next morning without a mark on it.

Two days later, the Russians started transmitting messages in a variant of the code Coomb had got from Valentski. The messages flowed between Khabarovsk, headquarters of the Far East Military Region, and the front line along the Chinese border. Some even appeared to come from inside China. At first, the messages were few. The British crypto-analysts worked day and night, but they couldn't break the code.

Chapter Thirty-five

Maguire looked down at the shadows of the helicopter's
scything blades skimming over the oily sheen of the waveless
sea below. They were only a hundred feet or so above the
water. Sampans and junks slipped past silently, blurred faces
flipping up like cards to stare at the ungainly machine
clattering over them. He swallowed down his old inevitable
fear of falling. The pilot pointed ahead to a curving sandy
bay with steep hills behind it, stone cottages crouching along
the edge of the beach. Maguire nodded. It looked smaller
than he remembered it, but he could see Coomb's house
clearly. The helicopter slid downwards, hovered, settled onto
the beach.

'One hour, all right, sir?' the pilot asked him.

'Yes. Thanks.'

Sand flew up all round him as he ducked away under the
blades. The Whirlwind lurched clumsily, then soared
upwards. He felt the white heat of the sun on his back, felt it
glaring up at him from the sand.

Ragged children stared and giggled behind their hands at
him. A few old women watched from the cottages, their
wrinkled faces shadowed by wide straw hats. The same four
or five sampans were moored off the shore, the same
wrecked hull half-buried in the sand.

He walked quickly onto the stony path towards Coomb's
house. It looked the same, or, rather, as he would have
expected it to look in the heat of the day, dazzlingly white
and promising coolness. As he approached, the dalmation

bounded out towards him as before, but this time it didn't bark. Maguire let the dog sniff his hand. Its black, wet nose just touched his skin while its almond eyes looked up at him unfathomably; then it bounded away.

He followed it towards the door, which was open onto the welcome dimness of the hall. But it was from the veranda that he heard his name called.

'Mr Maguire.' Suk-Yee was sitting in the shade; he could see only her head from where he stood. She was wearing sunglasses. Her face looked, at first, unchanged.

'I'm sorry to intrude like this – '

'The door's open. Come in.'

Into the cool shade of the house. The rugs on the white walls, the stone floor, the plain cane chairs – nothing had changed. Except that there seemed to be an even greater stillness in the air.

She came to meet him, taking off her sunglasses. He felt her hand limp and cool in his, saw, or thought he saw, more shadows in her eyes and began another apology which she cut short, leading him out onto the veranda.

'John'll be here in a minute. Someone rang to say you were coming.'

'The political adviser, yes.'

'John must have seen the helicopter. He's out walking.'

She offered him a long, cane chair, and sat down again herself, putting her sunglasses back on. A doll with a broken arm lay by the foot of her chair. Her bare foot tapped the stone floor beside it. She was wearing thin, blue trousers and a sleeveless white blouse. Her hair was pulled back severely and tied with a pink ribbon at the nape of her neck. He noticed a slight tenseness at the corners of her mouth.

'I was very sorry to hear about . . .'

She nodded briefly, then said, irrelevantly. 'It's absurd for him to go walking in this heat.'

'It is very hot.'

'There's a typhoon coming.' Her voice sounded strained, almost clipped. 'It's always hottest before a typhoon.'

'Yes?'

211

'Would you like a drink? Coffee? Tea?'

'Er, no, thanks, I – '

'No? Can you stay for lunch?'

'I'm afraid not. Thanks very much, but the helicopter's coming back for me soon. I've got to fly straight back to London.'

'I see.'

He watched her foot as it toyed with the doll by her chair. Almost absently, it seemed, she was caressing the lifeless plastic body with her toe. The dog watched too, cocking its head, then lay down beside her. Maguire felt the weight of his tiredness heavy on his eyes and limbs.

They sat silently now – she'd stopped trying to converse. He found himself watching her breasts rising and falling regularly as she breathed. He watched the shadowy pulse in her throat, her tapered, motionless fingers, her bare foot stroking the dead little doll. The sound of a mouth organ came from the back of the house. The dog's ears twitched at it, then lay still.

Maguire recalled the servant sitting in the dark courtyard only a month ago, and it seemed not a month, but a year. There was no sound from the village. Everything lay crushed under the heat. Only the lapping of the sea on the sand and the rambling melancholy of the mouth organ. Then he saw a tear trickling down under her sunglasses, down her high-boned cheek.

'Is there anything I can do?' he asked helplessly.

'It's all right.' She stroked the tear away with her finger. It seemed suddenly a beautiful finger to Maguire, a beautiful hand. One he would want to touch.

The dog lifted its head, pricking its ears again.

'Here he comes,' she said. She breathed in and swallowed.

Coomb's unruly hair passed just above the veranda. Maguire felt a pang of guilt at seeing him first without being seen – as if he were getting an unfair advantage. He stood up.

Suk-Yee went to meet Coomb.

'Mr Maguire's here.'

'Mm. Saw the helicopter.' He came in, sweating profusely.

'I'm terribly sorry to intrude on you again,' Maguire started once more. 'Especially – '

'Hmph.' Coomb ignored his tentatively offered hand and slumped into the rocking-chair. 'I've said no ten times. How often do I have to repeat myself before it sinks in?' His lips, too, seemed tighter than before. He looked a little thinner, his stare a little stonier.

Maguire unlatched his briefcase. 'There's a letter for you here from Brigadier Stuart. And a whole file.'

'Anything to drink, is there?' Coomb interrupted him.

'Coffee?' Suk-Yee nodded and went out.

'I don't understand it all of course, but . . .'

Coomb took the envelope, tore it open and read the letter through, dropping the crumpled envelope on the floor.

'We're not asking you to come to London now. Only to work on it here if you would . . .'

'Thank you, Mr Maguire,' Coomb held up his hand, frowning. 'I can read perfectly well.'

Maguire flushed and stood waiting, then, unasked, sat uncomfortably in the nearest chair.

'And where's the file?'

'Here.'

'Hmph.' Coomb opened it on his lap and skimmed through the pages. He got up abruptly. 'Let's go into the study.'

Suk-Yee followed them with Coomb's coffee, placed it on the desk and went out, closing the door. Maguire imagined her sitting on the veranda again, toying with the doll on the floor, a silent tear moistening her cheek.

Coomb sat down, nodding Maguire to the other chair. The typescript of his book lay in a neat pile on top of the desk, pencilled corrections in the margin of the first page. He gazed at the pile of paper thoughtfully for a few seconds, then pushed it aside to make room for the file.

'They've changed the code and they're using it – '

'I'm sure the file explains everything.' Coomb swallowed the coffee in one gulp. A few drops splashed onto the file. He dabbed them clumsily with his sweat-stained handkerchief and started reading.

213

The pages rustled over. Coomb propped his head on his hands and frowned. Maguire looked round the bookshelves and the walls. There was no picture of Coomb's daughter. He was at first surprised, then surprised at his surprise. He tried to read the top few lines of Coomb's typescript upside down, gave up, gazed out of the window at the sea again. An old freighter, black and rusty, was cruising slowly across the bay. He wondered idly where it came from, watching the dark smoke threading up from its dirty, red stack. A plaintive tune on the mouth organ drifted in faintly from the courtyard.

'Mr Maguire,' Coomb looked up, leaving his finger on a line on the page. 'Did you know that man Johnston didn't tell me about my daughter until six hours after I arrived in Tokyo?'

Maguire nodded.

'Do you think that's why I've refused to go back to London?'

'Well, partly, yes.'

'You're damned right, Mr Maguire. You're damned right. I will not go back to London.'

Maguire looked down at the polished stone floor. 'But wouldn't you have done the same?' he asked at last.

'What?' Coomb stared at him, then away out of the window. 'I see you've got a knack for politics, Mr Maguire.' He bent over the file again. The mouth organ stopped, then started another tune. Maguire gazed out of the window. His skin was sticky with sweat in the warm, still, midday air; his eyelids were drooping with weariness.

Coomb leafed through to the flimsy pages at the back of the file. They contained all the messages that had been intercepted in the variant code, with time, date and estimated place of origin. Coomb turned them over slowly, then leaned back.

Maguire looked up expectantly. Coomb's eyes were closed, but his frown remained. His cheeks looked gaunt.

'They've changed the transposition key.' Coomb's eyes were still closed. 'You've got a wife, Mr Maguire?'

'A wife? No, I . . .'

214

'Well, don't get one.' Coomb's eyes opened suddenly and he looked down his nose at Maguire. 'Or if you do, don't get a child. Don't get a child.'

Maguire was about to chance some useless word of sympathy again, but Coomb lifted his hand forbiddingly.

'If I have any ideas, I'll let you know.'

'The army's signals installation here is at your service. All you have to do is ring the political adviser and he'll arrange it all. They've got some very sophisticated stuff – '

Coomb shook his head. 'You've got to know where to start.' He pursed his lips. 'All that machinery's a waste of time if you don't know where to start . . . Useless.'

The clatter of the returning helicopter sounded through the open window.

'That thing coming for you?'

'Yes. Can I say you'll be working on it?'

'You can say if I have any ideas I'll let you know.'

'The political adviser's number is on the file.'

'It's also in the phone book.' Coomb leant back, clasping his hands behind his neck. Maguire noticed two large, wet patches of sweat under the arms of his shirt.

Maguire stood up. 'We were terribly sorry to hear about . . . about your daughter.' It had seemed impossibly callous not to mention it, despite Coomb's menacing discouragement. But now he regretted doing so.

'Keep your social hypocrisies for people who appreciate them, Mr Maguire.' He stood up, again ignoring Maguire's hand, glancing at the wall behind him.

Maguire followed Coomb's glance to a bronze Chinese urn on the bookshelf. It was a tripod, high up on the top shelf, the books held away from it on each side by ugly green metal bookends.

'Those are her ashes, Mr Maguire. Would you mind seeing yourself out? Oh, and tell your people to send me all the messages they receive, would you? I take it there's no objection to that? The more I get, the more likely I am to have an idea.'

Maguire looked back as the helicopter lifted off the beach.

The ragged children had appeared again and were staring up, shielding their eyes. A man in a conical straw hat watched from a sampan moored by the shore. Coomb's house diminished rapidly. The Whirlwind swung away over the sea.

'Typhoon coming our way,' the pilot said chattily. 'Won't be here for a day or two, though. You leaving straight away, sir?'

A few hours later the VC10 was a glittering arrow high over the starving plains of India and Maguire was lying back dozing in his cushioned seat.

Chapter Thirty-six

Peking, Friday, 10 September 1971

Small, slightly stooping, but neatly dressed, Lin sat writing at the plain wooden desk in his bedroom. The large characters plodded laboriously along the page stroke by stroke, then slowly dried as he leaned back to read the sentence he'd just written or think of the next. There were many changes and crossings-out. Writing had never come easily to him and this was the hardest of all. It was to be his speech at the October the first National Day parade. By then he would have taken Mao's place.

'It should be known to all soldiers, commanders, cadres and party workers, to all the broad masses,' the peroration stumbled along, 'that the correct line is still' – with a frown, he changed that word to 'always' – 'is always to study Mao Tse-Tung's thought and implement his policies. Our great leader has been taken from us, but we shall not waver in our determination to resolutely follow his course. We must strengthen our vigilance against the right-wing opportunists who are still lying low waiting for their chance to team up with the imperialists. Those who oppose the trend of history are swimming frenziedly against the tide. They are merely lifting up a boulder to drop on their own feet . . .'

Yeh-Chun brought in a bowl of fried yellow beans and Lin pushed his chair back, sighing and rubbing his tired, weak eyes under his glasses. One of those metaphors would have to go, he realized that, but which – swimming against the tide or dropping a boulder? He sniffed the beans and reached for the chopsticks. Yeh-Chun rested her hands on his bony

217

shoulders and read what he'd written. He sensed her indulgent smile as she spoke. 'You can't lift up boulders while you're swimming against the tide.'

'I know,' he raised the chopsticks thoughtfully and picked out two of the largest beans. 'But which one should I keep in?'

In answer, she leaned over him, picked up the pen and crossed through the words 'are swimming frenziedly against the tide'. Her body felt warm and comforting against his. He leaned his head on her arm in an unusual surge of tenderness. 'Sometimes I wonder whether I have the strength for all this,' he said broodingly.

'We can't go back now,' she answered in a firm voice. 'Anyway, in three more days it will all be over.'

'I didn't mean I was afraid,' he reproved her quietly. 'I meant my health.'

She glanced down at his frail body, more like a scholar's than a great commander's. 'You won't get any stronger as you get older.'

He chewed his beans and swallowed. 'In three more days it won't all be over, it will only just be starting.'

'The worst part will be over.'

'Hm.' He picked up some more beans with the chopsticks, then pushed the bowl aside. In three days' time how many people would be dead, he wondered, and who would they be? He thought of the Korean he'd had killed. It wasn't like killing in war. And there'd be a lot more of that to be done. Dirty, treacherous killing. He swallowed and sighed. Well, there's no going back now. He licked his thin lips and took up his pen again.

Chapter Thirty-seven

The First Chief Directorate of the KGB includes two units which had become very interested in Coomb by this time. The first, Special Service II, was the counter-intelligence service. Officers of this unit made an immediate investigation of Coomb as soon as Valentski's confession reached them.

He was watched in Japan and watched in Hong Kong. His biography was hastily obtained and analysed. Documents from secret British files, which had long ago been photocopied by a blackmailed homosexual cipher clerk, were retrieved and scanned. They hinted at Coomb's role as a cryptoanalyst. Cables sent to Coomb were monitored by the Chinese agents through whom Russia operates in Hong Kong. Maguire's visit was observed and its purpose easily inferred. Clearly, Coomb was not only an agent, but also a valued cryptoanalyst whose assistance was being urgently sought by the British government.

It was when this inference had been made that the interest of the second unit was aroused – the executive action department, Department V, in charge of 'wet affairs', or liquidations. Because of the importance of Engineering Project 571, Department V suggested Coomb should be eliminated. The British had obviously seen through the diversionary ruse of Russian military activity on the Persian border and were working on the variant code. Coomb was apparently a cryptoanalyst by whom they set great store. It was vital to the success of Project 571 that the code shouldn't be broken in the next two or three days. Finally, Coomb was, it seemed, unprotected, and there were gangsters available in

Hong Kong who were ready and disposable instruments for murder. The recommendation went up to the highest authority. Down it speedily came with 'Act Immediately' marked above the required initials.

In the three Russian military regions of the Soviet Far East, all leave was cancelled without explanation. Defensive positions were reinforced, missile silos and nuclear bombers placed on full alert.

At the same time, border patrols were reduced and forward outposts only lightly manned. Things had never been so quiet along the Amur and Ussuri Rivers. Chinese soldiers jeered at the Russians skulking in their dugouts and pissed across the border in full view.

In Peking, Old Kang and Chou watched and waited.

In the South China Sea, a large typhoon was drifting towards Hong Kong. It had passed over the northern Philippines from its breeding ground in the Pacific, smashing buildings, flailing its way through forests, sinking ships and flooding plains. That had wearied it a little, but, moving out to sea, it gathered strength again. Two hundred miles from the centre of the storm, a sturdy Hong Kong fishing junk had its teak timbers pounded to pieces by the huge, relentless waves. The crew cut down the main mast and tied themselves to it as the ship broke up. One by one they drowned. Only a woman survived, picked up after three days in the water. The rest of the crew had been her husband, his brothers and her children. Two hundred miles from the centre of the storm, in the foothills of the waves.

Hong Kong, Saturday Morning, 11 September 1971
The wind moaned and whistled at every crack, shaking the windows and doors so that the house trembled all the time. Sudden gusts made the glass in the windows bend and the doors shudder against their bolts. And all the while the rain swept down, in long wind-driven sheets and washed like a

flood over the roof of the house. Water ran down from the window frames, spread under the doors, dropped steadily down through the roof.

Outside, dark grey cloud masses staggered before the invisible wind or exploded against the hillside, where the few trees that could bend were flattened and the few that could not were snapped and broken. The sea in the bay looked strangely calm, protected by the headland from the full force of the wind. But, underneath, it stirred and heaved. The boats, tied fore and aft in shallow water, moved uneasily, like animals with the scent of the slaughterhouse in their nostrils.

Suk-Yee paused by Coomb's desk, a bundle of towels in her hands. 'More coffee?'

Coomb shook his head, frowning down at his work. Sheets of paper with mathematical calculations and impatiently crossed-through grids of letters lay all over the desk or, balled up and tossed away, on the floor.

The window rattled dangerously with another sudden gust of wind. Suk-Yee glanced at the pane bending before its force. She'd stuck lengths of tape in a broad lattice across the glass, to lessen the danger from flying splinters if it did break. But he'd still be lacerated, sitting there. 'You shouldn't sit by the window like that.'

'Shh.'

She tried to fasten the window more firmly and stuck some more tape on.

'For God's sake, what are you doing now?'

'It's coming nearer.'

'What's coming nearer?'

'The typhoon.' She used the towels to mop up the rain seeping through the cracks in the window frame, spilling over the ledge and running down into a widening lake on the floor. 'The radio says it may pass right over us.'

'Hmph.' He glanced out of the window at the opaque sheets of rain sweeping over the beach towards them. 'Any more coffee, is there?'

'I just asked you.'

'Did you?' He was frowning down again, lips pursed, head in hands, 'I didn't hear.'

She took some old newspapers off a stool and spread them out over the expanding lake on the floor. Everything she did seemed to be done slowly and deliberately. She had time to spare, she thought, as she watched the paper soak up the water; now she would always have time to spare. 'This room's going to be flooded again.'

'Shh! Shut up, can't you?' His frown deepened. Then a moment later, 'Where's the boat?'

'They brought it in as far as they could and tied it up.'

They both looked out at the little junk, twenty feet long, nervously riding the swelling sea.

'When the wind changes – '

'If it gets smashed up,' he interrupted her, 'we can charge the government.' He went back to his calculations frowning and chewing his thumbnail.

She spread more paper on the floor beneath the windows, wringing the soaking towels out in a red plastic bucket that stood in the hall to catch drips from the roof. With every door and window bolted shut, the house smelled of warm, mouldy air, stifling to breathe.

Suk-Yee checked the veranda doors again. They had heavy metal bars screwed across them to prevent them from swinging open under the force of the wind, but the incessant shaking had worked one of the bolts loose. She gripped the brass butterfly end and twisted it tightly into place again. The door shuddered continuously against her hand, almost as though it were alive. She mopped up the water seeping across the floor and spread more newspapers. The rugs were all rolled up on the chairs, the scrolls and ornaments carefully put away inside drawers and cupboards. Dim, oblong shapes showed on the bare walls where the scrolls had hung. It looked as if they were packing up to leave. But they would never leave now. There'd be no need.

She went upstairs. Sarah's room faced her. She stood looking at the glossy white paint of the closed door. She could see her own faint, shadowy reflection, shaking as the door shook with the wind. She pushed down the dulled brass handle and went inside.

She gazed at the wig lying on the chest of drawers, at the violin case behind it. She gazed at the closed wardrobe, at the bare mattress, at the little case of Sarah's last clothes and belongings, still lying on the mattress where John had left it when they'd brought it from the hospital. She fingered the little metal catch of the case, but didn't press it down. She didn't want to look inside, to touch the last things Sarah had touched, to indulge the morbid appetite of grief. Still, her throat tightened and knotted.

She went to the window and checked the catch. It was fast, and the ledge still dry. The storm was battering against the front of the house, but not here. She looked down into the courtyard. The banana tree's ragged leaves were tearing and streaming in every direction as the wind swooped over the house and rioted wildly round and round the walled space. The drains were blocked already in the gutter and the swirling rainwater was rising up to the kitchen threshold.

She heard John's heavy steps on the stairs and turned round.

'Isn't there some squared paper somewhere in here?' He jerked the top drawer of the chest open, started rummaging inside, then paused. He looked up at her. She was watching him with an incredulous, distant reproachfulness.

'You were just going to use her books for scrap paper?' she asked ruefully. 'Without even remembering?'

He looked away, down at the open drawer. An old reading book stared blankly up at him. The corner of the cover was torn and bent. He gazed down at the picture of a jolly Englishman with two jolly children in a jolly English car in a jolly English suburb.

'It had gone out of my mind,' he said slowly. 'That's all . . . It had just gone out of my mind. How could it?' He pushed the drawer shut and went heavily back down the stairs to the study.

She gazed numbly round the room again, then left it, closing the door on the emptiness. She went into the bedroom and checked the windows there. She emptied the bucket which stood collecting drips from the roof in the bedroom. The house shuddered in a sudden fiercer gust of wind. She went downstairs to the kitchen.

The dog crouched on the stone floor, chin on paws, eyes watchful, ears twitching at the howling bluster of wind and rain. She checked the bolt on the back door and laid some towels along the threshold. 'The water will be coming in here soon,' she said to the servant in Cantonese.

The old woman shrugged sullenly. She was lighting a joss stick in an empty jar in the corner.

'And another cup of coffee, please.'

'I'm cooking lunch.'

'Lunch can be two minutes later.'

She sighed and grumbled sulkily, but filled the kettle. She hadn't forgiven Coomb for having Sarah cremated instead of buried, nor Suk-Yee for having allowed it.

The steam of cooking mingled with the humid air. The walls were sweating. The door quivered constantly against its frame and a little river of water began to flow under the towels Suk-Yee had laid down.

The servant switched on her red portable radio to hear the half-hourly typhoon report. Suk-Yee listened as a crooning Cantonese love song faded and the announcer read the bulletin from the observatory.

'*The eye of the typhoon is expected to pass over Hong Kong very shortly. Places which have been protected will then feel the full force of the winds. Sustained wind speeds of a hundred and twenty knots are now blowing from the northeast quarter, with gusts in excess of a hundred and seventy knots. All transport, schools, government and business offices are closed. It is dangerous to expose yourselves to windows or to leave your house or dwelling.*

The tide is expected to be fourteen feet above normal and there will be severe flooding in low-lying areas. Landslides have occurred in various parts of Hong Kong Island and Kowloon. Four ships have reported they are in difficulties

*as their anchor cables have broken. Marine Department
tugs are unable to go to their assistance because of the
heavy seas. The –* '

The self-important voice was suddenly silent. The servant
fiddled with the volume and tuner controls, shook the radio,
held it to her ear and put it down. 'Blown away,' she
muttered peevishly. 'Serves them right.'

Suk-Yee took the coffee, put it down wordlessly on
Coomb's desk, picked up the dirty cup and saucer, took them
to the kitchen and went back to the living-room. She sat
down in the rocking-chair and watched the veranda doors
quivering and rattling under the violence of the wind. The
water was spreading out steadily over the floor past the
sodden dyke of newspapers.

*From now on I shall only watch life. There's nothing else
for me to do. I shall only watch.* And she grew still in the
hollow room as she listened to the howling, rushing wind, the
shaking doors, the pelting rain hurled in wave after wave
against the windows.

She gazed out at the tumultuous sky, but saw instead Sarah's
empty room, still and closed, already smelling of disuse. How
Sarah had liked to watch typhoons, as if she could somehow
draw into her own body some of their abundant strength and
force. Suk-Yee sat still, as she would always sit, watching the
driven rain, listening to the shouting wind.

Coomb drew yet another grid and started plotting the letters
of Russian alphabet onto the thirty-two spaces. He wrote
them carefully, and tensely, like a man playing chess who
believes he is about to checkmate a wily opponent. And
before he was half-way through, he knew he'd succeeded. He
stopped, leaned back almost breathlessly, swallowed a
mouthful of cold coffee and put the cup down on the edge of
the saucer, gazing all the time narrow-eyed at the grid.

After a moment, he leaned over the desk again and plotted
the remaining letters in their places. He had the key. He had
it. Nervously he took three Russian messages, all sent within
a few hours of each other only two days ago. Step by step he

decoded the first one, writing it out beneath the grid. The string of letters went across the page and separated themselves into words before his eyes. He put a pencil stroke between each word to make sure, then read.

REPORT UNIT READINESS 1200 HOURS.

The message had come from the Russian military headquarters in Khabarovsk. The other two messages had been sent within four hours of the first. Coomb felt certain they had been encoded with the same key. He read the letters off the grid and wrote them down, smiling as they transformed themselves into words. The first was also from Khabarovsk:

SUPPLY FORWARD UNITS BY NIGHT ONLY.

The third was from the Russian embassy in Peking. It had been monitored by the Chinese and Old Kang had sent it at once to London. Coomb read it out.

ESSENTIAL AVOID BORDER INCIDENTS BEFORE ENGINEERING PROJECT 571. IMPLEMENTATION NOW PLANNED DEFINITELY 0100 HOURS 13 SEPTEMBER.

He leaned back again, his pulse beating faster, and swallowed the rest of his coffee. For a few seconds he closed his eyes; then he opened them again and read the messages once more. He didn't hear the fury of the wind and rain or notice the little lake of water approaching his feet.

His hands and arms were sticky with sweat. He wiped them on his handkerchief before he copied down the two transposition keys, the substitution key and the three messages on a clean piece of paper. Underneath them, he wrote in his spiky hand:

Political Adviser, Hong Kong Government.
   Russian substitution and double transposition keys for 8 September 1971, with three decoded messages sent on that day. Deciphered by J.C. on 11 September after twenty-one hours continuous work. The principles of this code are now clear. J. Coomb.

He scraped back his chair, got up and found he was walking in an inch of water. Suddenly he was tired. His eyes burned, his head throbbed and his legs were stiff and heavy. He opened the door and went into the hall.

There was a sudden loud crash and tinkle of glass. The door slammed violently shut behind him, bursting the plaster loose from the jamb, and he heard the wind hurling and smashing everything in the room. The windows had blown in. For a moment he tried to open the door again, but the pressure was far too great. Suk-Yee pulled his arm.

'Look at your foot!' she shouted above the tumult.

A sliver of glass had slid under the door and cut his sandalled foot. It was bleeding freely yet painlessly. The wind pounded against the door and shrieked beneath it. They heard more glass breaking, bookshelves falling, the rain pelting against the quivering door. Suk-Yee pulled him away.

'I've done it!' He slumped down in the hall beside the phone. 'I've done it!' He showed her the paper.

'What does it say?' She cupped her ear.

'Don't know. I mean, don't know what it means,' he shouted. 'Something about September the thirteenth, anyway. Where's the political adviser's number? I knew it was a double transposition key. I knew it. Where's that bloody number?'

'Here.'

'Hmph.' He lifted the phone, started dialling, stopped, listened, replaced the receiver, picked it up, listened, slammed it down again.

'It's dead.'

Suk-Yee was trying to stem the water flooding underneath the study door with another bundle of towels. 'The lines must be down,' she shouted back above the din of the rattling doors and the frenzied wind. 'The radio's gone dead as well.'

Coomb cursed, trying the phone again and again. 'I've got to get through somehow! The thirteenth's only two days away.'

She was kneeling down, pushing the towels tight against

227

the door. Already they were sodden. Coomb called out to the amah.

'It's no use, she won't leave the kitchen in a typhoon!' Suk-Yee got up. 'Isn't there a radio transmitter in the police post at Sok Yue Wan?'

'How the hell am I going to get there in this?'

'The eye's supposed to be passing over us soon!'

Coomb slammed the receiver down for the sixth time. 'Give me a Band-Aid, can you?'

She gave him the flat red tin. He put one Band-Aid over his foot, then emptied the rest out onto the floor.

'What are you doing?'

He folded the paper with the code keys and the messages on it inside a plastic envelope which was lying by the phone and put it inside the tin, pushing the lid on firmly. 'Safe keeping! It would get soaked in the rain!' He put the box in his hip pocket.

'You can't go out in this!'

'When the eye comes, I'll try the police post. They must be able to get in touch.' He leaned back with his head against the wall and closed his eyes. 'My God, I'm tired.'

She hadn't heard; his voice had sunk. But she looked at his drawn cheeks and unshaven chin. 'What's it all about?'

'What?'

'What's it all about?' she shouted again.

'Something to do with China! The Russians are planning something!' He shrugged. 'God knows! I don't really care any more!'

They sat there listening to the wind buffeting the study door. The rainwater washed out under the towels and spread towards them. Each of them thought of the urn holding Sarah's ashes. It must have been tumbling over the floor. But neither spoke of it. The dog came slowly down the hall from the kitchen, sniffed at the study door and the towels, then lay down beside Coomb, its heavy head on his knee. He scratched its ear idly.

'What are we going to do now?' Coomb opened his eyes to look at Suk-Yee, then let them close again.

'What?'

'What are we going to do now?' he shouted.

'What do you mean, now?'

'Now that . . . Sarah's gone!'

She shrugged. 'Carry on living, I suppose!'

'Hmph!' Mentioning her name had brought her face back into his mind. For the past day and a half he hadn't thought of her at all.

'Why, what do you want to do?'

He didn't answer, lifting his head abruptly. The winds were falling. The house was growing suddenly still and quiet. They could hear the amah stirring something in the kitchen and the heavy pounding of the sea on the beach. Yes, the winds had died and the house was strangely calm and hushed. The eye of the storm.

'All right, I'm off,' Coomb said. His voice seemed unnaturally loud.

'Stay at the police post if the winds start again.'

'Won't have much choice.'

'I'll see what I can do in the study.'

Again each thought privately of Sarah's urn. Their eyes met, but they didn't speak. Coomb called the dog and unbolted the door. A soft, calm rain was falling. The air smelled fresh. He nodded to Ah Lai, the fisherman from the nearest house, who had also come out and was securing the ropes of the boats. Coomb noticed the flotsam thrown up on the beach, the heavy, threatening swell and his own boat still safely moored.

He turned up the hill towards the police post on the other side of the island. The dog loped along in front of him. The path was flooded and strewn with debris. Branches, trees, mudslips and boulders had obliterated it. The whole hillside looked as though some giant had wallowed on it, crushing or breaking everything in its way. Coomb started climbing, splashing and stumbling in the mud, moving as fast as he could. When the eye passed, the great winds would come again, but from the other side, with even wilder violence.

Ah Lai's ancestors had lived in the village for generations.

All had been fishermen; some had been pirates. Once it had been a large village, but now it had dwindled. Many had left the sea for factory work in the new towns of Hong Kong or had emigrated to England, where they worked in laundries and restaurants. A few had become sailors for the big cargo lines and came home once in five years, to find everything changed.

But Ah Lai had stayed. He went fishing every day of his life, grew a few vegetables on his small plot of land and did odd jobs, such as looking after Coomb's boat. He was forty-seven years old and had eight children, each of whom left school as soon as they were eleven to help him fish and farm. He'd had bad luck. Two boys had died within a year of their birth. When the next child was born a boy, he'd given it a girl's name, to deceive the spirits that must have wanted to kill his boys. And the boy with the girl's name survived, his youngest child.

Ah Lai frowned as he watched Coomb clambering up the hill, the dog bounding ahead, pausing, bounding ahead again. He tightened a knot in the rope holding Coomb's boat and started towards his hut. He knew the eye of this typhoon would be a small one; soon it would pass. Coomb clambered on over the trees and boulders. Ah Lai wondered why he was acting so strangely.

He was nearing Coomb's house.

Suddenly there was an air-shattering blast and the whole building seemed to lift then bulge, then sag and slowly collapse into a pile of rubble, dust and smoke while the blast still echoed off the hillside.

Coomb looked back over his shoulder, at first incredulously, then with a sickening leap of fear. For one second he stood numbly, thinking *No*, *No*, then he started running back, stumbling, falling, cutting himself, to the pile of bricks and smoking plaster that had been his home.

Ah Lai and the dog were before him. The dog was sniffing uncomprehendingly, Ah Lai pulled at a lump of broken masonry. He heaved it aside, dropped it and muttered, staring down and shaking his head.

Coomb knew from Ah Lai's face what he would see. His

fist clenched as he stepped forward. Suk-Yee lay with one arm thrown across her eyes as if in sleep. But she was not asleep. Her cheek was torn open from mouth to ear and a heavy girder had crushed the top of her head. Coomb had never seen anything as distorted and ugly as the broken-doll expression on her lifeless, blood-spattered face.

The dog sniffed at her, nuzzled her, licked her blood. Coomb kicked him savagely. The dog yelped and jumped away, then lay down, watching with hanging tongue and cocked head as Ah Lai started clearing the rubble off Suk-Yee's body. Coomb felt giddy and sick. He hoped he was going to faint, but no, he had to stand and watch as her crushed body was gradually uncovered. In her other hand was the empty, battered urn.

Coomb tapped Ah Lai's shoulder numbly and shook his head. 'The old woman,' he said dully, 'In the kitchen.'

Ah Lai's children were there now and several women from the village. They were heaving at the rubble in the back of the house, grunting and shouting. Coomb sat down dazedly. Surely he would faint now, black out and cease to feel. But he was still conscious, Suk-Yee's mutilated face there beside him, and somewhere an indifferent bird was singing obscenely on the indifferent hillside.

His body started shaking. He cursed the dog, which had come nearer again, and shoved it away weakly. Someone shouted loudly and he looked round with a surge of absurd hopefulness, half-believing they had found Suk-Yee was still alive after all. But the shout had come from Ah Lai, who had collapsed on the rubble, coughing and clutching his side. As if in a trance, Coomb saw blood trickling out of Ah Lai's mouth and, as his hand grew feebler and slipped away, the widening stain of blood on his checkered shirt.

Then the dog was barking wildly, the villagers were all running away and Coomb saw two men coming towards him with revolvers in their hands. He watched bemusedly as they aimed at him. A chip of cement flew up by his knee and he heard the screaming ricochet of the bullet, then the report of another shot.

Suddenly he felt fear again. He was alone; they were walking steadily towards him; they were coming to kill him. He gasped and jumped up, dashing blindly away towards the sea. The dog raced beside him as if they were playing some game. The sand spurted up in front of him and he swerved aside, his shoulders braced for the bullet that would crash into his back.

But it was the dog that suddenly yelped, stumbled, rolled over and lay still. Coomb swerved again, realized he was heading towards his boat and splashed into the sea. As he climbed frantically on board, he noticed out of the corner of his eye that the men had stopped to reload their guns. No time to undo the knots. He seized a chopper from the cabin and struck at the ropes until they parted, then turned the ignition key.

He heard the men running down the wet sand, firing wildly. A bullet whined over his head and he ducked, then threw himself flat on the deck. On the second try, the engine started. He opened the throttle, gasping, and the boat rose to the swell. Bullets splintered the woodwork and hissed through the sea beside him, but the boat drew steadily away.

Coomb peered back over the stern. The two men were waist deep in the water, but they'd stopped firing. Behind them on the beach the dog lay inert on its side. Behind the dog were the still ruins of his house.

As casually as if they'd merely come to paddle, the men turned and walked back out of the water. They stood on the beach watching him. Nothing moved in the little village. Ah Lai's body lay clearly visible on top of the rubble where Suk-Yee too lay and the servant and everything.

The boat heaved and yawed crazily as Coomb lost his grip on the tiller. He caught it again and headed for the open sea. The waves grew heavier and his stomach turned when he saw them racing foam-flecked outside the little bay, so high they almost hid the peaks of Hong Kong.

Mechanically he felt for the box in his pocket, which still held the decoded messages. What was he doing with it? He tied on his orange life jacket and held the tiller tight with both arms, trying to think. *If the winds don't start again you'll have a chance*, he told himself numbly, and then, *Of course you haven't, you're going to drown*. That thought too was numb and detached. He steered towards the nearest point in Hong Kong and clung grimly to the tiller, waiting to meet the tumbling cliffs of waves. He thought neither of Suk-Yee, nor of Sarah, nor of the buried amah, nor of the shot Ah Lai. He thought only of the rearing, massive seas and the fragile boards beneath his feet.

The very first wave caught the junk nearly broadside, slewed it round and almost capsized it. Somehow, in the sliding gorge between that wave and the next, Coomb managed to right the boat, but as the towering green wall smashed down and thundered all round him, the tiller was plucked from his hands. The boat came up bravely, but the engine had died and it was powerless, wallowing and lurching, swept before the battering seas.

Coomb slid about the deck trying to grab the swinging tiller; he grasped it for a moment, then it was pulled out of his grip. It snapped back a second later and broke his arm. Then, as he sprawled there stunned, he heard the air begin to whistle past the mast, heard the fearful shriek and rush of the great winds returning. They reared down, snatching the breath out of his lungs, and pinned him down against the deck.

The eye of the storm had passed. The sky filled up with heaving, crashing torrents of water and blinding whiplashes of rain and sea. The mast splintered and broke, smashing in the cabin roof as it fell.

Coomb was swept overboard half-conscious as the shattered vessel shuddered and foundered.

Chapter Thirty-eight

Hong Kong, Saturday Evening, 11 September 1971

After the storm the dragonflies came. The great winds passed, the rain passed, the clouds lifted and the air was suddenly still and clear. Then the dragonflies rose above the wounded trees. Their brilliant bodies flashed in the failing light of the evening sun, their long, clear wings flickered busily. They darted and zigzagged crazily through the new, washed stillness of the air. And soon a bird cheeped from the undergrowth, a cicada whirred shrilly beneath a glistening leaf and a kite rose from its shelter, flapping with languid, ragged wings over the hill.

After a time, an RAF Whirlwind helicopter came skimming across the heavy sea, looking like some stiff, gigantic cousin of the dragonflies. At the controls, the pilot gazed down at the capsized hull of the Macau ferry, at a broken-backed freighter aground on the still-seething rocks, at the masts of a sunken steamer. He hovered dangerously lower, looking for survivors. The sea pounded over the wrecks. No boats, no rafts, not even a lifebelt. Nothing but the huge, running swell of the waves. He glanced at his winchman and shook his head questioningly.

The winchman shook his head too, pushing out his underlip and shrugging. 'Ping-pong ball in 'ell,' he said.

The Whirlwind soared upwards again and turned away, back towards Hong Kong.

The winchman suddenly tapped the pilot's shoulder and pointed. A body in an orange life-jacket lay on the rocks of a little headland, the sea which had tossed it there still lifting and throwing it, as if in some savage game.

The helicopter slid downwards and hovered twenty feet above the rocks.

'What's he like?' the pilot asked as they winched the body in.

'Bloody knackered. But 'e's still breathing.'

Coomb was moaning faintly, his lips cut and bruised, his lids fluttering. The winchman put one ear to his mouth, covering the other with his hand against the clatter of the engine.

Coomb's voice muttered hoarsely and urgently, but the winchman couldn't make out a single word. Then he saw Coomb's hand fluttering feebly towards his hip pocket. He reached down, saw the squarish bulge and pulled out a Band-Aid tin. Inside, wrapped in its plastic envelope, he found Coomb's message, sodden but still legible.

Chapter Thirty-nine

Peking, 1600 Hours, Sunday, 12 September 1971

Tiger Cat Lin sat in his office coughing again and again, his pale hands pressed uselessly against his chest. As the fit subsided and, flush-faced, he got back his breath, he reached for the fresh copy of the *People's Daily* which lay neatly folded on top of the pile of documents in front of him. Prominent on the front page was the announcement of a set of fifty photographs of Chairman Mao – one for each year – to commemorate the fiftieth anniversary of the founding of the party. Many of the photographs reproduced in the newspaper showed Lin himself beside the Chairman, diminutive, but loyal, Mao's chosen successor. His 'close comrade in arms' the text extolled Lin, 'a brilliant example for the whole army, the whole party and the whole people all over the country'. Lin pored through his spectacles at the smile on his face as he stood beside his master. He wondered what might be read from it.

He blew his nose, wiped the phlegm from his mouth and looked away, blinking and watery-eyed, at the large map of Peking on the wall. Uninstructed except by habit, his gaze focused on the radio station and the Chairman's residence in Chungnanhai. His thin, frail hands folded and refolded the handkerchief, then stowed it away in his pocket.

On the other wall, Mao's obligatory portrait looked down at him, larger than life, the shrewd eyes gazing at him with that sardonic, knowing expression Lin could never quite fathom. He looked away uncomfortably, pushed the *People's Daily* aside and began going through the routine papers left over from Saturday – as if his mind were not distracted by unruly thoughts and images, as if his old chest wound were not aching, as if his pulse did not keep thudding erratically.

The orderly came in with his green tea, and Comrade Lin smiled his usual polite thanks, his tufty, grey brows rising over the glasses which had slipped down his narrow, curved nose. When the door shut, he looked at his watch. Nine more hours. At one o'clock in the morning, he would lift the phone and say the single sentence which would commit him to assassination and rebellion – no, which would restore the true revolutionary line. But despite its swift erasure by the after-thought, the traces of the first, *assassination* and *rebellion*, lingered in his mind. He wished it was all over, wished he could stop it, resented his own weakness. The tea steamed in front of him. He sipped it, then pushed it away. It made him feel sick. When he was younger, his nerves had been better. Before Pinghsingkuan, thirty-four years ago, he could have eaten or drunk anything. But then all his enemies had been outside him. He hadn't had to fight the intangible guerillas of guilt as well.

He forced himself to read the next document. The orders for the National Day Parade. He glanced through it perfunctorily and signed – an empty, if necessary, ritual. Tomorrow those arrangements would be superseded. Today they must seem fixed and secure. He turned to the next document and the next. Work calmed him and stilled his mind.

London, 0810 Hours, Sunday, 12 September 1971
Stuart sipped some strong, sweet tea from a chipped mug and leaned back, rubbing his unshaven chin. He was sitting on a raised dais in the operations room that hadn't been used since the Cuban crisis in 1962. Beside him sat Maguire, Johnston and a man from the China desk at the foreign office. Below them was a large horseshoe table. Twenty intelligence analysts sat in pairs round it, writing interpretations of freshly decoded messages as they were brought in from the cipher room. At the head of the table, two

controllers assessed the interpretations and wrote recommendations to Stuart.

They'd been up all night. Coomb's information hadn't come in until eleven-thirty the evening before. It had taken three hours for it to trickle up through the hands of incredulous duty officers in Hong Kong – first to the military, then to the police and finally to the political adviser, who had to be tracked down to a Chinese restaurant where he was entertaining the editor of a local communist newspaper.

Coomb's key and the decoded messages were flashed to London. A fuller report came a couple of hours later when the attack on his house had been discovered.

Stuart's cryptoanalysts were several stages behind Coomb. It would have taken them another thirty-six hours to break the code. As it was, they were at once able to check his conclusions and use the principles he'd established to decipher other messages that had been intercepted in the last few days. Coomb had worked on a conjecture which he'd plucked out of a hundred possibilities – that the Russians had varied their code as little as possible by simply doubling the number of transpositions. Having three messages sent on the same day, he'd been able to make the start which led him to their key. Given that, the rest was easy.

Stuart sipped his tea again and shuffled through the pile of decoded messages in front of him. Maguire, glancing sideways, noticed that the stubble on his chin was a metallic silver. Soon his hair would be going grey all over, not just at the sideburns. He caught himself wondering ridiculously why people's hair went grey from the chin up instead of from the head down.

'Shouldn't we pass some of this stuff over to the Chinese now?' the foreign office man asked.

'There isn't much in this lot.'

'We know something's planned for one o'clock on the morning of the thirteenth.'

'We don't know what, though.' Stuart nodded at the horseshoe table. 'They're working on a new batch. Let's see what they make of that first.'

The foreign office man glanced at his watch but said nothing. Maguire noticed the two controllers leaning their heads together at the top of the table to confer over some papers that had just been brought up to them.

'Would you like some more tea?' Stuart asked him.

'No, thanks. I'll wait.' He rubbed his sore eyes round and round with the heels of his palms. For some reason, the action reminded him of Suk-Yee stroking away that single tear the last time he saw her. He looked at his stubby, pink hands and thought of her slender almond ones.

'You may have to wait a long time,' Stuart was saying as he sipped from his mug again.

The foreign office man glanced at his watch once more and once more said nothing. Stuart filled his pipe from a shabby leather pouch. He packed the tobacco shreds down in the blackened bowl carefully and deliberately with his spatulate finger.

'Any more news about Coomb?' Maguire asked.

Stuart's slightly protruding eyes considered him coolly through a bluish drift of smoke. 'Dying, I'm afraid,' he said. 'Or dead already.'

The two controllers were going round the table now, talking with their analysts one by one, checking their papers, reading new cables.

'This looks like something,' Johnston said, speaking for the first time in an hour.

The four of them watched the controllers' progress, watched the heads turn and shake or nod. At the end of the horseshoe, the two conferred again, then nodded. One of them was dark and bald, the other fair, with a gingery moustache drooping over his mouth.

They climbed onto the dais together and laid a number of cables in front of Stuart. 'We have a clue, sir,' the bald one began.

'Yes?'

'All these cables have the same message – Engineering Project 571 to be implemented at 0100 on September 13.'

'Well?'

239

'They all come from different regions of China. So far as we can tell, they come from places where Lin Piao's men are running the military. There's none from districts where he hasn't got any pull.'

'Hmm.' Stuart bit on the stem of his pipe a moment, then sifted through the flimsy papers before passing them across to the foreign office man. 'That's a clue all right.'

'Probably it's Lin Piao who's up to something,' the controller with the moustache prompted Stuart unnecessarily.

'Aye, we can see that,' Stuart grunted. He lifted the phone in front of him. 'He must be planning to take over from Mao – that's what it is. Chou En-Lai will be glad to hear about this.'

'If the message arrives in time,' the foreign office man murmured.

Stuart glanced at his watch. 'Half-past eight? That gives them sixteen and a half hours from now.'

'Not quite,' the foreign office man said precisely. 'Their clocks are eight hours ahead of ours.'

'Christ!' Stuart began dialling at once.

'I'm rather afraid,' the foreign office man went on with a touch of smugness, 'that we may be just a shade too late. In which case, it may well be goodbye Chairman Mao.'

Peking, 1830 Hours, Sunday, 12 September 1971

'No,' said Mao stubbornly, 'Not Lin Piao. Impossible.'

They stood before him, Chou with his hands behind his back, Old Kang with his extended, mutely holding out the report from London.

'The evidence – ' Chou began.

'Not Lin Piao,' Mao said again. 'I can't believe that . . .' He got up slowly, a full head taller than they despite his age. 'I can't believe that.' He loosened his collar, took the report from Old Kang's hands and read it through twice intently. His hand trembled slightly, shaking the paper. 'Lin Piao,' he breathed heavily at last. 'Why Lin Piao?'

'We must do something at once,' Chou's voice urged him. 'His forces are stronger than ours in Peking.' *Ours*, Chou was

240

thinking bleakly. *There's only Chan Tung-Hsing.*

'Why Lin Piao?' Mao stood there swaying slightly, like a heavy statue about to topple. But then slowly his eyes lost their dark vacancy. He was ready to listen now, to act. His sagging cheeks hardened perceptibly as his lips tightened. 'Get Chan Tung-Hsing.'

'I've already phoned him.' Old Kang blinked at the Chairman, 'In my capacity as minister of public security – '

'Never mind that. How can we get Lin off guard?'

'He's in the Defence Ministry now,' Chou said. 'We've been watching him for weeks. Send Chan to arrest him before he suspects anything. We've got to surprise him, otherwise he'll alert his forces.'

The Chairman's pouched lids slid down until his eyes had narrowed into slits. 'And suppose Lin has been watching us?'

The door swung open suddenly and Chan flung unceremoniously in. 'This is a hell of a mess, isn't it?' he blustered. 'Well, don't say I didn't warn you!'

Peking, 1930 Hours, Sunday, 12 September 1971

The standby signal had been given. Hung's force would be ready and waiting in one hour. Lin pictured the ammunition being doled out, the guns prepared, the tightening of buckles, the tense expectancy as the soldiers waited near their trucks and the drivers kept testing their engines.

They would all be wearing their red Mao badges – Lin's fingers strayed to the one he wore over his heart – platoon commanders would be carrying the little red book in their pockets, *Quotations from Chairman Mao, Foreword by Lin Piao*. They would believe to the last man that they were fighting to protect the great helmsman. It had been well planned; it was going smoothly. His nerves got better as the hours went by.

His direct-line phone shrilled. He started, then smiled at himself as he lifted the receiver. It would be Hung reporting he was ready. He was always early.

But it wasn't Hung. It was Wu. At first Lin didn't

recognize his voice, it sounded so hoarse and strangled.

'What?' he asked. 'What?'

'They're on their way to arrest you!'

Lin's heart seemed to stop instantly. His breath caught in his chest. Then his whole body thudded with the returning gallop of his pulse. 'Arrest me?' His voice sounded strange, as if it weren't his own.

'Chan and two truckloads of men – they've come from Mao. Chou and Kang were there.' Wu's voice sounded strange, as if he were breathless from running. 'Public Security – two trucks – '

Lin clenched his puny fist, trying to think while Wu's hoarse voice jerked erratically on and his own pulse thudded and bounded in his ears.

'We've been found out, then?' he asked slowly.

'Of course we have!'

'What shall we do?' He was thinking aloud as he weighed the alternatives – fight or run.

'Get Hung going,' Wu's voice urged him.

'What?'

'Start the whole thing now! They're ready, aren't they? Hurry, you've only got ten minutes! Give Hung the signal and hold out there until we can get to you. They're only two truckloads – '

'Get off the line,' Lin interrupted curtly. 'I can't think with you shouting in my ear.'

'Well, hurry – '

'I'll ring back in one minute.' He put the receiver down, covered his face with his hands and tried to think. The image of two green trucks whining towards the Defence Ministry loomed behind his eyes. He had his bodyguard, a few sentries . . . Could he hold out? He listened to his heart pounding while he wavered uncertainly, second after precious second. Fight or run? He had to decide. Suddenly he lifted the receiver again, dialled the secret number to Hung and listened with quivering nerves for the ringing sound. He would fight.

But there was nothing. No ringing sound, no busy signal –

242

only utter blankness. A choking, cold numbness gripped his throat and chest. He put the receiver down and dialled again. His arm trembled slightly. He watched his pale, thin fore-finger moving the disc round, pausing, moving it round again.

Nothing. Dead. They must have cut the line. He was too late.

It's over then, he thought suddenly and, *How can it all collapse so quickly?* A great weight was dragging him down while his chest shuddered numbly with the racing of his heart. But he made himself dial yet again. Just once more, once more. How long it took to dial a number!

And again the same unspeakable deadness, dead as the grave.

It's over. It's all over. For several seconds he sat there stunned, while the weight dragged him further down and his thudding heart urged him up. They were coming for him, two truckloads, and there was nothing he could do. He sat there, paralysed with despair, while another twenty, thirty seconds slipped away.

Then, suddenly, his clarity and decisiveness returned. He must escape. He looked at his watch. Only five minutes or so before they'd be here. He dialled Yeh-Chun on the internal line, in the office immediately below his, where she worked as his assistant.

'Yeh-Chun?'

'Yes?'

He drew the top drawer of his desk open as he spoke and took out his pistol. 'We've been asked to Wu's for dinner. I forgot to tell you this morning. Can you have the car pick us up at once? At once – we're late.'

She seemed not to have heard at first, but then her voice sounded almost matter-of-factly in his ear. 'Yes, all right. At once.'

He dialled Wu again on the other line. Wu answered immediately. Lin pictured how his manicured hand must have been hovering over the phone, willing it to ring.

'Hung's line is dead. They must have cut it.'

243

'It's all up then!'

'Yes.' Lin shoved the pistol into his pocket. It was large and bulky.

Wu cursed hoarsely. 'Can you get away?'

'I'll try. We're leaving now.'

'We?'

'Yeh-Chun.' It hurt him to breathe, and when he spoke again his voice was almost gasping. 'Is the plane ready?'

'Yes, of course, but hurry.'

'Give us half an hour, then leave without us.'

'Half an hour, right. Until five past eight.'

The orderly came in as he replaced the phone.

'Comrade Lin, Yeh-Chun is outside.'

'Yes, I'm coming.' *It's finished, then.* He kept thinking numbly. *It's finished.* And suddenly it seemed as though it never could have succeeded.

'You didn't like your tea?' The orderly frowned reproachfully at his cup. 'It's cold now.'

'My cough . . . I feel a little sick.' Tiger Cat Lin took his cap, put it on with exaggerated deliberation and forced himself to walk unhurriedly out of the room, stoop-shouldered, hands behind his back. 'Leave it there. Perhaps tomorrow . . .'

The orderly stared after him puzzledly. How could Lin drink it tomorrow? He hated cold tea.

Yeh-Chun sat in the ante-room, her fingers laced together, her eyes strained. One look at his face and she knew. His glance warned her not to speak. They walked silently downstairs to the waiting black car. The driver stood chatting to the bodyguard, the two straightened as Lin and Yeh-Chun approached.

'Drive to the airport as fast as you can,' he said blankly to the driver and bodyguard. 'Don't stop for anyone. Some of the 8341 Legion have been causing trouble.' One hand felt for the butt of his pistol, the other slid across the seat and squeezed Yeh-Chun's. Her palm was cold and moist.

Red banners fluttered in Tien An Men Square, red slogans hailed the Chairman and Lin Piao, docile families strolled along the wide streets in the evening sun. A troupe of acrobats was performing in Pei Hai Park. It was an ordinary dull Sunday evening, like the Sunday before and the Sunday before that. Lin's car passed unnoticed in a whirl of dust. It wasn't until they were near the airport that a straggling cordon of policemen tried to wave them down. The driver hesitated, his foot rising slightly off the accelerator.

'Drive on!' Lin ordered tensely, and the driver pushed his foot down again. The policemen scattered, one aimed his gun, the bodyguard fired and the policeman reeled away. Yeh-Chun's lips were trembling, but she made no sound.

The plane had already taxied to the end of the runway when they reached the airport. It was the British-built Trident jetliner, equipped as an emergency airborne command post for Chairman Mao. They whined away into the northern sky fifteen minutes before Chan and his trucks arrived.

The pilot set course for Russia. Wu had prepared the way well. No Chinese fighter rose to intercept the unarmed plane, no anti-aircraft missile reached out towards it from the ground. Tiger Cat Lin sat by the window, watching his country slide away beneath the quivering wings. Yeh-Chun spoke to him comfortingly, Wu bitterly, the others with respect or fear or shame.

Lin scarcely answered. The altitude aggravated his chest wound, and he was racked by spasms of coughing. In any case, he was thinking of how he would end his life now as an ailing, useless Russian puppet, hidden in some Moscow suburb. That was all he could have told them, and he didn't want to speak of that.

But then, over Mongolia, one of the plane's engines failed. Wu swore, the flight engineer sweated, and the pilot struggled to keep the plane flying as it steadily lost altitude.

'Land anywhere!' Wu screamed hoarsely.

For answer, the pilot pointed down at the ground below.

Nothing but desolate rocks and peaks. The altimeter needle swung relentlessly lower, whatever he did.

Yeh-Chun broke down at last. She was sobbing and whimpering as she pulled her useless safety-belt tighter. Wu was wide-eyed and grim. The others screwed their eyes shut or stared out in terrified fascination at the rising mountains with their indifferent, jagged teeth. Only Tiger Cat Lin looked down with numbed acceptance. He didn't really want to go on living anyway. He'd had enough.

His pale, tenuous fingers brushed against the Mao badge he was still wearing over his heart. He unpinned it and held it in his palm, gazing briefly at the golden outline of the head he could not topple. Then he tipped his hand and the badge tumbled off onto the floor. He didn't want to die wearing that emblem of his failure and defeat.

Suddenly the ground was rising faster. Rocks and boulders from some long-past avalanche lurched sickeningly up towards them. The pilot shouted a wordless scream and covered his face; Lin too shut his eyes and turned away. There was a thud, then the grind and crash of tearing metal. And then nothing.

It was two days before the Mongolian border guards reached the burned-out plane. The charred remains of eight men and one woman were found among the wreckage.

Chapter Forty

Coomb's skull had been fractured, his left lung punctured by a broken rib; he'd been torn and bruised on the rocks and before that he'd been in the sea for several hours. He fell into a coma soon after the helicopter found him and never fully recovered consciousness. In flickering moments of pain-dimmed half-awareness, he asked for Sarah, asked for his book and muttered something incoherent about a rose for Suk-Yee. The dainty Chinese nurses couldn't understand him and shrugged their dainty shoulders. After a few days he died, in the hospital where his daughter had died three weeks before.

No trace was found of his assailants. Police ballistics officers reported that the bomb which blew up his house had been 'a sophisticated device, not likely to have been made in the colony'. However, after surprising instructions from Whitehall, where, after consultation with the Chinese, they'd decided to play things down, the bomb report was quietly filed away. A story was circulated that Coomb's stove had exploded, bringing down the house, and that he'd subsequently been attacked by robbers, whose stray shots had killed Ah Lai and the dog. There were letters in the *South China Morning Post* for weeks afterwards about the need for more police protection and for stricter controls on the installation of gas stoves.

In China, meanwhile, all army leave was cancelled for weeks, all planes were grounded and urgent meetings of the Politburo held. It was announced that the National Day

Parade would not take place. The names of Lin Piao and several high officials ceased to be mentioned in the press. Lin Piao's protégés were gradually replaced, demoted or transferred. Careers that had been stunted and withering under Lin's reign as defence minister suddenly began to blossom and grow.

The investigation of what was to become known as the Lin Piao incident went on for a year before any public acknowledgement of it was made. One of the investigators was Comrade Hua Kuo-Feng, then little-known except as the man who had helped to foster the Mao cult at the Chairman's birthplace, Shaoshan, in the fifties. There were whispers that he might be one of Mao's lost children. But the rumour was never endorsed – nor denied.

As for Mao himself, his confidence in everyone seemed to have been broken. He never appeared in public again.

In Moscow, the chairman of the KGB did not, after all, gain a seat on the Politburo. After the failure of Engineering Project 571, the Russians couldn't agree on what to do about China. So they did nothing at all.

It didn't take them long to decide what to do with Valentski and Smetanka, though. Within a couple of months they were tried and sentenced at a closed tribunal in Moscow. They were brought in one after the other to hear the verdicts.

Valentski was sentenced to death. He kept trembling and wiping his forehead with the back of his hand as if he couldn't understand what was going on, while the president of the court read out the sentence in a whining nasal voice. They led him away and shot him at once, two bullets in the back of the head. Before the executioner fired, Valentski sniffed at the sleeve of his jacket in what had become a habitual gesture. It still held the faint comforting smell of tobacco, of home, of the life he had lost. Perhaps those were the last images to pass across his broken mind.

Smetanka was treated leniently. He was dismissed from the army and sent to a labour camp for ten years. Lydia, his

248

coarse and pampered wife, Valentski's disappointing daughter, was lucky to get a job in a brick factory in Siberia.

Valentski's stupefied widow was moved to a shabby room in a shabby Moscow suburb. She had to look for work and eventually was taken on in a food store. The KGB kept an eye on her and Lydia, just in case.

After many months, the British Intelligence Service realized they owed Coomb some money. As there was no one else to give it to, they gave it to his father. Brigadier Stuart brought him the cheque in person, explaining that it was for certain advisory services Coomb had rendered the government. Coomb's father took the money gratefully and even proudly, but never quite understood what it was all about.

Hong Kong, 18 August 1972

Maguire was visiting Hong Kong a year later, for talks on trade with the European Common Market. To the surprise of the financial secretary and the chagrin of the financial secretary's wife, he excused himself from the final dinner for representatives of the textile industry and went instead to Lamma Island. Accompanied by the same cool, agile detective, he stepped ashore from the same police launch and walked in the same moist, clinging heat of twilight over the hill to the little village where Coomb had lived.

The white stone huts threaded along the bay were blurring in the dusk. Oil lamps gleamed in the open windows, dogs barked, children in the shadows shouted. Three sampans rocked gently on the barely moving surface of the darkening sea. The hull of the old wrecked boat was still there, only deeper in the sand now.

The rubble had been carted away from the ruin of Coomb's house, and the low, broken walls stood out stark and clear in the dimming light. Thick green plants sprouted everywhere through cracks in the cement and stone. Soon they would cover everything with a luxuriant green shroud.

The detective spat, lit a cigarette and leaned on what had been the veranda. Maguire stood where the living-room had been, stood where the study had been, stood on what had been the kitchen floor. He remembered Suk-Yee's hands, Coomb's spiky hair, their daugher's smooth, bald skull. Somehow the banana tree in the courtyard had survived. Hidden in the dimness beneath its long, ragged leaves, Maguire thought he saw a cluster of green fruit. He listened to the children's voices echoing from the beach and heard, or thought he heard, the plaintive wailing of a mouth organ.

The light was fading quickly. He turned and gazed out across the bay at the mauve, hazy hills of Hong Kong. Their peaks were still glowing in the last rays of the sun, but lower down it was already dark. As he watched, the dark edged slowly up the highest slopes, until only the last peak still dimly glowed.

A door slammed in a nearby house, a pot banged and scraped. The children's voices seemed to grow small and faint, as if the dusk were smothering them. A cicada began its monotonous chirping somewhere in the ruin, and then another and another, until it seemed they shrilled their harsh yet calming chorus under every leaf and stone.

The next morning, in the departure lounge at the airport, Maguire felt a hand on his shoulder. Turning, he saw a familiar face. It was Tom Cramley, Coomb's colleague at Magdalen. A little plumper, a little more grey, but as rosy-cheeked and sensual looking as ever.

They talked of Coomb as they shuffled towards the boarding gate.

'I never heard exactly what happened,' Cramley blinked inquisitively at Maguire. 'Been in California all year. I wouldn't have known at all, but for a letter I had returned, marked *Addressees Deceased*.'

'They were attacked by some robbers apparently,' Maguire examined his boarding pass unnecessarily. 'And their house caught fire. It was in a typhoon.'

Cramley pursed his lips while his eyes smiled incredulously behind his glasses, but he pried no further. 'And Sarah?'

'The little girl? She died a week or two beforehand, I believe.'

Cramley clucked his tongue. 'Well, at least that was expected.'

As the plane banked over the harbour, Maguire smothered his customary fear and looked down at the stiff-ribbed sails of the junks. They reminded him again of the paper boats his grandfather used to make.

'I think that's the island where Coomb lived,' he pointed through the window.

'Really?' Cramley peered past him. 'I thought of taking a look yesterday, but apparently it's hard to get to. And besides, there doesn't seem much point now. Not much of a place, is it? What on earth could he have seen in all that rustic idiocy? But then again, he always was an eccentric. What became of his book, by the way?'

Maguire shrugged. 'Went with the house, I suppose.'

Cramley took out a cork-tipped cigarette and lit it musingly. 'Just as well, perhaps. It sounded like a lot of nonsense to me anyway.'

They had been flying for several hours when the radio officer brought Maguire a folded message. 'Thought you might be interested in this, sir,' he said.

Maguire read it, sensing Cramley's barely concealed interest. 'The Conservatives have held the marginal seat at Preston.'

'Oh?' Cramley's curiosity drained away, but he tried to dissimulate. 'Does that mean the omens are good for your seat, at the next election?'

'I'm not sure I'll contest it,' Maguire said slowly, as if he hadn't yet decided.

'Really? Why not?'

But Maguire only shrugged.

At lunch Cramley recommended the white wine as travelling better than the red, although both were almost undrinkable. 'Did anyone ever read his manuscript, by the way?' he asked suddenly.

'Coomb's? I read a few pages once.'

'What did you think of it?'

'I . . . couldn't really say,' Maguire muttered evasively. 'It did seem very well written, in a way. It was very . . . intense.'

'Mm . . .' Cramley sipped his wine and put it down again. 'All the same, he should have stuck to logic. All that doomsday stuff was just a morbid obsession after all. Wouldn't ever've thought of it if it hadn't been for his daughter.'

The plane drew four long, graceful vapour trails above the barren plains of India, where half a million people looked up vacantly and starved.